EARRINGS

for a **BLACK DAY**

EARRINGS

for a BLACK DAY

Surviving Perestroika in Russia

A Novel

Mila Austin

iUniverse, Inc.
New York   Bloomington

EARRINGS FOR A BLACK DAY

iUniverse books may be ordered through booksellers or by contacting:

iUniverse
1663 Liberty Drive
Bloomington, IN 47403
www.iuniverse.com
1-800-Authors (1-800-288-4677)

ISBN: 978-1-4502-1467-4 (sc)
ISBN: 978-1-4502-1468-1 (ebook)

Printed in the United States of America

iUniverse rev. date: 04/28/2010

This book is dedicated to my dear parents, Nickolai and Zinaida, whose endless love, wisdom, and sacrifice helped me through my entire life. I will always love and remember you.

Introduction

"Don't be born beautiful, but be born fortunate," the Russian people say, believing that fate exists. This conclusion matured in Russia based on centuries of observation, and has been passed from generation to generation in the form of folk sayings, fairy tales, and legends.

The folk belief in a beautiful girl's wretched destiny originated during the time when Russian people were suffering and surviving endless brutal wars for freedom against the Turks and Tatars, and then against the Mongols in the thirteenth century. The most desirable trophy that every invader dreamed of was to bring home a captured young, tall, slim, beautiful Russian girl.

The same tragic story was repeated in the wars against Sweden in the eighteenth century, France in the nineteenth, and Germany in the twentieth. The huge territory of the vast Russian empire stretched from Eastern Europe, across northern Asia, and into North America, and attracted attention of many rulers in neighboring countries. In addition to the desire for land, the beauty of Russian women made foreign men's hearts beat faster and the blood race hot through their veins. During the wars, poor Russian people smeared their daughters' faces with soot and hid the girls inside dark rooms dug under the floor.

When most people speak about fortune they seem to be referring to a force that is beyond their control. Being born with beauty is considered an advantage, and, if a girl has the ability to cultivate her charm and wit, it is even a greater one. On the other hand, if one is born in the wrong place and time, beauty may cause harm and a broken heart, leading to an unhappy life or even death. Just as colorful butterflies become an easy target for silly kids who try to catch them, unprotected beauty of attractive women makes them an easy prey for evil men.

The modern Russia is different. Many women refuse to be victims. They fight for their freedom… and for a more fortunate life.

Prologue

December 1989, Russia

Lena GRABBED HER FUR coat and fled from the dorm, driven by the uncontrollable need to escape the confinement of the stuffy room. For a few hours she wandered aimlessly through the streets of the small town. She moved mechanically, passing crossroads and turning corners. Flashbacks of the most horrible day of her life filled Lena with unrelenting secret guilt as she remembered slipping into the factory's shower room and locking the door behind her to make sure no one could enter.

Unanswered questions flooded her mind. *How long was I unconscious? Why did my baby die? Was he alive when I delivered him, or did he die in my womb?* By evening, she had wandered onto a dark road in the suburbs. *If he was alive, could I have possibly rescued him if I'd noticed the cord was looped around his neck before I passed out?*

Lena did not notice a crowd of drunken men in the shadows ahead until she nearly bumped into a huge man's chest. He railed, "Hey! Are you blind or drunk?"

She reacted with a violent shudder that shocked her back to reality. Lena tried to go past the man, but he spread his arms wide and gruffly said, "Got caught, tiny sparrow?"

Lena looked around in hope of seeing helpful passers-by, but found only the grim faces and staring eyes of hoodlums encircling her like predators on a hunt.

They are prisoners! The horrific thought flashed in her mind. Surrounding her was a crowd of drunken, filthy men, with unshaven rough faces. All of them were dressed in identical jerseys and cheap caps with earflaps.

Lena remembered the sewing factory administrator's warning to female workers to avoid going out on the streets, especially at night, since the town would be full of recently released criminals who had received amnesty. Hoping to appeal to their humanity, Lena tried to sound unafraid. "Guys, my mother's ill," she lied. "I had to go to the central drugstore for medicine."

The big man laughed, "Ha-ha-ha! She's rushing home to her mom."

Lena answered in a soft voice, "Yes, I was in a hurry, because my mother's waiting. I didn't notice you, so please excuse me..." She started to walk around him.

The big man spread his arms out to block her passage, and his friends imitated him. "Such a sweet girl! And where does your mommy live? Over there, in the woods?" He nodded toward a stand of trees by the road. "Where, in the hen-house?"

Another hoodlum began to guffaw and gestured toward the deserted road. "Okay, show us!" The crude men now formed a cage around Lena.

"I, apparently, got lost," Lena's voice trembled. She knew she was in trouble.

"Now you'll have to go with us, beautiful maiden!" said the huge man, looking down at her like a wild bear rearing up on its haunches. "We will even bless the occasion with holy water." He took out a bottle of vodka from his jersey and with a sweeping gesture exhibited it to his circle of friends, who pulled their own bottles from their pockets.

"Let's go to that woodpile on the roadside. We'll be shielded better from the wind there," a mustachioed man shouted.

"Good idea!" the bear-like leader agreed, squeezing Lena's elbow and pushing her toward the woodpile. "Go, go, go, girl!" Seeing that some of his cohorts were groping Lena, he gave them a threatening glare. "She's mine! I found her, so I get her first..."

Chapter 1

June 1975
Village Rizovka, Northeast of Moscow

IT WAS A SUNNY summer day, and Lena Petrova, a pretty nine-year old little girl with long black braids, ran in a meadow covered with bright flowers, enjoying the hot summer weather.

Her parents rested on a nearby blanket, chatting and watching Lena pick wild daisies which opened their golden hearts toward the sky, like a million miniature reflections of the sun. She tried to find the biggest ones, and jumped from one flower to another until she had her hands full of them.

Lena approached her parents and sat down. A big smile crossed her face. She plucked one petal off a blossom, talking out loud, "He loves me, he loves me not…" The petals fell down one after another. "He'll spit, he'll kiss, to his heart he'll press, to hell he'll send, he'll call me 'his'… He loves me, he loves me not…"

Lena's mother, Varya, grabbed her daughter laughing. "And who do you have on your mind, dear?" Varya was thirty-seven years old. Her refined and aristocratic facial features were very attractive and visibly contrasted with those of the average rough-skinned peasant women in the village.

"Who is on my mind? I don't know," Lena replied, "I heard the big girls say it this way." She continued to pull off the petals.

"You are a silly girl. You need to think of someone special when you are doing this," Lena's father said, tugging at one of her long black braids. "Now tell us, who are you in love with?"

Lena squinted at her father, blinking against the bright sun. "Well, *Papa*, I'll ask the daisies about you!"

"All right, go ahead!" Kyril nodded.

Lena took another flower. "He loves me, he loves me not..." more petals fell on her lap.

Kyril burst out laughing, and embraced his wife, rolling with her on the grass. "Why don't you ask about your fortune, darling?" He looked into her dark-blue eyes.

"I know it, without flowers," Varya answered in a soft voice.

Kyril smiled and gave her a long sweet kiss. He was a good-looking man, in his early thirties. From even the slightest glance anyone knew he was a gypsy: dark-skinned, thin but athletic with lean muscles, similar to ones that long-distance runners have, with black curly hair, a hooked nose, and burning deep-brown eyes.

Lena finished pulling off the petals, "He loves me, he loves me not... HE LOVES ME!" she shouted joyfully.

Her father jumped up, and seized Lena in his strong hands, to spin her around. He whirled and whirled, until, becoming dizzy, he fell with his laughing daughter onto the grass. Kyril looked at Lena's face inquiring playfully, "Loves? Of course, loves! What else could these daisies say about your father?"

Varya joined her loved ones in their hug and the three lay close together, embracing each other for a few minutes longer.

"Let me show you how to make a wreath from these flowers," Varya said. She put the flowers on her lap and started to braid them together.

Lena watched and then began making her own wreath. Varya finished hers first, tied the ends together, and put it on Lena's head as a crown. Lena also finished her wreath and, bowing, as if her father was a king, put the wreath on his head.

Kyril laughed, "Hey, these things aren't for men. Men are supposed to wear helmets, not flowers." He took off the wreath and put it on his wife's head. "Here is where this crown belongs. Now your mother looks like a queen, doesn't she?"

"Yes, she does! My mother is so beautiful."

"Don't be born beautiful, be born fortunate," Varya said with the stern voice of a teacher. "Why do you think people say that, Lena?"

"Because it's better to be smart?"

"True. Happiness is not found in beauty. *'Beauty may open the door, but only virtue enters,'*" Varya answered.

Kyril smiled, listening to them, then turned to Lena, "Look at your mother. She is not just beautiful, but also very intelligent. Traits that came from her family." He looked into his wife's eyes, as if seeking permission to share a secret, then blurted, "Your great-grandmother was born in a noble family—"

"What?" Lena looked at her father, amazed, thinking she had heard something wrong. "What did you say? Nobles are *bourgeoisie!*"

"Stop, stop!" Varya put her palm on Kyril's hand. "Sometimes it is better to forget who you are, and just be like everyone else. Forget where your roots are, simply mix with the *proletariat* in one gray mass. It will make our life much easier, darling."

She turned to Lena, "I'll tell you that story when you are a little bit older, my daughter, when you are grown up."

Lena bit her lips, shrugged her shoulders, and nodded.

Varya looked at her watch. "It's time to go home."

The three of them left the meadow to walk down the road to their village. Lena was between her parents, each one holding her hands. She tried to swing. Kyril said, "You are too tall for that now, Lena."

"OK," Lena straightened up, still holding her parents' hands, quietly singing to herself.

"Ri-zov-ka," she read aloud from a sign on the wooden plate nailed to an ancient oak tree. "Why is our village named this way?"

"The name Rizovka came from the word *'rizik',*" Varya said.

"Remember those red pine mushrooms I brought home last year? They grow in the forest around the village," Kyril added. "It is named after them."

"How funny! Father, we have a boy in our class, named Volodya, and his hair is red. So the boys call him *'Rizik'*. Now I know why." She laughed, relieved that her father smiled too.

"It's not good to call people by nicknames," Varya said. "We must use their real names."

"I know," Lena answered. "But he is just funny, and so freckle-faced!"

"Hey! Now we know who you are in love with!" Kyril winked at his daughter, laughing.

Lena blushed, not replying, and continued walking sedately, only now with a shy smile on her lips.

Chapter 2

LENA'S MOTHER WAS THE elementary school teacher for their village. She taught all the subjects from first through fourth grade. The school had an annex that was assigned as living quarters for the teacher's family.

There was a living room and two bedrooms in the annex. The living room had the same furnishings every village house had: a huge, red-brick wood-burning fireplace, or *pech*, that served for cooking and for heating the house. The brick top of the *pech* was covered with blankets and was wide enough for two adults to sleep on, which many people did during the cold Russian winters. A wooden dining table with two benches stood in the center of the room, and a nap-bed was hidden behind the curtain by the wall, next to the *pech*. There was a bookshelf full of textbooks and teaching materials stacked behind the two glass doors, with a wooden cabinet on the bottom, where cups and dishes were kept.

When they got home, Lena filled a clay vase with water and put a bouquet of fresh daisies in it. Then she took a book from the shelf and sat by the table to read. Varya put on an apron and went outside to feed the pig and the chickens. Kyril got out his tool box and sat on the wooden stool by the window to repair his boots.

Gypsy music wafting down the street reached his ears. Kyril looked out from the open window. A young gypsy woman was singing and dancing near carts that moved slowly up the street. Lena put her book down and stepped to the window. Hugging her father's neck, she asked, "Who are those people, *Papa*?"

"They are Romany people who like their freedom." Kyril put down the boot he was repairing and sat Lena on his lap.

Lena leaned out the window to get a better look at the gypsy women, dancing in their long, bright-colored skirts.

"Their skirts are so beautiful! I've never seen anything like this!" she exclaimed, pressing her face to the window, trying to see more.

"My parents were Romany people," Kyril said. He paused. "They were killed during the war with Germany. That's why I was raised in an orphanage." Kyril gently touched Lena's curly black hair. "You've got your mother's deep blue eyes, but the rest is all my gypsy blood."

"And that's why I like to dance! Let's dance, Father!" Lena jumped down from his lap and started to imitate the gypsy's women's dance. She spread her arms apart and shook her shoulders in a snake-like movement. Kyril danced with her, lifting his hips and rolling his belly. They both laughed.

"Could you tell me more about these people, Father? They look so different, but I like them."

Kyril nodded, and then admitted, "But I don't really know much, except what I have found out in books." He went to the bookshelf and took out one of Varya's textbooks. He sat by the table, and Lena stood beside him. "Here," Kyril said, turning the pages and reading aloud.

"The origin of gypsies in the Soviet Union is tied to their earlier migration from India via Persia into Eastern Europe during the 15th century. After the October Revolution of 1917 the nomadic gypsies didn't want to break with their established way of life, with their centuries-old traditions and habits. They didn't accept the Soviet law of collectivization. They never cultivated the land, never were able to build, nor read or write."

Kyril turned the pages, but the topic of the textbook had changed. He looked down the page and read the note:

"In 1974 there were about two hundred thousand nomadic gypsies in the Russian Federation territory (about 0.07% of the Soviet Union population) who still followed their traditional occupations of metal working and music making."

Kyril closed the textbook with a sigh.

"I don't understand it, Father," Lena said sadly.

"It says here that after the Soviet Revolution gypsies were afraid to meet with the new, still unknown, way of life. The groups of gypsies traveled from one town to another."

"Don't they work?"

Kyril fingered the book, watching the crowd of people following the caravan out of the village. "The women make a living by fortune telling and the men by suspicious operations in the horse trading market," Kyril replied. "That's what people say."

"What do 'suspicious operations' mean?"

Kyril picked up his boots, he felt ashamed of his heritage. "Many people complained that their money disappeared after they stopped and talked to gypsies. That's why the *milicia* advises people to avoid any contact with gypsies."

"How sad," Lena answered quietly, sitting down on the bench. "Does that mean they are bad people?"

"In other countries, somewhere on another side of the planet, such an attitude toward the minor nationality could be called racism." Kyril looked at Lena's wide open eyes and realized that Varya wouldn't like that he discussed this topic with their daughter. "But there is no such word in our country. All these people want is to be free," he concluded.

Lena was ready to ask him something else when the door opened and Varya stepped in, holding a clay jar full of fresh and still-warm milk. She put it on the dining table and turned to Lena, saying, "Get the glasses and some bread, daughter."

Kyril went back to fixing his boots.

Varya glanced at his guilty face. "What were you talking about?"

"We talked about freedom," Lena answered, putting the empty glasses on the table.

Varya poured the milk and repeated, "Freedom? Freedom is consciousness of necessity. You'll learn it later in middle school history, Lena. Our freedom is in following the Communist Party that leads us to the great goal—Communism, when every member of our society will have a happy life."

"And what about gypsies?" Lena asked quickly.

"What about gypsies?"

"Why don't gypsies follow the Party?" Lena looked at her mother, and Varya frowned at Kyril.

He glared back. "Because the freedom of 'following the Party' is not real freedom." Kyril didn't like arguing with his wife, but he wanted to prove his point. "Would you call the horse that is tethered to the rear of the carts 'free'? Probably not. Gypsies don't want to follow the Party's direction, because it ties up their freedom. They understand freedom differently than we do."

"I saw a little foal. He ran beside his mother, who was attached to the cart!" Lena exclaimed joyfully. "I wanted to pet this foal, Father! He looked so cute…"

"It's time to sleep!" Varya announced sharply, cleaning up the table.

"Okay, okay," Lena answered, lowering her head and slowly drinking the warm milk. When Varya went to put the jar of milk outside to keep it cool, Lena jumped closer to Kyril and asked quietly, "Could we go to talk to these people some day, Father?"

"I might go there myself tonight," Kyril whispered back. "But I don't think your mother wants you to go, Lenochka." Lena sadly nodded her head, because her mother's authority was inviolable. He kissed her cheek. "Good night, my beautiful, sweet daughter."

Kyril and Varya went to bed, and Varya, tired from the long day, dozed off quickly, hugging her husband's chest. Kyril lay on his back with his eyes wide open, unable to sleep. The soft sound of gypsy music played in the distance, disturbing him, touching something deep within his soul. He always wanted to know more about his own people. He wanted to know what his mother looked like, and he wanted to find his relatives. But how would he do so? He even didn't know his real name.

There was a short note in his personal file at the orphanage which stated that he was born in 1944, during World War II. His mother was killed while shielding him from the bombing with her body. A Soviet soldier found him in the ruins, and gave the baby his own name, Kyril Petrov.

Kyril was raised in an orphanage and then he went to serve his duty in the Soviet Army. Afterwards he came to Rizovka to celebrate an army friend's birthday and met Varya at the party. Kyril and Varya fell in love at first sight and were soon married. Being raised in a Soviet school, then going through the army, Kyril didn't give much thought to his ethnic origin. The kids were told in school that all of them were *the Soviet people*, a new historic nationality, regardless of the ethnicity they belonged to.

After the wedding, it didn't take long for Kyril to realize that the old stereotypes people had about gypsies were still alive. It wasn't easy for him to live among people who wondered why a teacher, who was the moral role model for the whole village, had married a gypsy. He sincerely loved his wife and daughter, but at the same time he felt an inexplicable pain and an overwhelming desire, hidden deep in his soul, to learn about his people.

Kyril took Varya's hand off his chest to free himself, and kissed her on the cheek. She smiled in her dream.

"I'm going to go and take a look at the gypsy camp, darling," he whispered.

"It's late, time to sleep."

"You sleep, dear. I'll be back soon." He pulled on his pants and slipped quietly out the door.

The night's bright moonlit sky welcomed him. Billions of stars covered the earth like a saffron silk quilt, and they appeared so close that Kyril wanted to straighten out his arm and touch them. He felt an immediate surge of recognition that he was a part of the endless universe, part of something greater than himself.

He walked down the dark village street toward the lovely sound of guitar music.

A few minutes later Kyril approached the gypsy camp. Several fires were burning, and people were sitting around them, playing guitars and singing. A beautiful young woman noticed him. She stood up, and with a welcoming gesture, smiling teasingly, she invited Kyril to join them.

Chapter 3

VARYA WAS AWAKENED AT dawn by the crowing of roosters in the village. She turned to hug her husband, but touched Kyril's empty pillow instead. Still half-dreaming, she moved her hand down the sheet. It was cold. Varya's eyes snapped open. *Kyril's not here! He must already be up and out.* She lay on her back, quietly listening to familiar morning sounds outside the house.

The old cowherd Danila was hollering to the neighbors' cows, gathering them together while passing through the village. "Hey, Burenka," he called the neighbor's cow, who didn't want to get out from its barn, "Get out here! Quickly. Quickly!"

Varya strained to hear Kyril's friendly voice greeting the old man, but the herd passed by, bawling cows moved toward the meadow, and the morning was quiet again. Instead of going back to sleep, Varya went outside to check Kyril's workshop. It was empty. She walked over to the school, checked the building and then stood by the fence. Nobody was there. The only sign of life were the cows moving in the distance.

Back home, Varya checked Lena's room—their daughter was sleeping peacefully. Her blanket had fallen down on the floor. Kyril wasn't there. Varya quickly covered her daughter, and went outside again, worried.

She remembered Kyril said he would walk to the gypsies' camp. She ran toward it, but all she found was smoke rising from warm coals where the fires were burned. She returned to the village and asked her neighbors if anyone had seen Kyril. They only shrugged their shoulders.

Only at dusk, when the cows returned home from the fields, the old cowherd stopped by their house and waved to Varya. When she came closer, Danila looked down, obviously uncomfortable as he cleared his throat and delivered the news that sent Varya into shock.

"I saw Kyril—" he avoided Varya's eyes.

"Where is he?" Varya interrupted impatiently.

"It was before sunrise…" The old man shrugged and stepped back.

"Look at me, Danila," Varya demanded. "Tell me what you saw!"

Danila didn't dare to look at the teacher. He turned his eyes away, watching the cows wandering into the neighbors' yards.

"I saw Kyril leaving with the gypsies. He was holding a young, pretty woman around her waist." Danila spat the words out and then quickly followed the herd.

*   *   *

"Why does a good life never last long?" Varya asked herself a week later, taking from the vase the daisies that Lena had picked in the meadow—daisies that had now become lifeless, dried and brown as if from grieving. Varya sadly looked out at the gray cloudy sky that seems to be mourning with her. "Just a week ago the three of us were so happy together," she thought. "Then those gypsies came, and put their camp in the field close by…"

Lena sat on the bed with an open book she was unable to read. From time to time she glanced at her mother's sad face and thought, *What if I never see my father again?* Watching her mother throwing the dried daisies away, Lena also thought about that sunny day in the meadow when she had shouted joyfully, "He loves me!" and how her father had spun her around. She remembered how they fell into the tall grass, and he held her tightly in his arms, inquiring cheerfully, "Loves? Of course, he loves! What else could these daisies say about your father?"

A photo of Kyril holding his five-year old daughter drew Lena to the bookshelf. She stood motionless looking into her father's smiling face, and bitter tears rolled down her checks. She whispered, biting her lips, "Loves..."

She remembered the fairy tale *The Stolen Sun,* in which the little birds and animals had been horrified when a greedy alligator swallowed the sun.

You are like that sun for me, Father, she thought. *What's going to happen now? Will this darkness ever go away?*

For the past week, burdensome heavy silence lodged in their house. Love seemed to dissolve—slowly, bit-by-bit, until it simply disappeared. There were no more jokes, or laughter, or fun. All Varya and Lena had now was emptiness, filled with the sound of the ticking clock on the wall.

All that week Varya had been completely lost in her own thoughts and almost didn't talk to her daughter. By habit, she silently cooked their food, placed one plate on the table, cut some bread, and then spoke softly, "Come, daughter. You can eat now."

Varya stepped to the window and sat down on the wooden stool beside it. She looked out the window to the street. Her head was covered with a scarf, the ends of which she was using to dry off her tears.

"Mother, why don't you eat?"

"You eat, I don't want anything," Varya continued to stare out from the window.

Lena ate, dropping tears into her plate. The monotonous ticking of the clock sounded like a funeral dirge. Suddenly Lena jumped up, approached her mother, and shook Varya's shoulders. "Mother, stop crying. Please! Father will come back. You'll see, he will return! He must!"

Varya pulled away. "I'm not crying, daughter. Go outside. Take a walk." She gestured toward the door. Varya needed to be alone with her grief so she could cry freely.

Lena left, and Varya remained seated by the window, looking outside, details of her life passed through her mind.

Varya was born in Leningrad in 1937, the only child of a factory worker and a nurse, Ivan and Olga Veronsky. The oldest generation of the Veronsky family was one of the *"bourgeoisies"* whose property had been nationalized by the Soviet government after the revolution. Now the Veronskys had as little as any average Soviet citizen, and lived in the same type of communal apartment as others.

When the blockade of Leningrad began in September 1941, Varya's father was mobilized to serve in the anti-aircraft defense. Her mother continued to work at the hospital, and her grandmother sewed uniforms while staying at home with little Varya.

Varya was too small to remember the war, but surviving the blockade, hunger, and cold of the winter of 1941 affected her health for the rest of her life. As an adult, she was horrified to learn from her school books how the heroic Soviet people had survived the devastating siege.

At the beginning of almost nine hundred days of the blockade, Leningrad's population was about three million people, including four hundred thousand children. The Nazis' bombing of the city was so heavy that on just one day in September almost two hundred fires had blazed at the same time. All the main food warehouses were destroyed. Huge amounts of stored food reserves, such as grain, flour, and sugar, were wiped out in the bombings and fires. Commercial restaurants and groceries had closed, and people could receive food only with ration cards, while the amount of food available with these cards was steadily reduced.

At the beginning of November the first snow fell, but there was nobody to clean it up, and the mountains of snow gradually stopped all public transport. By the winter of 1941–1942 there was no heat, no water supply, almost no electricity, and very little food. In December 1941, in the depths of an unusually cold winter, food rations in Leningrad were at only 125 grams of bread per person, per day. And it was all anyone could receive, just this tiny piece of bread, baked half-and-half with bran, nothing else. People could get water only from the frozen river, if someone was able to walk there. In January and February of 1942, two hundred thousand people died of cold and starvation in Leningrad.

On top of that, the darkness of the short days of winter, particularly terrible in December and January, left the people dispirited. Reports of cannibalism began to appear, after all the birds, rats, and pets were eaten by the starving.

The people could get to work only on foot. It was typical to see corpses lying exposed on the streets. Varya's mother was one of those who didn't make it. She died on her way home from work one evening after a 16-hour shift at the hospital. She was buried at the wilderness place called *Piskarevka,* to which most of the dead were carried.

Only many years later was Varya able to visit Piskarevsky Cemetery, hoping to honor her mother's grave. But all she found were hundreds and hundreds of granite tombstones with only the year of death, and a Hammer and Sickle engraved on them. Varya realized that she would never find her mother's grave. Circumstances caused by the war hadn't permitted regular burials—the most important thing then had been to avoid the spread of epidemics. Wood was too valuable for heating to be used for coffins. When the blockade was finally broken in January 1944, there were fewer than five hundred thousand people left in the "ghost" city that was once the thrilling, beautiful Leningrad.

Varya was evacuated in April 1942, together with her weakened grandmother, who died a few weeks after their transport. People told that her grandmother had saved Varya's life by giving the little girl her own rations of bread. Varya was placed in an orphanage in Sverdlovsk, by the Ural Mountains, where she grew up.

In 1955, when she was leaving the orphanage at age seventeen, a director called Varya to her office and handed her a little bag, hand-made from a sack and secured with a linen cord.

"This little hand-made bag was tied around your neck when we brought you here," the director said. "Your grandmother made it. There was a note with your name in it, and this..." The director untied the cord, opened the bag, and took out a small golden cross and a pair of gold earrings. "I kept it in the safe all these years, Varya. You know, children are not supposed to have things like this. Now that you're an adult and starting your own life, I am returning what was given to you by your grandmother." The director paused. "Varya, I advise you to keep it out of people's view. You're a member of a *Komsomol* organization, and you know that an atheist can't have such symbols like this cross."

"I know," Varya said. "Thank you, Natalia Ignatievna." For the rest of her life Varya warmly remembered this elderly woman, who was a proud member of the Communist Party, but who had broken the rules for a child's sake.

Varya worked at the Sverdlovsk grocery store for a few years and studied at the university in the evenings. After graduation, as a young teacher, she was sent to work in Rizovka, where she met Kyril.

Kyril had never known his parents, and Varya also had no family. Only after many years of corresponding with the military commissariat had she found out that her father had been killed in the last days of the war and was buried in German territory, so she wasn't even able to visit his grave.

Kyril and Varya needed each other and they made a good family. Varya loved Kyril's joyful and cheerful character, and he respected her intelligence and good sense. But now, this night, she found herself sitting alone by the window, waiting for him.

What happened? Varya asked herself. *How could Kyril simply trade us for a gypsy woman and float away in a stranger's arms?* Varya desperately searched her mind for answers.

Where did he go? Why? How could he possibly leave me behind with our precious daughter, whom he adores so much? Varya felt breathless, airless, sunless.

Again and again, she tortured herself with the same questions, *Why? How could it be? How did it happen in an instant?*

With a freezing fear Varya realized that Kyril might have abandoned her. *He was taken by another woman, perhaps by an idea, one unknown to me. Even so, how could he have been so deceitful to have just run off, without even saying good-bye? He flew away, and now we are left on earth without him,* she thought.

Varya's heart squeezed from pain. *Is this how I must live out the rest of my life? What would happen if he should return one day? Could I forgive him and let him back in? Would I…?*

All of a sudden Varya came to her senses. She looked around the now dark, empty room.

"Lena?" Varya's voice was wheezy and cracked, her throat dry. No answer. She stiffly rose from the stool where she had sat for several hours. Her muscles were numb. She moved slowly, took an aluminum cup, scooped up water from the pail, and soothed her dry throat.

She turned on the light and went to Lena's room: "Are you in bed already?" The bed was empty. "Where are you, Lena?" Then she remembered sending her daughter away after dinner. Chills began to rise along her spine. Varya went out to the porch, peering hard into the darkness. "Lena?" No sound. "Lena!" More silence. "LENA!!"

Chapter 4

Lena RAN DOWN THE street toward the road, through the fields, wiping the tears from her face. She ran barefoot under the hot July sun but didn't feel the burning ground beneath her feet. She could feel nothing except the throbbing pain in her chest.

Finally tired, she slowed, but continued to go forward toward the forest far ahead. The fields ended, and now tall and wide pine trees bordered the road, hiding the sun behind their heavy, green-needled branches. Lena had never gone this far from the village on her own, but she didn't have any fear. Her father had told her that she shouldn't be afraid of animals, and Lena always felt herself a part of nature.

As she was looking at the hill in front of her, far away on the road she noticed a small figure slowly moving toward her. There was something familiar about that person, and as she came closer, Lena recognized Granny Maria, their neighbor.

Granny Maria, a small woman in her late sixties, approached Lena and stopped, looking at the girl with amazement. "What are you doing here, child? Where are you going?" she asked, putting down her basket of herbs.

Lena looked at the old woman through tears in her eyes; her face was dirty from the road's dust. She cried out in despair, "I want to find my father! I want my *papa* back home!"

Granny Maria sighed and gently embraced Lena's shoulders, trying to stop the girl, both to comfort her and to stop her from going any farther.

Lena shook off the hug, and continued walking. "I must find him, and I will!" she murmured, swallowing tears.

Lena walked away faster, and then started running. Granny Maria sadly followed Lena with her eyes, then with a determined look on her face she sat down on the dirt and yelled, "Lena! Lena! Help me, child!"

Lena turned and looked back at Granny over her shoulder. When she saw the old woman sitting on the road, she stopped, pausing for a while. Then she turned and slowly went back, asking from the distance, "What happened, Granny?"

"I hurt my foot, and I can't walk on it. Will you help me to get home, child?"

Lena looked at the old woman, and the girl's face displayed her mental turmoil. She said regretfully, "Granny... I must go."

She took a few more small steps forward, looking back at Maria at the same time. Finally, her kind nature won the inner battle, and Lena replied, turning back, "Well, I will help you, Granny."

Lena took Granny Maria's hands and helped the old woman up. Maria pretended she couldn't walk on her foot. Lena lent her shoulder for support and took Granny's basket to carry. They slowly walked back toward the village. Granny Maria was glad she was able to stop Lena from running away. She hid a quick self-satisfactory smile, and then asked, "Are you hungry, Lena?"

"Just a little bit," the girl admitted, nodding while sobbing. "But it doesn't matter. I will help you and then I will go back. I must find him, Granny."

"I baked a cherry pie this morning. I think it is your favorite kind," the elderly woman said cheerfully. Lena didn't answer, just sighed, walking slowly under Granny Maria's weight.

Maria looked closely at Lena, "So, you want to find your father?"

"Yes," Lena said quietly.

"It won't be easy to do, and you might need some help. Would you let me be your friend and help you?"

Lena sighed again, "Yes, Granny Maria."

They returned to the village at dusk. Lena helped Maria to her house.

"Sit down, Lena. Rest." Granny Maria moved the wooden bench closer to the dining table.

Lena sat at the table, and Granny Maria poured milk into a mug and cut the cherry pie.

"Have some pie, Lenochka. But wash your hands and face first." She gave Lena a piece of soap and poured water on her hands, and then gave her a clean, home-made towel with bright flowers embroidered on its ends.

Lena sat back at the table, sadly looking at the pie, but not touching it. "My mother doesn't cook as well as you, Granny Maria. And she never bakes." She sighed. "I think my mother doesn't love me anymore." She shared her fear in a bitter whisper.

"That is not true," Granny Maria said, pushing the plate with the pie closer to Lena. "Eat. You should never think this way about your mother. Varya loves you." Granny Maria paused, as if she was deciding how best to say the next words. "She loves you, Lena. But in her own way, do you understand?"

Lena nodded and sipped some milk from the cup. She liked the way Granny Maria explained the things to her.

"I grew up in a big family. I always had both a father and mother, and many brothers and sisters around me. And Varya… your mother, was raised in an orphanage. No one loved her the way my mother loved me, and she simply doesn't know how to show you her love." Granny Maria poured more milk into Lena's cup and added, "And cooking and baking is not a big deal at all. I will teach you everything! And you will be the best bride in the village!" She concluded cheerfully, seeing that Lena was nodding her head, smiling.

Lena drank her milk, and then slowly, taking pleasure from every bite, ate the pie. She looked at the old woman's kind face and asked, "Granny Maria, where is your family now and why don't you have your own kids?"

Granny Maria took out the comb and began to unbraid Lena's hair. "Let me comb your hair, child." She carefully touched Lena's thick, tangled hair. "My family? We lived in Belarus and my whole family was killed in one of the night bombardiers' attacks. I don't have my own kids because of the war. We got married just before the war started, and then my husband was killed." The old woman sighed. "After the war… you know, not many men came back."

"Yes, I know. They told us at school that more than twenty million Soviet people were killed during the World War II," Lena replied.

"That's why we have many more women than men."

"Right, Granny."

Maria finished braiding Lena's hair and said with a smile, "But such a beauty as you won't have a problem finding a husband when you grow up!"

Lena didn't answer, tiredly bending her head down to the table.

"Do you want to sleep here tonight? I could put you on my bed. I sleep mostly on my *pech* anyway."

Lena gratefully nodded her head; she was too tired to answer. Granny Maria understood her better than anyone else. Maria put the girl on her bed, and a minute later Lena was asleep.

Maria stood by the bed, sadly looking at Lena's face and then turned to go out, murmuring, "Your mother must be going crazy looking for you."

She went out and was almost knocked down by Varya running up to her.

"Maria, have you seen Lena?"

Maria stopped Varya with a gesture, "She's all right now. Let's sit down here on the steps, Varya."

Varya obediently sat down, feeling relived that Lena was safe, but she was angry at Lena's behavior and said harshly, "She will be punished for not coming home before dark! Where is she?"

The old woman looked at Varya disapprovingly and answered in a firm voice, "You shouldn't be so hard on your daughter, Varya. I know you are a teacher and were taught how to discipline kids, but it won't work with Lena, not now at least. She's a good girl. She loves her father and feels heartbroken right now. She was hurt badly by his abandonment. She wanted to find him." Maria looked at now silent Varya, and added quietly, "I found her in the forest, far away from the village."

"In the forest?" Varya repeated, amazed.

"Yes. She was running away, trying to find her father."

Chapter 5

NEITHER VARYA NOR LENA knew how to react to Kyril's disappearance. He had always been the center of their little universe. Both his wife and daughter adored him unconditionally and unintentionally competed for his love, smile, and kiss. Now they felt as if he had suddenly died, although in truth, he could come back and show up at the house at any time. This uncertainty was worse than if he were dead.

Nothing could compensate Kyril's cheerful character, his laugh and joy for life. Varya felt betrayed, but she didn't want to say anything bad about Kyril. That is why she wouldn't talk with Lena about her father. Their grief was unbearable; it caused Varya and Lena to drift further apart, making their life even harder.

For years they'd been dreaming of building their own house, but now, without a man, it would be impossible. All their dreams they had shared together were gone.

In a small village like Rizovka, the school teacher was a person whose life was open to everyone's view and judgment. As the most educated person, the teacher was an example by which ordinary people measured themselves.

Before Kyril vanished, Varya was always beautiful and elegant, with bright lipstick on her lips. She was the subject of jealousy and envy of all the peasant women in the village. Tall and slender with her beautiful dark-blue eyes, the teacher had always dressed in the fashion of a city-dweller and talked as "a scientist," and for some inexplicable reason, she did not put on weight as they did. Probably because of this envy, Varya had no close girlfriends: people felt Varya didn't belong to them, wasn't like them, the ordinary village residents.

Now, after her husband ran away, Varya was pale, with her hair carelessly pulled back in a bun. Frequently she wore the same dress for a whole week. Varya looked tired, and much older than her years.

The teacher's life became the most frequent subject for the women's gossip. One day, walking by the well, Lena overheard the whispers of women talking behind her back, "How will the teacher manage her life without a husband? Even if she finds someone, she can't get married without being divorced first. And she can't be divorced without Kyril coming back."

Lena stopped and turned to the women, her eyes shining furious as she stared at them. "Stop talking about my mother!" she screamed. Ashamed, the women turned away from her.

Lena walked faster, not taking her eyes off the ground. She didn't want to hear anything bad about her mother. She loved Varya and wanted to protect her. Lena knew she had to become the same source of positive energy as Kyril used to be. She had his looks: curly black hair and his quick smile that would appear easily at any joke. She had his outgoing character and loved the simple life they had, with no complaints about anything.

The young girl took upon her tiny shoulders the enormous burden of comforting her grieving mother, and she was determined to carry it out. But what she didn't know was that every time she tried to cheer up her mother, telling her about the book she just read or new joke she had heard, this open happy smile on her face immediately reminded Varya of the man who betrayed her. This intolerable pain of having Lena as a constant remembrance living beside her was like a ticking mechanism placed inside Varya's body, waiting for its time to explode.

*   *   *

One year had passed since Kyril left them. It was the end of Lena's fourth year at the elementary school, the beginning of summer. The day was warm and sunny, and the pleasant smell of blooming purple and white lilac bushes drifted through the open window of the schoolroom.

Lena sat at the last desk, watching a couple of puppies playing outside in the school yard. For her age, she was far ahead of her schoolmates, often knowing the lessons before they were taught. Lena already had received all her grades, but had to remain in class anyway, as the school rules required.

Varya stood by the blackboard, writing down the math problems from the final exam and explaining common mistakes.

Suddenly the growing sound of gypsy music could be heard from the street, and gypsy carts appeared, moving down the road. Students ran to the windows to watch.

"Sit down! Get back to your seats!" Varya demanded, but the children stood by the windows, paying no attention to her. When all the carts had passed, they finally went to their seats, still talking about the gypsies.

Varya stood by the board watching the carts, too. Her face became pale, but she turned to the blackboard and tried to continue her explanations. She suddenly stopped writing, frowned, and raised her hand to her chest. Slumping forward, she lost her grip on the chalk, and stumbled to a chair by her desk, falling awkwardly into it.

Lena ran to her.

"Mother, what's wrong?"

"Chest pain. Get me some water. Call the doctor," Varya whispered.

Lena stormed out of the classroom.

The doctors said that Varya had suffered a heart attack. They kept her at the hospital for three weeks. Meanwhile Lena stayed at Granny Maria's house. They were lucky that it had happened at the end of the school year and all students' grades had been reported to the school district already. After returning from the hospital, Varya spent most of her time in the house.

Granny Maria visited them every day, bringing fresh milk from her cow. One afternoon she put the jar with milk on the table and turned to Lena's mother. "How do you feel? I brought you some milk and cabbage soup."

"Thank you. You're such a good neighbor, Maria," Varya replied quietly.

Granny Maria poured some milk into a cup and gave it to Varya.

"You shouldn't take it so hard. The doctor said we could lose you if you have another heart attack. Be careful. You have a daughter to raise."

Varya's eyes instantly filled with tears and she cried, "I know it. But I need my husband too. I can't live without him..."

The old woman looked at Varya strictly and declared in a firm tone, "You must. And you will."

*   *   *

Two years went by and they still hadn't heard anything about Kyril. When a gypsy tribe passed through the village again, Granny Maria went to their camp and asked if they ever had met Kyril. But the gypsies had never heard such a name, never seen him. "He was bewitched by a love potion," was the only suggestion she heard from them.

The neighbors continued gossiping. Lena didn't like hearing dirty hints about her mother, but it wasn't in her power to stop them. Gradually, the severity of her mother's character transferred itself to Lena: she also began avoiding people, hiding in her room and reading books.

Lena enjoyed reading fairy tales the most. She loved having the same name as a princess in a fairy tale: "Elena-the-Beautiful" and "Elena-the-Wisest." Lena knew she was pretty. She loved her long black curly hair, and she also knew that she was smart. No wonder it was easy for Lena to equate herself with a fairy tale princess. She expected that her life would also, one day, change from sadness and drudgery and develop into a fantastic scenario.

Lena was eleven years old when one of their neighbors had a big wedding. Everyone from their village was invited, and visitors came in from other places. Lena was helping in the kitchen, taking food to the table, cleaning and washing the dishes. There were so many guests that neighbors had to offer their houses for some visitors to stay in overnight.

"Mother, I want to go home," Lena said, seeing that Varya was still busy helping in the neighbor's kitchen.

"You go. I have to remain here and wait for the people who will stay at our house tonight," her mother replied.

Their home was close by, and Lena wasn't afraid to go alone. She didn't notice a man who was following her on the dark street.

Tired of vanity and the unusual cares of the wedding, Lena came home and fell into bed. She didn't have the strength to pull off her dress, and dozed off instantly. Suddenly, she was awakened from a nightmare, choking on something sticky and smelly that covered half of her face. Scared, Lena tried to free herself from the massive drunken body of a stranger who was pushing her down into the mattress.

The man was much stronger than Lena. He whispered, "Let me kiss you, my beauty, I've dreamed of that all day long." Lena choked on the man's saliva. The huge man lifted his head to allow Lena to breathe, then quickly closed her mouth with his palm. "You better be silent, if you don't want to get in trouble." Lena was unable to move under his heavy body. "I shall play with you for a little bit, and then you'll go," the drunken peasant assured her, thrusting his thick hand under her dress.

The dress Lena hadn't taken off saved her. The drunk, confused by the ruffles and ribbons, had to shift sideways to reach her underwear. Lena, taking advantage of his slowness, quickly slid off the bed and crawled under it.

The drunkard couldn't see anything in the dark. He stumbled out of the door, looking for Lena, who was nestled close to a wall, shivering. She stayed there until she heard Varya enter the house with the guests. Lena returned to her bed, and slid under the blanket.

Lena was afraid to tell her mother about this incident. She wasn't sure how Varya would react, and she didn't want to upset her mother, and cause another heart attack. Lena kept this bitter secret to herself. Her young girl's dream about a wonderful prince and her first kiss had been crushed, and lost forever. Lena matured visibly after this night. Her childhood had unexpectedly ended with that stinking, dirty kiss and she understood now why it was better not to be born beautiful.

Chapter 6

LENA TRIED TO HELP her mother as much as she could. She wiped the floor, fed the chickens, washed dishes, and did anything Varya asked her to do. Noticing that they had used all the water, Lena took the bucket and went out. Normally it was her mother who brought the water from the well, but this time Lena decided to try it on her own.

Lena hung the bucket on the chain, and dropped it down. She looked into the deep, dark well, making sure that the bucket was full, and then she started to slowly turn the well handle. She lifted up the bucket full of water and held the well handle, trying to grab the bucket with her other hand. Her small hand couldn't hold the heavy bucket, which suddenly fell down, splashing the water; the well handle sprang back up and almost hit her. She jumped back just in time, and then stood looking at the spinning handle until it stopped.

Volodya, a thirteen-year-old boy with a round, angelic face, and sky-blue eyes, whose red hair turned to a straw-like color under the hot summer sun, was passing by when he saw Lena struggling at the well. He rushed to help her. The two of them managed to pull out the bucket, and then carried it together to Lena's home.

"Do you want to go mushroom hunting with us tomorrow morning?" Volodya asked, helping Lena put the heavy bucket onto a bench.

"Sure I do!" Lena answered excitedly. "Who's going?"

"Just three of us guys."

"Guys? No adults? Aren't you afraid of getting lost?"

Volodya smiled. "No. We have been there so many times that I know every path in the forest. We'll go at dawn; can you wake up that early?"

"Sure I can!" Lena was glad to get a chance to bring home some mushrooms. "Please come over and knock on my window. I'll ask my mother. I'm sure she will let me go with you."

The northern Moscow region normally has warm, somewhat humid summers and long, cold winters. The warmest months are July and August, with temperatures reaching into the high twenties in Celsius. The cold winter, when the land is covered with snow up to two hundred days a year, is followed by a short summer, which is greatly appreciated and loved by everyone.

There are up to forty varieties of edible mushrooms commonly found in the Moscow region. The best of them are *belie*—the white ones. Also common are *chernushki,* black ones, and *lisichki,* which mean "little foxes." Others have picturesque names like *podosinovik*—"under-the-aspen-tree," *podberezovik*—"under-the-birch-tree," and *maslyonok*—the "slippery" one.

Mushrooming is hard work. People get up early in the morning and go deep into the wild forest—the farther the better, as there are always many competitors all going out with the same goal, and as usual, the quickest one is the winner. Those who sleep late will find only low-cut mushroom stems sticking up from the ground.

The next morning Volodya knocked on Lena's window. The curtains moved, and she waved excitedly to him. The next minute Lena appeared outside. She was wearing an old sweater with long sleeves—absolutely necessary to protect against angry mosquitoes. Her head was covered with a kerchief, and she wore waterproof boots. She carried a big basket with a knife, a sandwich, and a bottle of water in it.

Volodya critically observed Lena's "ammunition," and nodded with satisfaction. "It's good. I'll make you a stick when we get to the forest." Two other boys waited for them on the street.

"Why do I need a stick?" Lena quivered, almost running, trying to match Volodya's pace.

Volodya looked at her with a supercilious smile. "I can tell that you have never mushroomed before. You don't want to step on a snake, do you?"

"Snake?" Lena asked fearfully. She had forgotten about the snakes.

"Don't worry; they aren't too bad. I'll show you how to recognize the poisonous ones, and I will be close by."

They walked for about two hours on a road between the fields and then finally turned onto a narrow path which was hidden by high grass.

"Not so many people know this path. My father showed it to me," Volodya said proudly. He looked at Lena and added, "I don't show this path to just anybody. It will be our secret place, promise?"

"Yes," Lena nodded agreeably. They picked their way through swampy wet thickets, crouching to avoid getting jabbed by dry branches. Finally Volodya stopped, took out a knife from his pocket, and went closer toward an alder bush. He reached for the branches, chose the strongest, cut it off, and quickly peeled off the leaves. He gave the stick to Lena, and then made one for himself. The other boys were making sticks, also.

"We can eat our breakfast now. There are so many mushrooms this year that you better have your basket ready," Volodya said, as they all sat on the grass to eat.

A green frog jumped in the grass, and one of the boys grabbed it in his hands and began examine it.

"Has anyone ever tried to fry the frogs?" he asked his friends, and saw their faces twisted in squeamishness.

"I read that it is a delicacy in France. People there eat fried frog's legs," Lena said.

"No way!" another boy exclaimed, spitting in disgust. The others laughed at him.

"You don't know the forest, so stay close to me," Volodya told Lena as he stood up. "I am not worried about the boys—they've been here many times. You do know how to recognize poison mushrooms, right?"

"Of course. Every child knows that. Do you think I'm stupid?" Lena raised her eyebrows.

"Okay, okay!" Volodya smiled, effortlessly tossing his hair over his shoulder. "I just didn't want you taking home a basket full of fatal *poganok*."

Volodya moved forward, poking the fallen leaves with his stout stick. Lena followed him, looking on the ground and under the trees.

"Here! I found one!" one of the boys yelled from behind some trees, and immediately another one replied, "I've got three of them here!"

Lena saw Volodya kneel and she rushed to him. He stopped her with a gesture, "Be careful! Watch under your feet!"

Lena looked down and couldn't suppress her gladness. "Ah!" A small sturdy white mushroom was right at her feet, and she had almost stepped on it. Lena knelt and plucked off the brown leaf that hid the mushroom top.

"It looks so lovely!" she whispered to herself.

Volodya glanced at her, "Cut off the stem with a knife carefully. We have to leave the roots in the ground for new mushrooms to grow."

"I know that," Lena answered, clipping the stem. She brought the mushroom to her nose and smelled it, closing her eyes with pleasure. "Oh. It smells as fresh as early dew on the grass, and as damp as old moss at the same time!"

Volodya cut a few mushrooms and put them into his basket. "It's a white mushroom family here. Walk around and look carefully; I'm sure we can find more."

Lena, still on her knees, looked around and immediately saw two small mushrooms hidden under the fallen leaves. "Yes! I see them!" she replied, quickly jumping to her next trophies.

"Hey!" one of the boys yelled, checking on his friends.

"A-u!" his friend shouted.

"Here!" Volodya yelled back to them.

A few hours later, all the birch-bark baskets were full. "We've done well today!" Volodya concluded. He looked at the empty bottle in his hand and asked, "Does anyone have any water left? I'm so thirsty…"

His friends shook their heads, "No."

Volodya led his group out of the forest. "My father once showed me a little brook; it's on the way home. I hope it didn't dry up yet."

The others trailed behind Volodya, bending down under the heavy baskets on their backs. Minutes later Volodya stopped and knelt down at a narrow gully with muddy water in it. He started ladling out water with his hands.

"You can't drink this water! It's dirty and full of germs!" Lena yelled.

"Germs?" Volodya's blue eyes twinkled. "Where?" He ladled water into his palms and observed it closely. "Hmm. I don't see any!" He watched Lena as he sipped water from his hands.

His friends laughed and followed his example. Lena sighed, looking at the boys, but said nothing more and refused to drink.

"So, how do you like to eat your mushrooms?" Volodya asked his exhausted friends on the way home, trying to cheer them up.

"I like mushroom soup the most, I think," Lena answered.

"With potato, pearl-barley, onions, and carrots in it," one of the boys agreed with Lena. "My mother makes such a tasty soup! And she also marinates and pickles mushrooms for the winter."

"My parents save mushrooms for winter, but we dry them," the other boy joined the conversation.

"With our long winters, you'll have to make dozens of trips, not just this one," Volodya answered. "And my favorite meal is potatoes, fried with mushrooms and onions!"

Everyone nodded, "Oh, Yes!" The boys rubbed their stomachs and grinned at each other.

"We are almost home!" Volodya said, as the village came into view. Now on the sandy road they could take off their heavy boots—it was so much easier to walk barefoot.

Later that day Lena and her mother sat together sorting and cleaning the mushrooms.

"You did a good job," Varya said.

"It's because of Volodya. He knows really good places. But it's our secret now."

"Really?" Varya smiled. "And you won't tell me where this place is?"

"I promised not to," Lena answered.

"It's okay, don't worry. You can keep *that* a secret. I don't mind." Varya patted Lena's shoulder.

"Mother, Volodya told me that he is also going to work in the collective farm field tomorrow and asked if I wanted to go. May I?"

Varya looked at Lena. "In the field? But you're only twelve, daughter. Volodya is at least a year older, and he's a strong boy."

"He said they will get paid for that job at the end of summer. He is working to buy books and clothes for school. And I need those too, right?"

Varya sighed. "That is true."

"May I go to work tomorrow, please?" Lena looked into Varya's eyes, begging. "I do need a school dress, and books, and a coat."

"Well. I can't argue with you. You can go!"

"Thank you, Mother!" Lena hugged Varya and kissed her on the cheek. "Are we making my favorite mushroom soup tonight?" she asked.

Her mother nodded. "If you wish."

"And potatoes fried with mushrooms and onions?"

"Are you so hungry? Yes, of course, why not? You deserve it, Alena!" Varya laughed, looking at her smiling daughter.

Lena felt happy hearing her mother laughing again. *Maybe now things would get better,* she thought.

Chapter 7

THE NEXT MORNING LENA and Volodya signed up to work in the collective farm fields. The teenagers, together with other peasants, sat on the back of the truck that took them to the fields. There they were divided into groups that spread out across the land where the cut grass had been left on the ground for drying.

The teenagers walked with rakes, spreading out dry hay, and putting it into piles. Men and women followed them, picking up the bundles with pitchforks and making a huge haystack.

The peasants had been working non-stop for several hours under the burning sun, when a man's voice finally yelled, "Break time!"

The people dropped their tools, walked to the haystack, and sat in its shade. Someone spread out a clean linen cloth, making a common table, where everyone put their food to share. There were rye-bread sandwiches with salted fatty pork, boiled eggs, fresh cucumbers, and green onions. Volodya sat beside Lena. Lena drank from her glass bottle and then spat it out with a grimace.

Volodya looked at her. "What did you drink?"

"I brought some milk, but it turned sour."

He smiled. "It's too hot for milk to stay fresh. I have some tea left, if you want it."

Lena took his bottle and drank. A few people lay down around the haystack to relax. Volodya pointed to the nearby forest, and suggested to Lena, "Let's go there. Maybe we'll find some berries."

"All right, I'll go with you," Lena agreed. They got up and went toward the woods.

Varya was lying on the bed when the door opened wide, and Lena ran toward her mother, holding two baby rabbits.

"Mother, look what we found in the forest!"

Varya looked at the rabbits. "They're so small! What are you going to do with them?"

"We want to keep them. Volodya said he will make a cage for them…"

Lena looked at Volodya, and he nodded, "Yes, I will."

Lena continued, "Volodya said they grow so fast that we might have more of them in a few months!"

"When they are big enough, we'll have meat to eat, and fur to make the hats!" Volodya added.

"They're so cute! Can't we just keep them, not kill them?" Lena asked, petting the rabbits.

Volodya didn't answer, but turned to the door. "Let's go outside to make a cage."

Lena followed him.

In the back yard Volodya, working with a hammer that he had brought from home, made a cage. Lena sat on the wooden step-ladder, holding the rabbits on her lap.

"Now I'll fix a little door here… it's done! You can put them in." Volodya placed the cage on the ground, holding its door open. Lena let the rabbits in but didn't close the cage's door in time; one rabbit slipped out and ran away.

"Oh! Volodya! He ran away! Catch him!" Lena screamed.

Volodya ran behind the rabbit and fell down on the ground, trying to catch it.

"He ran here, behind the bush!" Lena followed the rabbit. Volodya ran too; they both jumped behind the rabbit, laughing.

"I've got it!" Volodya stood up, holding the rabbit by the ears. Lena smiled happily at her friend.

Lena worked the whole summer, and at the end of August she proudly brought home her salary. "Mother, look! Here are twelve rubles and fifty-six kopeks I've earned!" She handed her money to Varya. "Would it be enough to buy me a new school uniform?"

Varya hugged her daughter with tears in her eyes. "The dress costs around four–five rubles, and we also need two aprons, the coat, and the books. It's a huge help for me, daughter. I'm so proud of you." Varya kissed Lena. "We'll take a bus to the district store tomorrow and will try to buy everything you need for school."

The next day Lena stood in the middle of the room in a new school uniform: a brown dress and a black apron, which were two to three sizes bigger than necessary. Lena looked in a mirror, and pronounced with tears in her voice, "I look ugly in this dress, mother!"

Varya stood up from the bench, approached Lena, kneeled, and tried to fold up the bottom of Lena's dress. She checked the long sleeves, and pronounced in a soft but firm voice, "I'll sew it up, and nobody will see it. This dress will be good for the next year and maybe even longer."

Lena sighed. She didn't argue, only pouted. She had worked so hard for the money and she wanted to look pretty for Volodya. *He loves me... I feel he does,* she thought. Maybe he was that special boy she had been dreaming about—could he be her Prince?

Lena liked her new school, although it was located in another village, and she had to ride a bus every morning that required getting up at six o'clock. They had a separate teacher for every subject, and there were thirty-two students in their class. Lena became the best student; teachers liked her for her good behavior and advanced performance. She often helped other students, explaining math to them or the most difficult rules of the Russian language.

As always in autumn, the students of the middle and high school were assigned to work in the fields, helping the adults gather the potato harvest. Everyone knew that winter would be coming soon, and people could be found nowhere else but in the fields picking up potatoes behind the tractors.

Winter was an especially hard time for the students, as the arrival of the school bus became unpredictable. No one ever knew if they would be able to get to school in the winter time—the driver might not show up to work, or the bus might be broken down, or the weather might be so cold that the water froze in the radiator.

On one such winter morning Lena stood waiting for the bus. She wore an old topcoat that she had grown out of, and she had a new rabbit fur hat on her head. Volodya stood beside her; he also wore a new rabbit fur hat with ear-flaps. Two other teenagers stood on the side of the road waiting. Volodya shifted from one foot to another, rubbing his hands and ears, then looked at his watch. "It's very cold this morning. The bus might not come at all..." he said.

"Great! Let's go home!" one of the boys offered.

Lena also looked at her watch, "Yes, we've been waiting for thirty minutes, but we could walk to school, and if we went fast, we could be on time for the second hour."

Volodya looked at Lena with wide eyes. "Lena, it's six kilometers away! And we don't even know if the road was cleaned up—it was snowing the whole night!"

"I know how far the school is, but I don't want to miss my classes. I am going." Lena turned and marched down the road. The boys stared at her. "What?" One of them twirled his finger by his ear. "She's crazy!"

"Lena! Wait!" Volodya ran after her.

The other boys looked at him with ironic smiles. "And he's crazy too. I'm going home," one of them said, and his friend nodded. Both turned and went in the opposite direction.

Chapter 8

August 1979, Yalta

CENTRAL MILITARY SANATORIUM WAS one of the oldest health centers and the most prestigious vacation place where only well-paid people could afford to stay. The sanatorium was located in the small town of Gurzuf, eighteen kilometers from Yalta, on the shore of the picturesque Gurzuf Bay. The building was comfortably hidden from curious views in the nineteenth-century town park, behind tall cypresses and blooming magnolias, among fountains and sculptures. The sea was right there—just one hundred meters from the residence.

Victor Nevorov, a thirty-year-old Soviet Army officer, proudly brought his young, lovely wife Tamara there for their honeymoon. He had recently returned from four years of service on the Soviet military base in China, and was enjoying his long-anticipated and hard-earned vacation.

He had met Tamara five years earlier, after his graduation from the military academy. Tamara was a student at the music conservatory at that time, and couldn't go with Nevorov to China. During Victor's time of service, the two young people sent hundreds of letters to each other, and now, finally, could enjoy their marriage.

Although one could never know where his military duties might send him, Nevorov hoped that this time he might stay in Kiev. Both he and Tamara wanted to have a child soon.

It was their third day in Gurzuf, and Victor couldn't get enough of the beautiful summer weather and the warm water of the Black Sea. He woke Tamara early, saying "Darling, let's go to the beach before it gets too hot there. You're not used to this climate, and I am afraid your skin might get burned in the sun."

"But I've gotten sunburned already," she answered, stretching out her reddened arms.

Victor observed his wife's skin and said, "You can stay in the shade under an umbrella today." He looked at his wife with begging eyes. "I really want to swim!" He jokingly kneeled on one leg, and took Tamara's hands in his, "Please! Go with me, my love!"

"Okay, okay!" Tamara laughed at his overly dramatic pose.

They left the room and walked to the beach, holding hands. Tamara had long black hair, as do most Ukrainian girls, and soft, peach-like skin. Her big brown eyes, fringed with long black eyelashes, twinkled as she laughed happily, listening to Victor and glancing with admiration at her tall, well-built husband. They looked so happy together that even people in the street turned and stared at the handsome, carefree couple.

Victor loved to swim and fully enjoyed the waters of the Black Sea. He was getting out of the water and walking toward his wife, waving to her and smiling, when he noticed a young soldier whose face was red from the heat. The soldier was sweating, unable to take off his uncomfortable uniform. He walked slowly, and his heavy boots sank in the wet sand. He was looking attentively at the people in the water, and at those lying on the beach, searching, trying to find someone.

The young soldier finally spotted the two-meters-tall commander with shoulders as broad as two men. He rushed toward Nevorov, saluted, and then asked, "Comrade Captain, may I speak?"

Victor took his towel from the sand, dried himself off, and then nodded, "Yes. Speak."

"I have an order for you to return to the Base, Comrade Captain." The soldier opened his bag, took out a brown package, and gave it to Nevorov.

Nevorov looked at the envelope, then back at the soldier. "What's going on?"

"Urgent training."

Victor glanced at his wife, knowing that she wouldn't like what he was going to tell her.

*   *   *

Two days later Victor Nevorov arrived at the military training base hidden deep in the wide forest on the north of the Ukraine. The base was full of young officers waiting to be interviewed by a representative from Moscow. They laughed, talked to each other, and were very relaxed.

Dozens of green-brown military tents were set up under the trees and each served a different purpose. One of them was being used as an office for the representative from Moscow. During the week, two thousand young officers would be interviewed, and special commands would be formed. The officers had no idea what they were being prepared for. Everything was conducted in strict secrecy.

Nevorov sat on the grass under the tree and observed the officers who were coming out from the tent after being interviewed. "I am wondering what this is all about," he addressed a young lieutenant, who was passing by.

Lieutenant Sergey, a handsome twenty-two-year-old man, with black-hair, dark brown eyes, and a lean athletic body, sat down next to Victor. Quick to smile, he was the kind of person people instinctively liked and trusted. Sergey looked at Victor and shrugged his shoulders, "I wonder too. They asked such strange questions, as if this training was somewhere overseas."

"Shall we buy black sunglasses, white shirts, and cream trousers?" Nevorov asked jokingly, and both men laughed. "It would be nice to serve as advisers in a resort in a southern country, maybe at the ocean," he continued. He closed his eyes, dreaming of the place where he could continue his interrupted honeymoon with Tamara.

Later that day all the officers stood in a line in front of another tent, filled with military ammunition. Each of them received spotty-colored camouflage uniform, automatic weapons, and ten hand-grenades, which the soldiers called "lemons."

Nevorov exited the military tent, the Kalashnikov automat hanging on his shoulder. He held a belt of cartridges in one hand, silent and special night-vision war devices in another. He approached Sergey, who sat under the tree studying his weapon.

"So what do you think, Sergey?"

Sergey put down the AK-47, reached for a pack of *Belomor*, and offered the cigarettes to Nevorov. They smoked silently, watching the others getting their ammunition. Then Sergey stood up and slung the Kalashnikov over his shoulder. His face was serious. "I'm afraid we are going to Afghanistan, Comrade Captain."

*   *   *

That night four heavy military-transport planes "IL-76" landed in Kazakhstan. The Soviet Army soldiers in full gear jumped out of the planes. A few minutes later they sat in the truck which delivered them to the Kazakhstan military air-forces base. There, officers were trained in conditions that approximated those where they would be sent in the near future. During this time the officers' families knew nothing about the location of their loved ones. The Army's command wouldn't tell women the truth, saying only that their husbands and brothers were out for the regular military training exercises.

Preparation of a command was intensive. The commanders studied new, just recently received automatic weapons, and practiced how to use hand-grenades by throwing them into the target. They trained in tactical exercises, such as how to neutralize leaders of gangs in settlements, putting special emphasis on shooting.

Each commander was checked for his stability and courage. They were also tested on psychological preparation for extreme situations. Not all of them were able to pass such checks. One of the high-ranking officers refused to fly at the last minute. His comrades called him a coward. They might not have understood his fear of leaving his wife a widow, and his recently born daughter an orphan.

Captain Nevorov and Lieutenant Sergey passed the quality round. Now would come the real test, as measured by Generalissimo Suvorov, who had won the war with Napoleon, and used to say, "It is hard in training, but easy in fight." The future would tell if the words of the Great Russian Commander would come true this time.

Chapter 9

December 1979, Moscow

PEOPLE OFTEN SAY IT is hard to understand Russia and the Russian character, as it seems to be filled with contradictions. The Russian character can be servile and imperious, warm-hearted and cruel, hospitable and xenophobic, emotional and restrained, suspicious and fatalistic, fearful yet reckless. Indeed, many national policies can only be understood by reference to the "ubiquitous Russian character."

Patriotism in the Soviet Union had no boundaries. Children were brought up from kindergarten to honor the motherland, to respect their leaders, to treat Lenin with religious reverence. Russian people joked about the Party, the leaders, and the communist system, but they did not make fun of their country.

It is not the Russian soul that must be blamed for its mysteriousness, but rather the incentives and actions of the dozen men entrenched behind the high Kremlin walls in the center of the Russian capital. These members of the Politburo were obsessed to the point of paranoia with secretiveness, as with something indispensable to their continuous existence. The most important and often tragic decisions, which affected lives of thousands, were made in such conspiracy that simple people never knew about them.

In the period from March to October 1979, the Politburo of the Communist Party held several meetings discussing the situation in Afghanistan. They exchanged opinions regarding the requests from the

Afghan government to send in Soviet troops, and every time the leaders came to the consensus that such a step would be impermissible.

However, in October, following the physical removal of the President of the People's Democratic Party of Afghanistan Nur Taraki, by another member of the party Hafizullah Amin, the situation has changed. The push to change their former point of view about sending Soviet troops to Afghanistan came after American military ships were stationed in the Persian Gulf in the fall of 1979. Next followed the information about preparations for a possible American invasion of Iran, which threatened to radically change the military-strategic situation in the region, to the detriment of the interests of the Soviet Union.

The members of Politburo gathered for an urgent meeting in the Kremlin. "If the United States can allow itself to do such things tens of thousands of kilometers away from their territory in the immediate proximity of the USSR borders, why then should we be afraid to defend our positions in neighboring Afghanistan?" Dmitry Ustinov, seventy-one-year-old Defense Minister, asked other members of the Politburo.

Yuri Andropov, sixty-five years old, who at that time was Chairman of the USSR KGB, was tapping his pencil on the desk. He looked down at his papers and slowly answered, "By direct order of H. Amin, fabricated rumors were deliberately spread throughout the Democratic Republic of Afghanistan, smearing the Soviet Union and casting a shadow on the activities of Soviet personnel in Afghanistan, who have now been restricted in their efforts to maintain contact with Afghan representatives."

He browsed through his papers, put some of them down, and continued to read from the selected ones. "At the same time, efforts were made to mend relationships with America as a part of the 'more balanced foreign policy strategy' adopted by H. Amin. H. Amin held a series of confidential meetings with the American charge d'affaires in Kabul."

Leonid Brezhnev, seventy-three-year-old General Secretary of the Communist Party, took leadership and announced, "In this extremely difficult situation, which has threatened the gains of the April revolution and the interests of maintaining our national security, it has become necessary to render additional military assistance to Afghanistan, especially since such requests had been made by the previous administration of Afghanistan."

Andrei Gromyko, seventy-year-old minister of Foreign Affairs, the most respected by the ordinary people and all members of the Politburo, raised his hand. "I have to let you know, comrades, that among the leadership of the General Staff, the idea of sending troops to Afghanistan did not inspire any enthusiasm. Many of my colleagues refer to the American experience in Vietnam and warning that it will be hard for us to succeed in Afghanistan without bringing in additional troops. We won't be able to help the Afghanistan government without substantially weakening the Soviet military forces in Europe and along the border with China, which was not acceptable in all these years—"

"We shall disregard their opinion!" Marshal Ustinov interrupted.

These difficult deliberations of the Politburo over the problem of whether to send the troops or not, continued all through October, November, and the first part of December. On December 10, 1979, Marshal Ustinov acted on his own. He gave an oral order to the General Staff to start preparations for deployment of one division of paratroopers and five divisions of military-transport aviation, to step up the readiness of two motorized rifle divisions in the Turkestan Military District, and to increase the staff of a regiment to full staff without setting any concrete tasks yet.

However, the final political decision to send Soviet troops into Afghanistan was made two days later, December 12, 1979, by a small group of Soviet leaders: Brezhnev, Suslov, Andropov, Ustinov, and Gromyko. Thus the fateful decision was made by not even the full Central Committee of the Politburo, although a handwritten Resolution of the Politburo was prepared after the fact, and signed by almost all of the members.

On December 24, Ustinov convened the highest leadership of the Defense Ministry and made an announcement of the decision to send Soviet troops into Afghanistan without explaining the purpose of that mission. On the same day, the first printed document signed by the Defense Minister was prepared—the directive which said that the decision was made to "deploy several contingents of Soviet troops in the southern regions of the country to create favorable conditions to prevent possible anti-Afghan actions on the part of the bordering states."

At the meeting of the Politburo, Marshal Ustinov handed the directive to the General Secretary of the Communist Party and passed the document to the members sitting at the table. "Soviet troops are being deployed into the territory of the Democratic Republic of Afghanistan for the purpose of rendering international assistance to the friendly Afghan people."

Leonid Brezhnev, in full-dress uniform adorned with military awards, browsed through the document, then looked at the members of the Politburo and said, "We must send our troops into Afghanistan. But this mission must be kept in secret." He signed the directive, and then passed it to all the others. Everyone signed. Brezhnev looked at the document going around the table, and reassured the members of the Politburo, "We are going to end this war in two to three months. People don't need to know the truth."

Chapter 10

June 1982, Zarecie

GRADUATION DAY! THE TOP of the mountain she had been climbing for ten long years. Joy and tears, all mixed together with dozens of other emotions. Lena was proud of the great accomplishment and fearful about closing that door, leaving behind everything she had become so familiar with: strict teachers, and childish silly jokes over their strange habits; classmates, ones she adored and those she did not; routine schedules and the sound of the ringing bell; every room, every desk, and even the old, colorless walls felt like something she would always remember.

And a new life, new horizons. Her dreams were finally coming true.

All these thoughts, among many others, raced through Lena's mind as she stood with her classmates, waiting for the final ceremony. She couldn't help but smile, thinking about her school years, even though the tears were welling up in her eyes.

All exams and worries were behind her now, and she and the other pupils lined up in front of the school to receive their high school certificates. Everyone was dressed up, and by tradition, all students held bouquets of flowers in their hands, ready to give them to their favorite teachers.

The director of the school stood on a pedestal to give his speech. "I am proud to announce that our best student, the pride of the school, Lena Petrova, has been awarded the highest recognition of the Ministry of Education, the Gold Medal!"

Students and parents applauded. Lena, tall and beautiful, even in her brown school uniform dress and white apron, accented with white nylon bows on her long braids, went forward to the pedestal to receive her award. The director presented Lena a little box with a medal inside, and shook her hand. Lena flushed, and smiled happily. Then she turned and looked at the crowd of parents, trying to see her mother.

Varya caught Lena's eyes and smiled also. Her eyes filled with tears of joy, but Varya quickly swept them off with the back of her hand.

"Your daughter is beautiful," someone said behind her. Varya turned her head and saw an elderly gypsy woman, wearing old, colorless clothes, standing close to her.

"How do you know she's my daughter?" Varya asked, glancing suspiciously at the woman.

"I know it," the elderly woman replied firmly. "Neither you nor your daughter belongs here."

Varya wrinkled her face, disregarding the woman's words.

"But you are dead inside," the gypsy woman continued behind Varya. "And she—"

The elderly woman paused, looking attentively at Lena, who has returned to the students' line and stood beside Volodya. He smiled happily, unable to hide his admiration, and whispered something into Lena's ear.

"She is different from you. She has a spirit of freedom in her soul. She belongs to another world." The gypsy woman articulated her words slowly and clearly, as if she was reading a book. "Through her loss she will find the path."

"Why did you say I am dead?" Varya replied angrily, turning her head, but the woman had walked away.

"These gypsies…" Varya said to herself, shaking her head as if chasing away a noisy, annoying fly. She looked at her watch, and began making her way out through the crowd, not willing to admit that the woman's words had frightened her. "I could miss my bus," she mumbled.

When the ceremony was over, Lena and Volodya left together. They were late for the regular bus to their village, so they walked down the street, through the sewing factory territory, taking a short cut straight through the fields, onto their village road. Lena stopped and took off her high-heel shoes, standing barefoot on the dusty road. She looked around, stretching her hands apart, as if she wanted to hug the whole world, and then she looked up into the bright blue sky, and pronounced with a happy smile, "Look at this beautiful world, Volodya! Aren't you happy? I can't believe we won't walk down this road again, as we've been doing for so many years!"

"Yes," Volodya nodded his head, while also taking off his shoes and rolling his new black trousers up to his knees. "Life is good when you're young, smart, and beautiful," he added looking with joy at Lena. "What are you going to do now? Will you go to Moscow to study at the University?" he asked. They had talked about it so many times and he hoped that maybe after receiving the medal, Lena had changed her mind.

Lena sadly shook her head. "I wish I could."

They walked in silence, and then Volodya continued, "If your mother's heart is so bad that she needs you to stay with her, why won't the doctors give her disability?" he asked raising his eyebrows.

"My mother said that the government doesn't have money to support all disabled people. The doctors let people off work, only when they know that their patients have just a few months to live."

They walked by the road through the fields full of bright-blue flowers. Lena stepped from the road and went to the field, tenderly touching the tops of the flowers with her long delicate fingers, "I love *vasilki*," she said, smiling. "I love all flowers!" she corrected herself.

"Your eyes are blue as these cornflowers!" Volodya replied, picking a few blooms.

"Let them grow, please!" Lena protested.

"My father told me that in old times cornflowers were worn by young men in love." Volodya put a few flowering shoots into the front pocket of his white shirt. "Let's see what they will tell me."

"I didn't know you talk to flowers," Lena laughed.

If the flowers won't fade till I go to bed, it means she loves me, Volodya thought, making his secret wish.

They returned to the road, and Lena said, picking up where they had left off their conversation, "I think it is good that they don't give my mother a disability certificate. It means she's not so bad yet, right? They do check her at the hospital every year and they insist someone be with her, always. That is why I can't go to Moscow." She looked at Volodya and asked, "Anything new in your plans?"

"You know it. I can't avoid my military duty—"

"Two years away from home! Do you know when and where you will be assigned?"

"This autumn, but I don't know the exact day yet. Remember, I am a year older than you. And no, I don't know where they will send me."

"You will come back a grown-up man!"

"And after that I will decide what to do next," Volodya added. They were approaching Lena's home. Volodya stopped and looked at Lena intently, then he took her hand in his and asked very softly, "Will you be waiting for me, Lena?"

Lena paused, knowing this question was important to him, and she replied with a serious face, "Yes, Volodya, I will."

She opened the gate and asked, "Would you like to come in? We need to celebrate our graduation, don't we?"

"Yes, we should!" Volodya gladly agreed, and they both went inside.

Varya had prepared dinner, and it was on the table already. After so many years waiting for her daughter to come home from school, she was able to calculate precisely the time she needed to get ready for her. A big bowl, full of steaming boiled potatoes, and a pan with fried pieces of fatty pork, or *salo,* and golden eggs floating in grease looked so inviting to hungry Volodya's eyes. Smaller bowls with marinated mushrooms and pickles stood on both sides of the table to make this everyday food look like the "party dish."

Varya embraced Lena with a big smile. "Congratulations!" she said. "I'm so proud of you, daughter; you're the best part of my life." Then she turned to Volodya and hugged him also. "Congratulations on your graduation, Volodya!"

"Show your mother your medal!" Volodya exclaimed excitedly. "Is it really gold?" he asked while Lena handed a small cardboard box to her mother.

"No, it's not gold," Varya said, taking the medal in her hands. "It is just a symbol made from cheap metal, but it is a great honor to have it!"

"O-hh!" Volodya sighed in disappointment. "Not even gold!"

Varya turned to the table, took a little jewelry box that was sitting there, and said," I have a present for you, Lena!" She handed the gift to Lena, kissing her on the cheek. "This is for you, Lenochka, at this special time of your graduation, and your entering into adult life."

Lena opened the box and took out a pair of beautiful gold earrings, made in the shape of a crown, with tiny tear-like drops dangling down from the crown's bottom. "Ah! *Serezki!*" Lena exclaimed with excitement.

"Yes. These are your great-grandmother's precious earrings, *serezki* given to her on her wedding day. Now, it is your time to have them."

Lena kissed her mother and said, "They are so beautiful, mother! And so delicate!"

"You deserve that gift, my child. Please, be careful with them. It is your heritage. I wish you a very happy life. But, if a black day ever comes, use them as you need."

"May I wear them now, Mother?" Lena stepped to the mirror to try on the earrings.

"These *serezki* are too expensive for everyday use, daughter. It would be better to keep them away from people's eyes."

"Oho!" Volodya exclaimed, puzzled. "Where did you get such a treasure, Varvara Ivanovna?" By habit, Volodya continued calling his first teacher by her first and patronymic, or father's name as they did in school.

"It is a long and sad story," Varya answered, sitting down tiredly on the wooden bench beside the table. "My grandmother was from a very rich, noble family. They lived in Saint Petersburg. In 1918, after the October revolution, the Bolsheviks were taking over the homes of the bourgeoisie. They came into my grandmother's house and took everything: money, jewelry, food, clothes—anything they found that was valuable, even the wedding ring from her hand. It was so cold in the unheated house, and my grandma was wearing a warm scarf on her head, so the soldiers didn't notice these earrings... They are all our family had left. Factories, and homes, all the money in the banks—everything was gone. We became poor, as everyone else was."

"You never told me about this, Lena!" Volodya replied, wondering.

"It is because my mother told me we should forget who we are," Lena answered and turned to her mother. "But why did you say about the 'black day', Mother? We're building communism, our bright future, where every person will be a happy member of the society. Isn't that what you taught us in class?" Lena asked with the smile of a successful "finally-done-with-school" student.

"I teach the way I am supposed to," Varya answered, setting down on the table a teapot with freshly brewed tea. "But I also know our history. And I do know that bad things happen," she added.

"Nothing bad can happen," Volodya said resolutely. "The Soviet Union is the largest and strongest country in the world. We were first in space, we have nuclear weapons, we have the best Army in the world—no one can put us down. And your Lena—she's so smart and beautiful!"

"Volodya," Varya interrupted. "Do you know the old proverb *'don't be born beautiful, but be born fortunate?'*"

"Who cares what the old folks say?" Volodya disagreed, wrinkling his face.

"This is the wisdom of our people who believe that Fate does exist," Varya argued.

"I'll always protect Lena!" Volodya exclaimed, thinking that Varya underestimated him. "Everyone wants to be happy. But what does 'happiness' mean?"

"Happiness means well-being, delight, inner peace, health, safety, contentment, and love," Varya answered.

"But not everyone is born for happiness," Lena added, finishing her favorite marinated mushrooms. She had heard her Mother's lament many times. "There are places and countries where life brings people nothing but suffering, depression, grief, anxiety, and pain…" She was talking, picking on her mother's intonation, as if she was teasing her.

"Yes." Varya nodded, not noticing that Lena winked at Volodya as if they were playing and didn't take this conversation seriously. "That is why the old folks' depreciation of beauty is very reasonable. In our society we place a higher value on the human mind and soul, and not just on physical appearance."

"Would it be possible to correct 'the bad fate,' or must we simply have to agree that our future is predetermined?" Lena asked. "I don't want to be a victim of circumstances and live in constant expectation of some terrible 'black day' to come—"

"Struggling, and feeling smashed, as if between the hammer and anvil?" Volodya continued her thoughts. "Is there a way for a young beauty to become free from her wretched fate?" He was smiling teasingly at Lena as he spoke.

"I doubt it," Varya answered quietly, and both Lena and Volodya knew that she was thinking about her own life. "I wish we could do what we desire," Varya continued, but another proverb says that *'life is not a bed of roses'*, and both of you must know that reality might be very different from your dreams, or what you used to read in your favorite fairy-tales."

In small villages, people get up when the sun rises and go to bed early. Volodya left and Lena cleaned up the table. She went to her room and opened the window. The hot June day was cooling down, bringing to life thousands of insects, flying in the air and hiding in the grass. Lena couldn't sleep. She sat on the stool by the window, listening to the sounds of the living world outside and thinking about her childhood and her future—what would it bring her?

Chapter 11

THAT SUMMER AFTER GRADUATION Lena again worked in the fields of the collective farm. Volodya learned how to operate a combine and worked as a mechanic's assistant. He liked his job, and he thought that farming was probably a profession he would pursue after returning from the army. Military duty was a mandatory obligation for every eighteen-year-old boy that could only be avoided because of a disability, or postponed in order to attend college. Every Soviet woman who had a son lived in fear of the day when her beloved boy would be forcibly taken from her; it was inevitable.

Volodya and Lena's friendship was very sincere and had lasted for many years now. Because he was born in late September, Volodya had to wait an extra year to begin school and was older than the other kids. It gave him some advantage over the younger boys in his class, but now he was the first one among his classmates to go into the army. Volodya felt more than just friendship for Lena; he loved her deeply, but he had never talked to her about it.

When he received his draft notice from the military registration office, Volodya still wasn't sure if it was a good time to tell Lena about his feelings. He was a down-to-earth boy from a peasant family. His parents could hardly read newspapers, having had just four years of schooling, and he wasn't oriented toward higher education. Volodya liked to work and could do almost anything with his hands. He enjoyed the simple life and looked forward to returning to Rizovka and having a family someday, with Lena.

As Volodya read his draft notice, which stated he had to be at the military office in Zarecie the next Saturday at 8 AM, he thought of Lena. *She is so vulnerable; anyone could hurt her. How will she live without my protection?* Volodya's heart ached from worries. He was also jealous, and afraid that someone could steal this beautiful girl from him while he was absent. Volodya loved Lena, but being a responsible and honest person, he knew it wasn't time for them to be married yet. He wasn't ready to offer Lena a family life. Since their early childhood, Volodya had always treated Lena as if she were a princess: he did everything she desired, often even predicting her next wish, and he was the happiest when she smiled. Even as he adored Lena and was her best friend, deep in his soul Volodya felt that he didn't deserve her. She was so smart and beautiful. He sensed their differences, but hid this knowledge inside him, hoping that his kindness and admiration would make up for his peasant's origin.

Volodya knew that Lena thought of him as her older brother, and it was fine until he hit adolescence. For the last year or two he had had to constantly fight his desire to kiss her, to become closer to her. He knew Lena's character well enough to understand that his attempt to kiss her could put an end to the friendship he valued so much. He was even guarding Lena from the advances of the other boys in school, and Lena was grateful to Volodya for that. Lena's trust in Volodya was more valuable to him than fulfillment of his own desires.

He liked to go after work to Lena's house to watch TV together, or to go to the forest to pick berries, or go mushroom hunting. Everyone in the village thought of Lena and Volodya as "the bride and the groom," and expected them to get married. Lena accepted the situation; she liked Volodya, and not knowing anyone else better than him, she thought that her friendly feeling toward him was what people called "love."

"I have to talk to her and ask her to marry me before my 'sending-off' party," Volodya told himself and went to Lena's house.

Lena was standing in her yard, talking over the fence to Granny Maria when Volodya approached them.

"How are you doing, son?" Granny Maria asked. She treated all the village kids as her own. "Any news from the military office?"

"Yes, I received my call-up notice today. I'll be leaving next Saturday."

"Oh! So soon," Lena pronounced sadly.

"I want to talk to you, Lena," Volodya added.

"I have to milk my cow," the wise woman said, rushing away. "You, young people, talk."

"Don't miss my party, Granny," Volodya reminded her.

"I won't," Maria gestured with her hand.

Volodya turned to Lena and looked into her eyes with a long sigh, not knowing where to start. They gazed at each other; then Lena broke the silence, asking him in quiet voice, "Volodya, you wanted to say something?"

"Yes…" Volodya didn't know where to start, which phrase to choose, how to say that he loved her. He knew it wasn't a good time but feared that there might not be a right moment for him before his departure. The fence was separating them. Lena stood in her yard, and he was outside on the street. She looked at him with wide-open eyes, observing his face that clearly displayed all the mixed feelings Volodya was experiencing at this moment.

"Are you all right?" she asked.

Volodya shook his head and shouted out the last and most important thought, "Will you marry me, Lena?"

"What?" She grabbed the fence post. "Marry? When?"

"Let's go to the registrar office tomorrow and get married!" He looked at her and felt that his offer sounded incomplete, so he added, "Please."

Lena looked down, sighed, and took a deep breath. Then she looked at him and asked, "Is this because of your draft notice?"

Volodya nodded. "Yes."

Lena looked down again. Volodya felt he had forgotten to say something important, but he couldn't figure what it was.

Lena looked in his eyes and said quietly, "But I am not the legal age yet; I won't be eighteen until next year, Volodya."

He squeezed his fists in despair. "Who cares?"

"Lena! Where are you?" Varya looked out of the window. "I need you here!"

"Okay, I'm coming!" Lena answered, and turned back to Volodya.

"Mother has a bad cold. I have to make the mustard compresses for her." She stepped back.

"Lena, wait!" Volodya stretched his hand through the top of the fence trying to stop her, but he couldn't reach her. "I love you, Lena." His voice sounded quiet and hopeless.

Lena stepped back to him, and she touched his blond hair. Her strong and brave Volodya looked so weak and pitiful now, and she felt that it was she, not he, who was older at this moment.

"When is your party?" she asked.

"I don't know yet. Maybe on Friday."

"Lena!!!" Her mother opened the door and yelled impatiently.

"We will talk later!" Lena called over her shoulder as she ran toward the house.

It's an old custom in Russia to do the "send-off" party for boys departing for the military. Everyone in the village comes; if the weather allows it, tables full of food and drinks are set up outside. There are always one or two musicians who play the accordion and sing heart-breaking songs.

Varya sat beside Lena and turned her daughter's empty wine glass upside-down, signaling that Lena was not allowed to drink. "She's underage yet," Varya explained when someone insisted on filling Lena's glass. Lena's cheeks flushed; she was ashamed about her mother's harsh control.

"Just one drop. Her best friend is leaving, have a heart!" Volodya's father stood behind Varya with a bottle of home-made vodka, asking her permission.

Varya capitulated under her neighbor's pressure, and people's eyes turned toward her from all sides. "Just one drop. And you shall be home in one hour. I won't be sleeping, you hear me?" she said to Lena, standing up and leaving. "It's too late for me to be up. I have to take my medicine," she explained to the others.

Although religion was officially prohibited, the high morality of the Soviet people was based on long years of tradition and strict rules. It was the obligation for every family who raised a daughter to teach her how to cook, take care of the house, and be a devoted and honest wife. A husband expected to get a virgin; otherwise the family's good reputation would be lost forever. In small villages like Rizovka, where everyone's life was an open book, virtuous conduct was strictly guarded. Young people could step nowhere unnoticed, there always was someone who saw them; and the youth knew that it was better to behave well. Having no pre-school or after-school care, children grew up outside on the street, but with dozens of neighbors' eyes constantly watching them.

Exactly one hour later, just as Varya had instructed her, Lena rose from the bench and said, "I should go home."

"I'll go with you." Volodya stood up, and they left.

They walked in silence, and then Lena said, "I feel dizzy after drinking that home-made vodka."

"You didn't drink much, did you?"

"No, not much. But I am not used to it." She stopped and looked into Volodya's eyes. "You are so sad."

Volodya nodded and asked, "Remember, in *Romeo and Juliet* she says, 'Parting is such sweet sorrow?'" He paused. "I can't agree. It hurts."

"You're right. Parting isn't sweet at all." They approached Lena's home and she opened the gate. "I'll come to the military office tomorrow," Lena promised.

"Lena, wait!" Volodya said, following her and taking her hand. Now, after drinking some alcohol, he felt much stronger and wasn't afraid to tell Lena about his love. He turned to Lena and grabbed her other hand. "I love you, I love you, I love you!" he repeated, as he wanted to make sure she understood how much he loved her. They stood so close that Lena could feel how hot Volodya's body was.

"I love you too, Volodya," she said quietly.

All at once, he put his arms around her and kissed her on the lips. He breathed in the scent of home-made vodka mixed with a smell of pickles marinated with garlic.

"Let's go to your back yard. Just for a moment," he said softly, casting a look about to see if anyone had seen them. He gently pulled on Lena's hand and she followed him into the shadows.

Volodya impatiently pressed Lena to the wooden wall and kissed her fast and avidly, like a thirsty man drinking long-desired water. He was hungry for her, finally letting out his hidden, suppressed feelings, his love and admiration. Lena was shocked, and her usual guard was swept away with a hurricane of feeling that had suddenly overwhelmed her. Satisfying his first hunger, and noticing how quiet Lena was, Volodya stopped kissing her, looked into her eyes, and repeated, "I love you so much, Lena!"

"And I love you too," she answered again.

Now he kissed her more deeply and passionately, and through this kiss Lena could feel a strong desire that made her tremble in his arms and return his passion. Her kissing him was like starting a fire. Volodya's body began to shake, and he leaned against her, pressing her back into the wall. She could feel something hard, like a rock, pushing on her leg. That feeling of him brought her desire to a higher level, and she continued kissing him, unable to stop, not wanting to deny that pleasant feeling inside her.

The house door suddenly slammed open and Varya yelled, "Lena! Where are you?" Volodya and Lena heard Varya step down and walk to the fence looking for Lena. Volodya stood up straight, trying to cover Lena's white dress with his body and dark coat. They heard Varya go back in and close the door.

"I need to go inside," Lena said.

"Please, wait! It's our last night!" Volodya begged. He started kissing her eyes, her cheeks, her tender neck, whispering, "Oh, if you only knew what a pleasure it is to kiss you like that, Lena!" He unbuttoned her jacket, and touched her body through her dress. He did it passionately and cautiously, as he tried to remember every part of her, in order to take the memory of her with him. His arms went down, and he knelt in front of his beloved girl, with his head down to her knees, kissing the skirt of her dress, and hugging her legs; and then he suddenly grabbed her body, lifted her up and brought her to a nearby ladder.

"What are you doing, Volodya?" She asked, smiling.

"Let's go up to the attic, on the hay! Please, please!" Volodya held Lena in his arms kissing her.

"Volodya! No! Let me down!" Lena closed his mouth with her hand, stopping his kisses. "I promise you, I'll be waiting for you, and we'll get married. Do you believe me?" She looked at him strictly, and he obeyed, as he always did with her. He put her down, and she stood up.

"Do you promise me that?" he asked with great hope.

"Have I ever lied to you?"

"No, you haven't."

"I'll marry you, I promise. Especially now, after all your kisses, I know what I am waiting for." She smiled and kissed him once again. "Go in peace and serve well. Two years will go by fast. And maybe you'll get a leave somewhere in the middle, and come home."

"Yes, you're right. You will be eighteen next year."

"I should go now. You know, my mother…"

"Yes, I know. Good bye, my love."

"Good bye." Lena quickly went to the door, opened it, and the next minute Volodya saw her waving to him from her bedroom window. He sighed and turned toward home.

Lena stayed by the window long after he vanished from her sight, touching her burning lips with her fingertips, wondering at this new sensation she had just experienced and forcing herself not to run outside for Volodya so they could kiss more. *He loves me…*

Early Saturday morning, Volodya joined the line of new recruits in front of the district military building. The young men were between eighteen and twenty years of age. They were dressed in civilian clothing and carried back packs on their shoulders.

The military orchestra played a loud march. At the sound of the captain's commands, the recruits turned and marched away. Volodya turned back and waved to Lena, who stood among the other women. Lena waved to him, with aching heart. Volodya turned his head back one final time, trying to remember as much as he could of her, biting his lips and torturing himself with a nonsense question. *"Why, why have I been waiting so long to kiss her?"*

Chapter 12

AS A MILITARY RECRUIT, Volodya had three months of quarantine, a period of time during which newcomers were detained at a special training zone under enforced isolation to prevent any communication with the outside world. Even letters home were prohibited. The iron discipline was designed to erase memories of civilian life and make young men blindly obedient to, and an indispensable part of, the Soviet military machine. There were always cases of suicide during that rough time, especially among the boys from higher-educated city families, who were unable to sustain the hardship and bear the humiliation of losing their individuality. But there is an end for everything, and finally the new recruits, Volodya among them, flew out of the quarantine area in a military plane high above mountains they had never seen before.

They arrived at Kabul in January of 1983. The cold wet wind blew from the north, the land was covered with snow, and the new arrivals were glad to exchange their summer uniforms for winter apparel. At this point the young soldiers, who had become friends, were parted and sent to different locations. Volodya was assigned to serve in Captain Nevorov's command and, together with other recruits, was ordered to go to the helicopter that would deliver him to his destination.

The next morning the young soldiers stood lined up, listening to their commander, Captain Victor Nevorov, who read the *Instruction to the Soviet Soldier in Afghanistan:*

> "Soviet Soldier! Being in the territory of friendly Afghanistan, remember that you are the representative of

the Soviet country and its great people."

Nevorov looked at the young men standing in a straight line under the falling snow. He continued:

> "It is an honor to fulfill this great historical mission that has been assigned to you by our Native land. Remember that it is by how you conduct yourself in this country that the Afghan people will judge all the Soviet Army, all the great Soviet Native land—"

Nevorov stopped reading and again looked at the new arrivals before ending his remarks. "Everyone has to learn this Instruction and follow it strictly. Lieutenant Sergey Orlovsky will explain it to you in detail and he will also examine your knowledge of the Kalashnikov automat. Remember that we have been sent here to keep the international traditions of our fathers and older brothers, to guard the safety and territorial integrity of the Democratic Republic of Afghanistan and the southern boundaries of our great Soviet country."

The soldiers were released to have breakfast. Lieutenant Sergey gave them thirty minutes to eat. He pointed in the direction of the fire that was hidden from the wind behind a rock where water was boiling in a pot.

"You can warm up your cans of buckwheat *kasha* in that boiling water," Sergey told them. "I'll be back in thirty minutes."

Volodya and his friends rushed to the fire. Nothing could be worse for a soldier than to miss a meal, that truth the new soldiers had already learned. The small cans of kasha wouldn't satisfy the healthy appetites of the young men, but they could drink plenty of hot tea along with it, so no one dared to complain.

Half an hour later Volodya and his comrades sat on metal beds inside the military shelter. Lieutenant Sergey passed out a copy of "The Instruction" to each of them and waited while they read it.

"Any questions?" he asked after they had finished reading it.

One of the soldiers looked down at the piece of paper and asked, "I wonder, it says here, 'While being in the Democratic Republic of Afghanistan, remember to practice Soviet moral norms, orders, laws, as well as to respect the customs of the host country. By their character Afghans are trusting; they are sensitive to concepts of 'good and evil.' Does that mean we are not to kill?"

Sergey looked at the soldier and explained with patience, "There is a difference between the civilian citizens and the military. We are here to fight with an army, not against the civilians in the villages." Sergey read again from the Instruction: "It says here, 'When talking to Afghans, show respect to them. Afghans are very hospitable, but do not abuse their hospitality.'"

The young soldier looked confused. "Are we going to be in the villages?"

"Yes, when we receive an order to free villages from Taliban troops," Sergey answered. "And you have to be careful—the village streets are narrow and dangerous. Do not look into the courtyards, or windows. Any attempt to glance into a woman's face is considered the greatest insult in the Muslim world." Sergey paused, looked at the young men and emphasized, "Remember that. From our point of view those are innocent things, but they would arouse such rage in Afghan men that you could pay with your life."

Sergeant Andrey entered the tent and listened to Sergey, nodding in agreement. "Tell them about the market, Serega," he said.

"Yes, I will," Sergey answered the sergeant. He pointed his finger at the "Instruction" and continued. "It says here: 'Do not disturb Muslims during their religious practices. Do not visit a mosque, a tomb, or a cemetery without need.' Do you all fully understand that?"

The soldiers didn't answer, but several glanced back down at their copies of Instruction.

"Religion is very important for people here. They pray by schedule, at a certain time. They stop whatever they are doing and pray—"

"So, it's a great time to attack them," one of the soldiers exclaimed in excitement. That was quickly curbed by Sergey's strict look.

"No, it's not time to attack or to do anything else. We are here to protect, and although we are morally against religion, we still have to respect the Afghans' beliefs and traditions." Sergey stood up and continued. "Let me give you an example. We were passing a village at time of prayer, and a few of our soldiers stole some fruit they saw at the market—"

"They were punished hard for that!" the sergeant interrupted Sergey. The two exchanged glances.

"Yes, they were. You are warned." Sergey looked at the sergeant and then at the new recruits. "I know it won't happen again in our battalion."

He read the last few sentences:

> "With honor show what it means to be a citizen of the USSR. Be faultless in your behavior, and carry out your military duties honestly. Keep your comrades from acts discrediting the honor of the Soviet people. Develop with them a feeling of friendship and international solidarity with the people of Afghanistan."

Sergey folded up the Instruction and put it in his front pocket. "Questions?"

The soldiers had no questions, and they also placed their Instructions in their front pockets, as Sergey did.

"One more thing. Now, after giving your oath, you are allowed to write home, but you are not allowed to tell anyone where you serve and what you do. All your letters will be checked. Your return address will be "Moscow-400" and your name. That is enough for the postal service to deliver letters to you." Sergey turned to the door. "Now let's go to our duties," he said.

The soldiers followed him out of the tent to a hand-made wooden dining table. "You already know how to take apart your most important weapon—the automat Kalashnikov, right?" Sergey asked, placing his rifle on the top of the table.

The soldiers nodded.

"Any volunteer to show me how to do it?" He looked at the men.

No one answered. Sergey smiled, and then became serious. "Okay. I will show you how to take care of your weapon. Remember, your life or the life of your comrade may depend on its readiness. Now, look!"

Lieutenant Sergey sat on the bench by the table and demonstrated how to take the weapon apart. "Watch how I do it."

He removed the magazine and put it aside, then he moved the safety lever to the "fire" position, pulled back the bolt carrier lever, and ejected a round part from the chamber.

"While holding back the bolt carrier lever, you must inspect the chamber to make sure it is empty." Sergey quickly pushed the bolt carrier forward, pressed in a button, and lifted the rear, putting aside one part after another. The young soldiers looked with admiration at Sergey's quick actions.

In less than a minute Sergey had his weapon taken apart, its individual parts spread out in front of him. The lieutenant continued with a wide smile, "Assembly is the reversal of disassembly; you all know that." He quickly put his weapon back together. "Now you do it."

The new recruits picked up their weapons and started working on disassembling them. Sergey made them repeat the process until they could do it almost as fast as he did.

"How do you like our commanders?" Ivan, the soldier from Ukraine, asked Volodya when they lined up for the evening roll call. Captain Nevorov, Lieutenant Sergey to his right, and Sergeant Andrey to his left, stood in front of their battalion, looking straight in their soldiers' faces.

"They remind me of the *Three Bogatyrs,*" Volodya answered in a low voice. Ivan didn't reply, listening to Nevorov's report on the current situation in the area.

"Don't you remember? We learned it in school," Volodya continued talking to Ivan on their way to the tent. "My first teacher loved Russian history and literature. She would make us memorize whole pages from the Russian legends…"

"Really?" Ivan looked at Volodya with compassion.

"Yes, now I actually appreciate it. Thinking about our history helps me to be stronger. Serving in the Army will make us real men."

"Maybe like one of those Bogatyrs?" Ivan smiled teasingly.

"Yes." Volodya didn't notice the irony. "Remember Vasnetsov's painting? I really like his picture, *Three Bogatyrs*—three mighty men in full armor, mounting their horses—the legendary symbol of Russian military power, honor, and victory."

"Well… this name actually suits our commanders," Ivan agreed.

This nickname stuck to Nevorov, Sergey, and Andrey, and none of them really minded it, finding it even to be an honor. And those who had read Russian legends would admit that the appearances and even the characters of the three military commanders were as if they were offsprings of the great knights-errant.

His soldiers associated Nevorov with the epic Bogatyr Ilya Muromets, one who dedicated his life to defend fatherland, and famous for his physical and spiritual power and integrity.

By the legend, the second Bogatyr, Dobrynya Nikitich was a peasant. His mother told him not to go to the Mountains, not to trample dragons, not to rescue captives, and not to bathe in the enemies' river, but Dobrynya disobeyed his mother and actually went and did everything she warned him about. Sergeant Andrey was also a peasant who left his elderly mother at home in order to perform his military duty. Great courage was the main quality of Andrey's character.

And just as Alyosha Popovich, Lieutenant Sergey was the youngest of the three commanders. Fun-loving and easy going, he was loved by everyone. His bravery and creative mind made him one of the best soldiers, who would not shy away from defeating his enemies by trickery.

And in the same way as Bogatyrs and Knights united together, defending the land of Kiev Rus and the Russian people against the invasions of enemies and evil spirits, the modern Bogatyrs landed in Afghanistan to defend its people.

Chapter 13

MAIL TO RIZOVKA WAS delivered by Dunyasha, a middle-aged, tiny-as-a-bird woman, who wore the same warm jersey, a cap with ear-flaps, and knee-high soldiers' boots the whole year around. She sorted the mail in the largest post office at Zarecie, placed it into the huge canvas bag that she wore across her shoulders, and then delivered it to Rizovka and other nearby villages. She traveled in a squeaking cart pulled by an old horse that her father had left her upon his death. This horse was Dunyasha's best friend, and she was afraid she would lose her job when the old horse died.

Dunyasha knew all the news. She delivered the letters directly into the addressee's hands, and stood by while the person read it, expecting the news to be shared with her. After that, it wasn't private news any longer because Dunyasha shared it with everyone else on her way back to the post office.

"And who is going to dance for me today?" Dunyasha loudly inquired of Lena, who was walking in front of her down the street.

Lena turned and asked with excitement, "Do you have a letter for me, Dunyasha?"

"Dance! Dance!" the tiny woman said, stopping the horse, stepping to the ground, and holding an envelope high in the air, making Lena jump up to get it.

Tall Lena didn't need to jump; she snatched the envelope, looked at it, and exclaimed joyfully, "From Volodya! Finally! Thank you!" She ran to her house.

There Lena sat on the bench by the dining table, carefully inspected the envelope, read the date of the postmark, and opened it. A dried orange flower fell from the envelope onto her lap. Lena picked it up, and carefully examined it.

A beautiful flower, she thought, *but I don't recognize it.* She started reading the letter, and her face lit up with a bright smile.

Varya entered with a bag of groceries and saw Lena reading the letter. "Have you heard from Volodya?"

Lena answered joyfully, not taking her eyes off the letter. "Yes, it's from him. Finally, after weeks of silence, he sent it. But he didn't say where he is. He wrote, 'It's far away from home, and we have a lot of work to do.'" Lena looked at her mother. "Why wouldn't he say? Isn't it strange?"

Varya sat down beside her. She looked at her daughter's happy smile, and asked, "What else did he write?"

"Just about his fellow soldiers, how they are all doing." Lena folded up the letter, afraid that her mother wanted to see it. Volodya asked in it if she remembered their kisses, and Lena didn't want her mother to know about that.

Varya sighed, and pronounced after a pause, "Poor boy. I wonder if he's in Afghanistan."

Lena looked up at her mother, frightened. "Afghanistan?"

"Yes. At the war that no one is allowed to know about. But people know. They always do."

Lena stood by the bookshelf deciding on a good place to hide the letter. She turned to her mother. "What do you mean? Are we at war?"

Varya didn't answer and started to busy herself emptying her bag. She took out rye bread, then butter, and flour in a paper bag, placing it all on the table. Then she sat down on the bench and said, not looking at her daughter, "I was at the district meeting today. They told us, 'The country is going through a difficult time and we all have to tighten our belts.'" Her intonation sounded official, as she repeated what she had heard at the meeting. "They said there is not enough food, and that the government will have to use the distribution system soon. We'll buy our portion of bread, flour, milk and butter only with ration cards, the same as it was during the war."

Lena stood by the bookshelf holding the envelope in her hands, not knowing what to say. Afghanistan? War? Could Volodya be hidden away in some secret place in the vast foreboding desert, fighting in a war that no one, not even he, could tell her about? Would he be able to continue to send her letters? How would she know how he was doing? And, even if he was alive, or hurt? Suddenly she was struck with grief and anxiety for Volodya and for their future.

She glanced at her mother, who was sitting quietly with her hands crossed on the top of her long gray woolen skirt, gazing blindly down at the old wooden floor. Varya looked so tired and hopeless that Lena's heart squeezed in condolence for her.

"No food?" Lena couldn't comprehend what she had just heard. Their life had never been easy, and now it seemed it was going to get worse.

"You must get a job, Lena," Varya said.

Lena sighed. "Mother, you know there are no jobs in the village in the winter time. I asked every place I could, but people only laughed at me. They told me, 'We have more people than work'. I went to the nearby villages, too, but I heard the same answer: 'No job.'"

Varya looked up at Lena, "I talked to an old friend after the meeting today. She said there is a job available in Zarecie. A sewing factory is hiring seamstresses."

Lena gazed at her mother in doubt. "Do you think they will take me? I am not even from their town—"

Varya nodded, "Yes." She continued in a firm tone, "Go there tomorrow and tell them you're from Vera Ivanovna. It will help."

"Who is Vera Ivanovna?"

"She's the director of the grocery store in Zarecie that distributes food packages for the sewing factory."

Lena twisted her lips, but nodded, "I'll go."

*   *   *

The next day Lena arrived in Zarecie on the early-morning bus and went to the sewing factory, a three-story building on the town's main street. She stopped by the guard booth and asked for the personnel office, and was told to go to the second floor. Lena walked down the poorly lit corridor, and stopped by a door with the sign: "Personnel Office." She knocked. Nobody answered, so Lena pushed the door handle down and went in.

She entered a huge room, bright from light coming through the big windows covered with fancy white nylon curtains. Large portraits of all three proletariat leaders, Marx, Engels, and Lenin, hung on the wall above the desk. A woman in her thirties with blonde hair, well-groomed, and tastefully dressed, sat at a desk full of papers.

"Good morning," Lena said, closing the door behind her.

The blonde lady didn't answer, continuing to write. Lena waited, then went closer to the desk and said, "I'm looking for a job..."

The lady at the desk continued to write but answered in a loud voice, not looking at Lena, "We don't have any openings!"

Lena went toward the door, paused, then turned and pronounced quietly, "Vera Ivanovna sent me here..."

The hiring lady immediately stopped writing, looked at Lena, and then stood up from her desk. She approached Lena, "Why didn't you say that before? What's your name?"

"Lena Petrova."

"Very good. Sit down here and give me your passport."

The lady checked the passport, and then she gave Lena a blank form and asked her to fill it out. Lena wrote down her name. The hiring lady took the paper and picked up the phone. "Peter? I have a new worker for you." She turned to Lena. "A supervisor will show you your work place, and you can start tomorrow."

Peter, a man in his forties, with a rough-looking face, entered the room, observed Lena with curiosity, and then assured her with a smile, "We're always glad to have young, beautiful girls in our sewing brigade!"

"Just get to work, Peter!" the personnel lady gestured him out.

Peter opened the door, inviting Lena to follow him. "I'll show you around. Do you know how to operate a sewing machine?"

Lena stopped in embarrassment. "No."

Peter smiled indulgently, showing a missing front tooth. "No problem. We'll teach you." He put his hand around Lena's waist, gesturing with his other hand toward the hallway.

Chapter 14

THE SOLDIERS WERE ALREADY asleep in their bunks on the military base when Sergeant Andrey ordered them to get ready to board a helicopter. "Our men are trapped in the mountains!" he yelled.

Volodya and the other recruits grabbed their weapons and ran to the chopper. Their flight was short. The helicopter took their special operations group above the mountains, where they jumped to the ground via a rope ladder from the craft's door. They were to ferret out the Afghan soldiers hidden in the mountains.

The Afghans heard the sound of the incoming helicopter, waited while all the soldiers left the craft, and then opened direct fire. Volodya's friend, Peter, who was running in front of him, was shot and fell down onto the snow. Stunned, Volodya carried his wounded, bleeding friend on his back. The Afghans' fire forced them down. Volodya hid behind a large rock, and checked his comrade's pulse. Peter was dead.

A strong wind arose. The air was cold. A new, more terrifying attack started. The night lit up with exploding grenades. The Afghans fired from different directions; they threw five or six grenades, trying to shut down the Soviets' machine gun, and finally did.

The Afghans moved to within twenty-five meters, walking straight, and yelling something in their language. In this cold winter weather, they were attired much the same as they dressed in summer: a light jacket, baggy pants, a short canvas shoes on their feet; some of them were even barefoot. *They are not troops, they look like civilians!* The panic thought flashed through Volodya's mind.

The Soviet soldiers had to fire on them at almost point-blank range. All their grenades were used up, and the young, inexperienced soldiers had only a few spare magazines for their Kalashnikovs. When the guerillas were as close as five to six meters, Volodya could see their faces; he stood up and started firing at them with his eyes closed, fearing death at any moment.

Fortunately, the Soviet helicopter returned, bringing more soldiers. Taking their wounded and dead with them, the guerillas began backing off. There were many losses on the Soviet side, too.

Now, after this fight, Volodya huddled, pulling on his bedroll, freezing among the rocks. He turned from one side to another, trying to catch up on sleep, but sleep wouldn't come. His eyes were wide open, although he was terribly tired after the night fight. It was the first time he had seen Afghans up close, and he didn't even know how many of them he had killed. He felt horrible. It was unbearable and painful for him to know that he had taken someone's life, but the only alternative had been that his own life would be taken.

Exhausted, he tried to close his eyes and think of something pleasant. His home. Lena. Their kisses. Everything was so far away and so unreal now, as if he lived in a different lifetime.

Volodya hadn't realized how terrifying it would feel to kill people, and how easy at the same time. Only yesterday his friend had talked and smiled, and now Peter was dead. *What if I was killed too? What would happen to Lena? I promised to marry her, so I must return.* Volodya forced himself to close his eyes and think about home. Memories of his childhood and happy days spent with Lena came to him. He remembered their mushroom hunting, how they found the rabbits, and how both he and Lena cried when Volodya's father took the rabbits from them to make warm winter hats.

Volodya dozed off. He dreamed of a sunny day, and a sandy road; he saw Lena walking on the road far away from him… He ran toward her, yelling, "Lena, Lena!" and she stopped, turning toward him and waiting for him… Volodya ran toward her, closer, closer… And then, suddenly he saw a mine explosion and felt a bomb tearing his body into pieces, knocking out his teeth from their roots, spattering his brain.

Volodya woke up in a cold sweat. At first he didn't understand that he was still alive. He felt that his arms had become detached from his shoulders, his blood splattered, his brain scattered, and as if from a distance, he saw his body parts flying in the air. *What a nightmare!* He thought, slowly coming out of deadly, paralyzing fear. He tried to move his feet, but they were numb and motionless, his toes pointing up, like those of a dead man. The dream was so real that he had a hard time shaking it off. Volodya lay quietly for a few minutes, and then stood up. "What a horror," he whispered. "It's better to be awake."

He walked toward his comrades who were sitting in the cave, by a small fire, waiting for the helicopter to take them back to the base.

The young soldiers were talking about their girlfriends. Ukrainian Ivan read the letter he had received from home.

"Dear Ivan," his girlfriend wrote, "I know it has been only three months since you left, but I need your advice now. I know you will understand me as you always did."

Ivan looked at his friends and asked, "And what do you think she needs my advice for?"

"How to cook the Ukrainian borscht?" The young men laughed.

"Ah," Ivan dismissed their joke with a wave of his hand, stopping their laughter and continued to read, "I did promise to wait for you, but I met a man a few days ago, and he invited me to the movies. After the movie he accompanied me home, and he wanted to kiss me. I told him I have a boyfriend who is in the army now, but he told me he wants me to be his girlfriend.

"Dear Ivan, I need your advice. Please, tell me what to do. May I go to the movies with this man or should I stay home all the time? It's so boring to be home!"

Ivan stopped reading, and looked at his friends, "So what do you think I should answer her?"

"Tell her to stay home, if she wants you to marry her!" someone suggested.

Ivan stood up and spat through his teeth, "If three months seems too long for her, and she already went to a movie with another man, she won't wait for me for two years. And this is what I'll do!" He tore the girl's letter into pieces and threw it into the fire.

"Good! You're right!" His friends supported him. Ivan gave them a big smile, and took a few more letters from his inner pocket.

"She thinks I'm going cry for her? Ha-ha! Never mind! Here are Toma, Lora, and Dina. And each one writes that she loves me!"

"Wow!" Someone whistled with admiration.

"What a man! How did you do that? Tell us!" his friends demanded, laughing.

"Well," Ivan looked down, as an innocent boy does, but he couldn't suppress the smug smile that crawled from ear to ear on his face. "You know… Ukrainian girls ripen so quickly, like apricots almost… you can't let them go bad and fall off the branches!"

"Ha-ha," one of the men commented. "No wonder Ukrainian men are stereotyped as greedy, 'What I can't eat, I will nibble!'"

"True!" Ivan laughed with the others.

Sergeant Andrey, who had been sitting nearby listening to the soldiers' talk, cautioned, "A soldier, completely busy with his work, in which he has fully invested himself, and with which he is fully occupied, must be single-minded. We can think of home and love and women. But we must remember why we are here, and not allow ourselves to be distracted."

Volodya looked at his friends sitting around the fire. *How different we all are,* he thought. *We come from all fifteen Soviet Republics, representing different nationalities, but we all have the same goal: to serve our country. We left our homes, our beloved ones, to come here and to protect the Afghan people. But protect them from whom? We were told to fight the Taliban Army, but tonight we saw and killed people without uniforms, because they had weapons and they killed our soldiers.* Volodya sighed. He couldn't understand the politics. He didn't know what was going on, but he had given his oath to serve honestly, and he knew that he would.

Lieutenant Sergey came to the fire and sat beside Volodya.

"You have done a very good job tonight," he said to his soldiers. "I'm proud of you."

He turned to Volodya. "And you showed a special heroism during that attack, Volodya. I saw you standing straight up and firing right in their faces!"

"I saw that, too," one of the soldiers confirmed. "Volodya was furious at that moment. With his height and size I'm sure he made those guerillas shit before he even started firing!"

Everyone laughed, and looked at Volodya, who modestly smiled, not daring to confess how scared he was at that unforgettable moment.

"Do we have any drivers among you?" Sergey asked.

Volodya said, "I know how to drive. But I don't have a license. I was too young to get one. I used to be a mechanic's assistant."

"That's great. We'll need you then. After returning to the base I'll give you the map. We have to get food and military supplies from Kabul."

Sergey looked at the men, "I will need someone to go with him."

"I'll go," Ivan volunteered.

"How long does it take to drive from the base to Kabul?" Volodya asked.

"Normally about four to five hours. But in the mud we've got now, probably longer. And you never know what or who you will meet on the way. So we don't give any promises here," Sergey said.

"I understand."

*   *   *

Everything went as they had planned. Volodya and Ivan arrived in Kabul in good time. They loaded the truck with boxes full of food and departed from the city. The road was muddy from melted snow, and Volodya drove slowly, trying to watch carefully for holes on the road, not wanting to get stuck in the mud. Ivan sat beside him, observing the route, holding a gun, ready to fight.

They passed the first hidden security post point guarding the base location, and had spotted their tents just around the curve, when a mine exploded. Ivan was killed instantly, and Volodya's body flew into the air. He fell close to some bushes. The guerrillas, who were hiding there, quickly dragged him away. The Soviet soldiers fired from the camp, but it was too late.

"Captain, give us an order to attack the village! Volodya might be alive yet, or at least we'll get his body," the lieutenant yelled to Nevorov.

"Sergey, I just spoke with the Center. They have sent a peacemaker's team. They will be here soon to agitate the locals to take our side. We are prohibited from going inside the village."

Sergey went away, grinding his teeth. He knew any arguments were hopeless.

Later that day Sergey handed Nevorov his binoculars, and barked, "Look, what they're doing!" Captain Nevorov watched the guerillas' actions through the lenses, and his face became hard like steel. He returned the binoculars to Sergey. Sergey would rather die instead of witnessing this scene. He saw the guerrillas cut Volodya's belly open and fill his stomach with dirt. They ran a wooden stick through Volodya's body. Volodya was still alive and his face was twisted from the pain of the torture. He screamed. The guerrillas paraded him around the village. After Volodya died, the guerrillas cut his body into pieces and placed a pail filled with his body parts in the "neutral zone"—within firing distance from both sides.

After nightfall, one of the Soviet soldiers crawled out carefully to retrieve the pail. He almost reached it, only to be killed by a burst of gun fire. Nevorov looked through his binoculars at the dead soldier, and then turned to Sergey. "They knew we would want his remains, so they put him just out of reach," he said. "The guerrillas will shoot everyone who tries to reach the pail."

Throughout the next day Soviet soldiers lay on the battle line shooting at the crows circling above Volodya's remains. Sergey sat by a tent with a long cable in hand, fashioning something that might help him reach the pail.

By night his device was ready. He stashed a grenade in his chest pocket. Nevorov looked at him in astonishment. "What are you doing?"

"They won't take me alive!" Sergey stood up, grabbed his gun in one hand and took the cable in the other. He dropped to his stomach and crawled toward the pail, slowly, pressing his body tightly into the dirty snow. Nevorov watched him, ready to fire. Close to the pail, Sergey threw the loop and lassoed the pail. He waited for the inevitable burst of enemy gunfire, but it didn't come. He slowly pulled the pail toward him, and crawling backward, dragged it safely from the neutral zone.

*   *   *

It was a sunny winter day, and Lena was riding a local bus home. She worked at the sewing factory during the week, and returned home on weekends. She smiled as she looked out the window, thinking how nice it felt to be able to work and bring home some money. She opened her purse and counted the money she had in there. Lena was proud of herself.

In Rizovka she got off the bus, and walked up the street to her home. A military truck passed her and stopped at Volodya's house. Lena thought Volodya had come home, and she ran toward the truck with a joyful heart. Suddenly she stopped, scared: she saw the coffin two soldiers were pulling from the back of the vehicle.

"Mother! Mother!" Lena cried, opening the door of her home. "There are soldiers at Volodya's house… and a coffin…"

Varya hugged her sobbing daughter. Through the window she saw the neighbors running down the street toward the military truck. "How senseless," Varya said. "How unacceptable it is."

Lena didn't know how to react to what was happening. She went to Volodya's house. She saw the coffin. Someone said his body was in it, but she wouldn't believe them. Even when she saw the picture of him, dressed in his military uniform, nailed above his grave, she still wouldn't believe it. She simply couldn't accept his death. He was too young to die, and he had promised her that he would return and marry her. Her Volodya always kept his word, so how could he be dead now?

Lena decided she would always be waiting for him. No one would ever be as good to her as Volodya, who loved her simply for who she was, never judging, never complaining, always ready to be there for her, always ready to share, serve, and protect her...

Ah, Volodya, Volodya, where are you? How can I ever live without you?

Chapter 15

THE WAR IN AFGHANISTAN could not be kept secret forever. A rumor about the war began spreading around as more and more zinc coffins arrived home. Many people said that the greatest tragedy of the Afghanistan war was its senselessness. War might be understandable when protecting Fatherland and families, perhaps even permissible when new territories were won for the state. But who could reasonably explain the sense of a heavy, bloody, wearisome war in Afghanistan, that the average people were not permitted to discuss, even as more and more coffins arrived back home?

In Afghanistan Captain Nevorov asked his radio operator to connect him to a senior officer, Colonel Afanasiev. A few minutes later he spoke over the military radio: "I'll need transportation for Cargo-200, Comrade Colonel. We sustained severe losses. The dead are piling up..." He listened to Afanasiev's voice on the other end and then continued, "Comrade Colonel, we have found a huge cache of drugs... Yes, I think it is opium. The Afghans had a large supply of it hidden in the mountains. My soldiers found it... Yes, Comrade Colonel, we'll guard it." He paused again and then repeated as if he wasn't sure, "You will come here? Well, I'll see you tomorrow."

The next night Colonel Afanasiev and Captain Nevorov stood outside of the commander's tent at the military base and observed soldiers loading zinc coffins bound with wood into the transport helicopter. There were dozens of coffins in front of them. The soldiers were hauling out even more from a military truck, piling one coffin on top of another.

Nevorov couldn't suppress his bitterness, "We are losing more and more people. Can you tell me, for what?"

Colonel Afanasiev answered in a low voice, "Yes, we have paid a high price..." Suddenly he smiled to himself as an unusual idea came into his mind. Afanasiev turned his head away to hide his smile. The next moment he looked serious again, and said to Nevorov. "I need to call Moscow. It's urgent."

Nevorov went into the commander's tent to order a connection with Moscow, and then returned and asked the colonel to follow him.

Inside the tent a soldier stood up and saluted Afanasiev. "Moscow is waiting, Comrade Colonel!"

Afanasiev sat by the radio, and then both Nevorov and the soldier left the tent, he put the headset on and started speaking. "Hello, it is good you are still at work. I found out how to deliver 'the medicine' to Moscow." He listened to the voice on the other end, and then continued, "Yes, I know where you work. It's safe, I guarantee you." He listened, again, nodding. "I'll put it in hermetically sealed zinc coffins. No one is allowed to open them. Yes, it will arrive at a confidential address." As Afanasiev listened, the smile returned to his face. "Absolutely reliable and clean. Where do you want me to send these coffins?"

Afanasiev finished his phone conversation, left the military tent, and approached Nevorov. "Moscow has ordered transportation of all of the opium to Kabul."

"When do you need it to be loaded?" Nevorov asked the colonel.

"Right now!"

*　　　*　　　*

Shortly thereafter, on February 23, 1987, in the Kremlin, at a meeting of the Politburo, the Communist Party members sat around a long redwood table, listening to Mikhail Gorbachev, the new General Secretary of the Communist Party, who explained his view of the political situation:

"On Afghanistan. The reaction to our decision to withdraw is not simple. We did enter, how do we leave now? Yes, we can leave quickly, without thinking about anything, saying that the former leadership was to blame for everything. However we hear from India and from Africa that if we just leave, it would be a blow to the authority of the Soviet Union, that imperialism will start its offensive actions in the developing countries if we leave Afghanistan.

"Another issue. A million of our soldiers went through Afghanistan. We will not be able to explain to our people if we do not complete the war successfully. We have suffered such heavy losses! And what for? We have undermined the prestige of our country, brought bitterness. For what purpose?

"It is essential we help preserve Najib's regime. If we rush out now, the regime will fall. Najib's personnel are in panic. He even asks us to bring in five hundred thousand more troops; it is a bluff, of course. Otherwise, there will be bloodshed, a civil war, and Najib will be removed immediately.

"I believe we should continue negotiations with him, and maybe we will even have to give in on the dates of withdrawal. Maybe some of you have doubts about what I have just said?" Gorbachev concluded, looking at the members of Politburo. But no one objected.

"Then that is how we will act."

The decision was made. The members of the Politburo didn't mind delaying the end of the war. Gorbachev's vigor distinguished him from his doddering predecessors, whose artificial life-support systems and terminal "colds" were deathly metaphors for the decline of the system. The Soviet Union now had a leader who was younger than the state itself, and everyone lived in curious expectation as to how this new political experiment would end.

Only a year later after that discussion at the Politburo session, in May 1988, the first troop withdrawal from Afghanistan began.

Chapter 16

AS A PRIVILEGE LENA was assigned a room in the factory's dorm. She thought that the two magic words "Vera Ivanovna" probably had played an important role in the administration's decision about that. Two other girls, thirty-two-year-old Katya and eighteen-year-old Tonya, shared the same room with her. Tonya, a slim girl with long blonde hair, had arrived only a few months before Lena. They worked in the same department, spent most of their time together, became very close friends, and helped each other as sisters would do.

Katya, as the oldest and most experienced, was the mentor for all the younger girls at work, and she was amazed at how quickly Lena learned her job.

"In all my years here I have never seen anyone who could learn as quickly as you do," she told Lena with admiration. "You remember everything I tell you the first time; I have never repeated anything to you. With such a memory and ability to learn, you should be studying at the university instead of making uniforms in this run-down factory."

"Yes," Lena nodded in response to Katya's words. "Maybe one day I will."

Katya's family lived in a village about sixty kilometers south of Zarecie. Unlike Lena, she had grown up in a big family. Her mother had six children, and Katya was the oldest. Her father drove a tractor and worked on the collective farm. He liked to drink, and most of the time he was useless, sleeping drunk on his bed. Katya was the one who helped her mother to raise the other children. Just like Lena, she went home on weekends after buying bread, butter, and flour from the Zarecie store to take to her family.

Katya was very practical; she knew how to adjust quickly to new supervisors and life's obstacles, telling Lena and Tonya to follow her example. "My grandfather, who saw the czar, the revolution, and survived three wars, used to teach me," Katya shared the old man's philosophy with her friends. "My granddad was like a chameleon that can change colors: when a 'red' government came—he was red; when the 'whites' were here—he was white. 'Only this way a peasant can survive,' he told me. And it's the best way to be."

Katya knew everyone's tastes and preferences. If a seamstress bought shoes or a dress that didn't fit, Katya could always resell them to someone else in the dorm. She liked selling, and could sell anything that got into her hands. When food and clothes became hard to find in the local stores, she was among the first people who started weekly tours to Moscow, always returning with bags full of all sorts of goods. She offered the things she bought to her co-workers, and there were always people who wanted to buy, gratefully paying her "a little extra" for the delivery of food, clothes, and many other things.

Soon these trips to Moscow became Katya's second job which gave her additional income. From time to time she took Tonya with her because it made it possible for them to stand in several long lines at the same time. The girls would leave Zarecie on the Friday night train, arrive in Moscow in the early morning, and then take the subway to the center of the city where the biggest stores were located. They would get in the line in one department and write on their palms the number that would let them back in line.

Then they would go and stand in another line, returning to the first one periodically to check and confirm their places. People formed lines early, before the stores were open, although they didn't know what particular items would be sold that day. It didn't matter. Katya and Tonya stood in five or more different lines, and bought anything they could find in Moscow—with so many workers at their factory they always sold everything they brought back. Zarecie's store could offer people only a few products such as pickled cabbage, rye bread, and bottles of red port wine.

Food packages that included one can of condensed milk, one kilogram of sausage or kielbasa, four hundred grams of cheese, and a package of sugar were distributed at the factory weekly, but each person received it, by turn, only once a month. That was why people were happy to buy any additional food they could get.

Returning from Moscow, Katya always shared new jokes that she had heard from people while standing in line. It was always this way that the Soviet people would laugh about themselves and their government, but would feel offended if any foreigner said anything bad about their country.

"Here is a joke I heard in Moscow today," Katya said.

"At a meeting people asked Leonid Breznev, 'You have told us that we are on our way to Communism, when people will have everything they need, right?'

"'Yes.'

"'Then why are our stores empty?'

"'Because no one promised to feed you on your way there.'"

Katya smiled. She knew plenty of jokes, and she laughingly told another one:

"Leonid Brezhnev called the group of Soviet astronauts together. 'Comrades! The Americans have landed on the moon. The Politburo held a meeting and decided that you will fly to the sun!'

"'But we'll be burned, Leonid Il'ich!' the astronauts objected.

"'Do not be afraid, Comrades! The Party thinks about everything. You'll fly at night time.'"

Lena listened to Katya, laughing along with the others, and then she asked her older friend with some concern, "Aren't you afraid to tell these jokes?"

"Why should I be?" Katya asked.

"My mother told me that in Stalin's time people could be arrested and sent to a Gulag for that."

Katya smiled. "I know a joke about that too:

"A Soviet judge walks out of the courtroom, barely managing to suppress his wild laughter. A colleague asks, 'What is that you are laughing about?'

"'Well, I just heard a great joke,' the judge says.

"'A joke? Tell me!'

"'Are you crazy? I just sentenced a man to five years for that joke!'"

Both girls laughed.

"Why don't you go with us to Moscow next time and make some money too?" Katya offered Lena.

"Please don't be offended," Lena replied, trying to speak softly. "Even if I was dying from hunger, I don't think I would be able to make money by selling overpriced things to my friends and co-workers. I just don't think it is fair to them."

"Hmm." Katya shrugged her shoulders. "People in Moscow call it 'entrepreneurship'. You are just stuck in old-fashioned principles."

"I guess it takes a different kind of character than I have to be a 'new Russian' business woman," Lena answered.

Katya smiled indulgently. *Too bad, Lena,* she thought. *You will only be left behind.*

*   *   *

The women at the factory worked hard, trusting that things would change and the future would be better. Day after day passed, month after month, but life wasn't better, only worse. Nevertheless, people survived, new families formed, children were born—life continued in its natural and biological way.

Tonya cut off her long blonde hair into a popular "ala Murielle Mattie" style.

"I think our Tonya picked up a man from Moscow today," Katya proudly announced, putting down her heavy bags, and taking from her neck a garland of toilet paper rolls tied together by a long string.

"Really?" Lena asked in excitement, reaching out to help Katya.

"Yes. He traveled from Moscow on the same train with us and wouldn't take his eyes off Tonya. So… I started talking to him, and introduced Tonya and myself."

"She is a match-maker!" Tonya said, and her cheeks became pink. "But he's really a good man. I like him."

"He promised to stop in Zarecie and come to visit her on his way back to Moscow," Katya interrupted.

"Then we can go to Moscow on the Friday night train, together!" Tonya finished.

Lena smiled, and the girls hugged each other, happy for Tonya's good fortune.

A few months later Tonya and the man she met on the train were married, and she moved to Moscow. Every single girl envied her, because the dream of living in Moscow was the most desirable but one rarely achieved by poor and hard-working provincial girls.

The people were tired of their gloomy lives. There was no sympathy expressed when they watched on television the funerals of aging Politburo members, who passed away one after another, during a short period of time. The dark jokes could be heard, "Look how much money the Government spends on these funerals! For such money the whole Politburo could be buried all at once!"

Finally, a younger man, fifty-four-year-old Mikhail Gorbachev, was appointed as the Secretary of the Communist Party. The people looked to him with hope, listening to his speeches with high expectations of new energy. "Maybe now our lives will turn in the right direction. We have been struggling for a long time, but maybe our children will have a better future," some of them said, expressing thoughts of many.

"So, what do people in Moscow say about this new Secretary Gorbachev and his plans for *Perestroika*?" Lena asked Katya after her return from the capital one afternoon.

Katya became serious. "People in Moscow seem to like him. The simple workers hope that he will be able to make our life better." She paused. "But you know—"

"What?"

"The elderly people in my village say just the opposite."

"What do you mean?"

"Many believe that he is from Satan."

Lena stared at Katya in amazement. "What? Why?"

"They say that the unusual birthmark he has on his forehead is the stamp of Satan. Elderly people predict that Gorbachev has come to destroy our country."

Chapter 17

March 1989, Zarecie

LENA LOVED SPRINGTIME. IT felt so good to be outside on a bright sunny day after a long gloomy winter, when the sun was constantly hidden behind the low gray clouds. She had been working at the factory for almost six years, and had grown into a beautiful, slim, young woman. On one such sunny day, when the snow was melting, creating a mess on the road, Lena was walking down the main street in Zarecie. With a smile on her face, her long hair down her shoulders, in her unbuttoned coat, she tried to jump across the lumps of dirty snow on the road.

A young man in his thirties, tall and handsome, passed Lena. Suddenly he stopped, looked back, and quickly began following Lena, trying to catch up with her. The man approached Lena and asked with a smile, "I'm sorry... just wondering: what does such a pretty girl like you do in this gloomy town?"

Lena glanced at the man, smile still on her face. "Why is it gloomy? Look at this bright sun! It is springtime!"

"What's your name?" The tall man tried to stop Lena. "I'd like to get to know you a little better..."

Lena slowed down and looked at the man's face. "My name is Lena, and what is yours?"

"I'm Arthur. Are you busy tonight?"

"Yes, I'm taking dance classes." Lena checked her watch. "But I do have some time now."

Arthur looked around and gestured to the building across the street, "Let's go to that restaurant!"

Lena's face showed her uncertainty, as she delayed an answer. "Mmm.... I'm not sure."

"Don't worry, I'll pay!" Arthur insisted with a smile.

"I am sorry, but I don't know you well enough to accept your offer," Lena answered with confusion.

Arthur took Lena's hand and pulled her gently toward the restaurant. "But if you want to know me, we have to start somewhere. Just take it easy. Do you like ice-cream?"

Lena couldn't resist ice-cream, and nodded with a smile, "Yes, I do!"

At the restaurant Lena and Arthur sat at the table by the window. A waitress brought them a menu. Arthur started to read it, but Lena didn't. Arthur looked through the menu and asked Lena, "What would you like to eat?"

Lena shook her head, "I'm not hungry, thank you."

Arthur looked at her with a pleasant smile, then touched Lena's hand. "That's not true. Your beautiful blue eyes tell me that you are hungry." Lena turned her eyes away and then she looked down at the table.

Arthur offered, "I'll pick something and we both can eat. Would that be alright?"

Lena nodded with a shy smile, and then asked, "You speak with an accent. Where are you from?"

"I'm from Lithuania. I am doing some business here. And I do have money, so don't worry, please." Arthur paused, observing Lena. "Blue eyes and black hair—a rare combination. You are very beautiful!"

Lena was pleased with the compliment but tried not to show it, and asked, "What is your job? What do you do?"

"I'll tell you later," he said. He put down the menu. "So... you said you like to dance? I do too."

"Yes, we're having a dance party at our factory's dorm on Saturday night."

"It will be Women's Day, right?" Arthur noted, and added enthusiastically, "May I come as your guest?"

Lena again delayed her answer, and then said, slowly, as if in doubt, "I'm not sure if you'll like it there, Arthur. As you said, this town looks gloomy to you. And our women, they are very simple."

Arthur looked at Lena, observing her face carefully, and then almost jumped in joy from what appeared to be a sudden idea, "I know what you need!"

Lena smiled at Arthur's behavior.

"You need a nice long dress for that party!"

Lena frowned and looked down at the table again.

Arthur saw her reaction, and reassured her, "I'll buy you a dress! I will!"

"No, you can't!" Lena objected.

"I want to and I will. You are a real princess, and you deserve it!"

Lena shook her head again. Arthur stretched his hand over the table and covered Lena's hand with his. He looked into Lena's eyes and asked in a very low voice, almost whispering, "It would be my pleasure to give this little gift to you for Women's Day. Please, accept it. Don't think about the money. I have plenty, and you won't owe me anything. Please, be kind to me, don't refuse my gift."

Lena looked into his sky-blue eyes—they were kind and sincere. The color of his eyes, straw-like hair, his body type and the way he looked at her—all reminded her of Volodya. At this moment she felt as if she had known Arthur for a long time, and that she could trust him the same way she had trusted her Volodya. She thought it would hurt Arthur's feelings if she wouldn't accept his gift, so she simply agreed. "Yes, thank you."

The holiday party was held in the dorm's meeting hall. The wooden chairs were moved to the walls and stacked on top of each other. A red-colored banner nailed wall-to-wall read, "HAPPY INTERNATIONAL WOMEN'S DAY!" A tape recorder played patriotic music. The dorm administrator wished the workers a happy holiday, and then the dancing began. The waltz sounded from the tape recorder. Some women stood by the wall, and a few of them danced with each other.

Lena, wearing her long, dark, curly hair down, had on a tight bare-shouldered black dress that Arthur had bought for her. Arthur was dressed in gray business attire. They were a handsome couple and they looked like movie stars who somehow accidently found themselves in this gloomy and old dance hall. Their every move was followed by the jealous stares of many women standing by the wall.

"You are so beautiful, Lena! I have never seen a more attractive woman in my life. Let's escape from here." Arthur whispered in Lena's ear, and she laughed happily.

"Escape? Where?"

"I would take you any place you want. Would you go with me?"

Lena looked into Arthur's eyes. She didn't answer, just smiled.

"But, for now, let's just escape from this hall. There are too many curious eyes watching us."

"That is true. But I will need to get my coat from my room first. Then we can go."

They both laughed happily as they left the dance hall.

Arthur followed Lena to her room. Lena grabbed her coat from the wardrobe and was ready to go outside, when Arthur stopped her. "Please, wait," he said. He gently touched her hair, and asked, "May I kiss you?"

Lena smiled shyly, not knowing what to answer.

Arthur took her head in his hands and softly kissed her lips. His hands slipped behind her back, and he held her tightly around the waist. "You could make me the happiest man in the world, Lena," Arthur said, and kissed her again, but stopped, hearing the sound of people walking outside the door.

"Are your roommates coming?" he asked.

"No, my roommates went home for the holiday."

"What's all the noise about?"

"The party has ended."

"Let me kiss you one more time," Arthur whispered. They kissed again, and then again. Finally Lena gently broke away, "You should go, it is late." Lena put on her coat and opened the door. "I'll show you the way out, and then perhaps we could go for a short walk, if you would like that."

Lena and Arthur walked down the corridor, then turned and went down the stairs. As they approached the exit, Arthur tried to open the door, but it was locked. Arthur turned to Lena. "What's the matter?"

Lena also tried to open the door, and then she admitted in despair. "Oh, I forgot, they lock the door at night time. I am sorry."

Arthur looked upset, "And what shall we do? Who can open it?"

"I don't know. I may get in trouble if they find out that you're still here. We're not allowed to have guests in the room after 11 PM."

Arthur looked around, but there was no other exit from the building. "May I stay in your room then? I might be able to leave unnoticed in the morning."

Lena answered sadly, "It is my fault. You're right. Let's go back to my room."

After returning to the room, Lena put clean sheets on her roommate's bed for Arthur. He was watching Lena making the bed for him, and then he approached Lena and started kissing her again, whispering with admiration in his voice, "My Princess, my dear Princess. I want you; I love you. Be mine, Lena, mine alone!"

Lena gently pushed Arthur away. "I have to be up early tomorrow. If you want to stay here, you need to sleep on the other bed, please."

Arthur backed off agreeably, "Okay, as you wish."

Later that night, when Lena was already asleep, Arthur got up. He approached Lena's bed and quietly lay down beside her. Arthur waited, watching Lena as she slept. He slowly raised the blanket, and hugging her body tightly, started gently kissing Lena's face, her neck, her breasts, her body. Lena opened her eyes, whispering, "What are you doing, Arthur?"

"I want you to be my wife. Will you?" He didn't wait for her answer, covering her mouth with a hot, greedy kiss. The blanket fell down when his body started moving rhythmically. Lena tried to free herself, but Arthur was much stronger than she. "Don't be afraid. You will like it," he whispered and pushed hard his way through.

"It's all over now. It was good, my Princess," he assured her. Lena cried, as Arthur lay beside her, stroking her head.

When morning came, they didn't speak out loud. Lena lay on the bed with open eyes. Arthur stood up, went to the other bed, where his clothes were, pulled on his pants, and zipped them. "I should go, dear. And you shall go and do what you have planned. I'll meet you after work tomorrow." Arthur approached Lena and quickly kissed her.

As Lena stood, the blanket fell to the floor. Arthur looked on the bed and saw a bloody spot on the white sheets. He grinned, and with a satisfied expression on his face, quickly stepped to the door. "Tomorrow, baby, tomorrow!"

He opened the door and left. Lena sat back on her bed. She believed Arthur's promise, but something in his intonation made her cry.

Chapter 18

LENA AND KATYA WORKED in the huge and noisy sewing factory's assembly department. They sat among dozens of other women bending low above their sewing machines, making military uniforms.

Supervisor Peter pushed a cart with cut-out pieces of material between the rows, stopped it in front of the first woman in the row, and placed a stack of freshly cut sleeves on her table. Eighteen-year-old Olga, dressed in a low-cut bright blouse, sat in the first row. Katya was sitting next to her, and Lena was to the right of Katya. Olga gave the stack of pieces to Katya, who took the sleeves attached to the back and front details, checked them, and then turned to Lena, showing her Olga's work. "Look what she has done! It's all sewed backwards!"

Katya waved to Peter, who was moving his cart to the next row, distributing the next stack of material. Peter came over, checked Olga's work, and then grabbed the whole stack. He gestured for Olga to follow him.

Olga's face became pale with fear; she stood and silently followed Peter. The supervisor's office was a small messy room without windows. The desk was heaped with piles of all sorts of materials. Peter put the sleeves on the corner of his desk, and turned to Olga with an angry expression. "Do you realize what you've done? Do you want to lose your job?" he asked in a threatening voice.

Olga was so scared that she was afraid to answer.

"Now you'll have to stay after work and redo everything. Today our department will be behind the planned norm, and all because of you."

Olga began crying. Peter approached her, glanced down her blouse, and then said in a more friendly tone. "This is the most I can do for you in this situation. If you want to save your job…"

Olga looked at him with eyes full of tears. "Yes, I want…"

Peter went to the door and locked it. He returned to Olga, and started slowly to unbutton her blouse, revealing appetizing, big breasts. "Did you say you want to keep your job?" Peter pushed the fearful girl down on his desk.

A few minutes later Olga returned to her work table. Katya looked at her closely, noticing that Olga's hands were trembling when she pulled a piece of material from the stack on her table.

"What did he tell you?" she asked.

"He said I'll have to stay after work and redo everything," Olga whispered, unable to hold back the tears that ran down her cheeks.

When a signal for the end of the shift sounded, Lena stood up. "I have to go!"

Katya looked at a still sobbing Olga and said, "I'll stay for a while to help this poor girl. I know how bad Peter can be when he's angry."

Lena sighed, "Sorry, but I must go." She quickly went out and then downstairs to the exit.

There was a big booth, with windows on both sides to check the workers that were coming in and going out. Everyone had to stop by the guard and open up their purses for inspection.

Lena left the factory building and stood by the entrance, watching the other women getting out after their shift. She was waiting for Arthur. Soon the factory's entrance was empty, but Arthur still didn't come. Lena went out the factory's gate, looked down the empty street, and then returned back to the entrance. She didn't know where Arthur lived, nor his last name, or even his phone number. *If he doesn't come, I'll be unable to find him,* Lena sadly thought, walking back and forth by the entrance door.

Katya appeared at the door and approached Lena.

"What are you doing here so late?" she asked her roommate.

"Just waiting," Lena answered.

"Who are you waiting for?"

"A friend."

Katya looked at Lena with disbelief and repeated, "Hmm, a friend." She looked at her watch. "It's been almost two hours since you left after our shift. What kind of friend is that?"

Lena sighed. "You are right. There is no sense in waiting any longer."

They walked through the factory gate and turned onto the main street.

"I heard you danced with a handsome man at the holiday party? Who is he?" Katya asked.

"Just a man. We didn't have time to talk; he left early." Lena didn't want to continue this topic, but Katya already had the next question for her.

"Are you going to see him again?"

"Yes, he promised to come again. But, I'm not sure when. Do you need to buy groceries?" she asked, stopping at the intersection before crossing the street.

"Yes, I do. But the store will be empty, as always, I guarantee you."

It was a small provincial store, with only five or six shelves by the wall and glass displays that separated the saleswoman from the customers. Lena and Katya stopped and examined the half-empty shelves. There was only black and white bread, and cans with marinated tomatoes, pickles, onions, and coleslaw.

"Oho! Look, they are selling sausages today!" Katya exclaimed, noticing a saleswoman weighing some links she took from a small container on the counter.

The people began quickly forming a line to buy sausages that were rarely available. Lena stood at the end of the line, and Katya went to the counter to see if there would be enough sausages for them by the time they got to the front. She knew that every person could buy no more than one kilogram at once, so she could figure it out. She returned to Lena.

"It looks like we have a chance to get some." Katya opened her purse and counted her money. "I could probably buy two or three sausages with this," she said. Then she paused, thinking, "Well, we also need some washing soap." She closed her purse. "No sausages for me."

Lena also counted her money and said, "I'll just buy the bread. I have potatoes and cabbage, so I'll make a vegetable soup tonight."

*   *   *

An hour later Lena and Katya approached their dorm and entered. They went upstairs to the third floor, and then walked down the corridor. One of the doors was wide open, and they saw their new neighbor standing by that door, crying. Her suitcase was on the floor beside her. Loud yelling could be heard from the room. Lena and Katya stopped.

"What's going on?" Katya inquired.

Their neighbor answered, sobbing, "I went to the doctor... and she found out that I am pregnant. The doctor reports all pregnancy cases to the factory administration. Now they are throwing me out because women with children aren't allowed here."

Lena looked at the young girl with compassion. "But why now? We can't even see that you are pregnant!"

The neighbor answered, crying, "They don't want to show 'a bad example' to the others!"

The huge woman with dirty hair and an angry face, who worked as a dorm's guard, appeared from the room, carrying the bed sheets. She closed the door and locked it.

"Go ahead!" she gestured to the girl, and followed her closely, directing the pregnant woman to the exit.

Chapter 19

April 1989, Kabul

SOVIET TROOPS WERE FINALLY withdrawn from Afghanistan. The bloody war, which in Brezhnev's words, was supposed to last "no more than two to three months," had extended for ten years, and carried away 15,000 Soviet soldiers' lives, crippling even more souls.

Colonel Victor Nevorov stood dutifully in front of his soldiers lined up on parade in Kabul. He looked exhausted and much older than forty. His once youthful brown hair was generously gray. His tan complexion, drawn face, and cavernous eyes reflected tiredness from the sun, sand, and inhospitable conditions he had survived for a decade. The battle-weary Colonel dutifully read to the soldiers *The Statement of the Soviet Military Command*:

> "It is important to note that some people are trying to
> create an analogy between the presence of Soviet troops
> in Afghanistan and the American actions in Vietnam. It is
> not only unfair but even absurd to draw such parallels."

Nevorov looked up at the column of Soviet tanks with soldiers sitting on top. The soldiers' faces were tired, and the men were glad to go home. Colonel continued:

> "Starting with the fact that nobody invited the Americans
> into Vietnam, whereas the Soviet troops were sent to
> Afghanistan after numerous requests from the legitimate

Afghan government—"

"Start engines!" The command rang out from the head of the column, interrupting Nevorov. He folded the paper and put it in his pocket, running to take his place in the withdrawal.

The Soviet tanks moved toward the bridge through Amu-Darya. Victor Nevorov sat on the top of the last tank, looking back on the land of Afghanistan, and the words from The Statement he had just read to his soldiers resounded in his mind:

> "Withdrawal of Soviet forces, precise withdrawal, not flight, as was the case with the American troops in Vietnam, will be carried out according to plan, in strict compliance with the Geneva Agreements on Afghanistan, and according to the will of the Afghan and Soviet people with support from the world community."

Soon the tanks were on Soviet territory. The mountains of Afghanistan, a reminder of past nightmares, now could be seen far in the distance.

*   *   *

The next month Nevorov returned to Kiev but he could find nothing that he recalled leaving ten years ago. Life in the Soviet Union had changed completely.

It was hard enough for an active man to retire early and try to live only on his pension, but the transition from war to a peaceful life was twice as difficult. Nevorov had left one country—the Union of the Soviet Socialistic Republics—and returned to another, new country, which was now moving in unknown direction. Nevorov remembered how in Afghanistan, when his soldiers first heard about *"Perestroika,"* the men, who were already tired of the senseless deaths of their friends, would say aloud, even in his presence, "Let's go home! We did not swear to *this* new ruler. We gave our oath to the government of the Soviet Union!"

This protracted, unnecessary war, that had brought grief to thousands of families, was revealing itself to Nevorov as one of the major reasons for the collapse of the Soviet Union.

He walked into his one-bedroom apartment on the military base in Kiev's suburb, put his suitcase on the floor, and sat down on the sofa. He looked over at his wedding picture resting behind the glass on the bookshelf, and couldn't believe that the young, happy, smiling face belonged to him.

He remembered how after a few years in Afghanistan, he had received a letter from Tamara. She had written that she was tired of waiting for him and had asked for a divorce. Nevorov sighed, recalling how heartbroken he felt after receiving this news. He loved Tamara deeply but could do nothing in his situation, as he had sworn to serve his country and perform his military duties.

While in Afghanistan, Nevorov had tried to picture what his life would be like without Tamara after he returned home. When he filed the necessary papers for retirement, he suddenly discovered that no one needed him any longer. Alone, without a wife or family, having lost everything he had in the war, Nevorov felt he would rather return to Afghanistan. In reality all his feelings and emotions were still there, in the hot desert.

As a retired colonel, he could live in the apartment on the military base, but memories of his wife and their life together made his stay there too painful. Nevorov called every contact he had in Kiev, hoping to find a job, or at least to line up some interviews. He had a little savings, but now, with escalating inflation, his money was running out. Within the first months after his return to Kiev, nothing had worked out: people he knew before had moved, faces had changed; everything was different.

Day after day, Nevorov walked through the alleys in his favorite Maryinsky Park in Kiev, looking at used-to-be marvelous and now dried up fountains. Then he would sit on a bench smoking one cigarette after another, thinking of what he could do now.

Chapter 20

DESPAIR DIDN'T COME AT once. In the beginning there was fright, periodically replaced by hope, a mental consolation that everything would be all right, that 'it' could not happen to her. But as days went by, disturbing ideas became more obtrusive, and her doubts grew stronger. Like an iceberg building up in Arctic waters, becoming greater and colder with every new day, Lena's soul filled up, slowly and persistently, with an overpowering fear that gradually turned into a paralyzing state of depression.

At the beginning of May Lena arrived home—it was her mother's birthday. Holding a big bouquet of flowers, Lena approached Varya, who sat on the sofa watching TV.

"Happy birthday!" Lena kissed her mother on the cheek.

Varya accepted the flowers with a warm smile. "Thank you, dear."

Lena heard the noise of the gate opening and looked through the window, "There are some visitors coming, Mother."

Four women and Granny Maria entered. Varya stood up from the sofa, and warmly greeted their guests. Granny Maria gave Varya a home-made pie. Another woman offered *kielbasi* that she had made.

"Happy birthday, Varya!" Granny Maria hugged Varya.

"Oh, I stopped counting my years since I turned thirty, but thank you, and welcome," Varya answered with a smile. Lena and her mother moved the table to the middle of the room. They put the white tablecloth on it, and the vase with the flowers in the center, along with the pie, bread, and *kielbasi*. Lena brought marinated mushrooms, tomatoes, and pickles. Varya took a kettle with potatoes out of the *pech*. There was not much food in the house, but if guests came, in time-honored Russian tradition, people shared everything they had. Everyone sat around the table, and they began eating.

Granny Maria sat beside Lena. She reproachfully glanced at the untouched meal on Lena's plate. "Why don't you eat, child?"

"I have no appetite. I haven't been feeling very well lately," Lena quietly answered. For decency's sake she took a sip of cranberry juice from her glass.

"I don't like the way you look, girl," the old woman said.

As a little girl, Lena used to run to Granny Maria's house for a cup of hot milk, as they didn't own a cow. Often Lena would stay there late, listening to the old neighbor's made-up stories, combined with fairy-tales and real life adventures.

Granny Maria's entire family was killed during World War II. Not having children of her own, Maria indulged Lena, as if she were her own granddaughter, from time to time quietly cursing Lena's gypsy-father, "How could he abandon an innocent child? Impious!"

In the summertime, Granny Maria liked to bake pies with fresh berries. She would call Lena, "Come over, sweet child, I've got some treats for you. Have a piece of pie."

Lena also loved Granny Maria and she often shared her little secrets with the elderly woman. Lena felt comfortable in Maria's house, and it was much easier for Lena to pour out her heart to the old woman than to her own mother.

"We shall go to my house, child," Granny Maria said resolutely, getting up from her wooden chair. "I have some dried herbs. They will help your appetite."

Lena obediently rose from the table. "Mother, I'll go to Granny's house," she said. She took the hand of the old woman, whose body was twisted from long years of hard life, and they left.

Lena and Granny Maria walked slowly; they didn't talk. Lena slipped into her sad thoughts and Granny was saving her breath while walking.

In her house Granny Maria put Lena on the bench by the table, and placed a clay cup of fresh-milk in front of her. "Now tell me."

"What do you want me to tell you, Granny?" Lena asked, looking sadly into the old woman's face.

Granny Maria walked around the table, sat down on the bench beside Lena, and embraced the young woman's shoulders. "I see that something is bothering you. What is it, child?"

Lena, unable to resist the keen vision of the woman who had become wise with years, and who knew her so well, bowed her head. What to say? Lena had no one to share her problems with, and the fear of uncertainty had become unbearable, hanging above her head like a dark cloud, eclipsing her consciousness, and paralyzing her will-power.

Lena's cheeks became pink as she replied quietly, bowing her head even lower. "I don't feel well, Granny." Her face turned red and became hot from shame, and from the fear that her worst assumption might be true.

"Where does it hurt, dearest?" Granny Maria sympathetically looked into the girl's eyes. "Don't be afraid to tell me. I have herbs for any cause. With God's blessing they will help."

Lena could not say a word. Granny's compassion and her soft voice had caused a storm of emotions in the girl's soul, reminding Lena of her childhood, her years in school. For ten years she was the best student, the honor of the school, the most highly respected girl in their village. And what would happen now? How would she look into people's eyes?

She imagined herself six or seven months pregnant, walking down the street. The neighbors would stay by the well, scornfully looking at Lena as she passed them. "The best student! Honor of the school! Now look at her! Pregnant alley cat!"

How will I ever explain to my mother what happened? Lena thought. *In her eyes I will be an 'easy woman…'* Lena imagined her mother approaching her on the street; Varya's face was in tears. These fearful thoughts paralyzed Lena, and tears of shame and despair fell like hailstones from her eyes. She wanted to say something, but only an awful groan escaped from her chest, "Aaa-Aaa!"

The old woman rose, embraced Lena with both hands, and stroked her head with a shaking hand. Lena buried her head on Granny's chest. Granny whispered, "Do cry, cry, child. Tears clean the soul."

Having cried herself out, Lena wiped her face with Granny's towel which she grabbed from the table. She turned her red, swollen eyes to Maria and admitted in a quiet voice, "I am nauseated, Granny. I can't eat at all." Lena lowered her head again.

"Nausea? You probably got poisoned by something. You need to drink some chamomile tea. It will kill all the pain in your stomach…"

"It's been for two weeks now."

"Oh!" With a scared look on her face, Granny Maria put her hands on her chest. "Oh, my dear child, you aren't pregnant, are you?"

Lena whispered, covering her face with her hands: "I don't know, Granny. I didn't have my period."

"For how long?"

"Five-six weeks probably. I don't keep a calendar."

"Ohh." Maria glanced at bunches of dried herbs, hanging from the ceiling all over the house. "Ohh… I hope it is not too late."

Maria climbed on the top of the *pech* and removed a bunch of herbs hanging there. "You must take a steam bath. Then I will make you a drink, with one very rare, treasured herb. You will stay with me overnight. With God's will, I will help you, child. Who is he?"

"Who?"

"Who is the father of your baby?"

Lena's face blushed bright red and then became hard. "Nobody. There is no father. And please, don't ask me this question again, Granny."

The old woman nodded in agreement, then stood up and went to the door. "I shall go to prepare the steam-house for you." She glanced once again at crying Lena and whispered, "Ohh… you poor child."

Chapter 21

LENA HAD FORGOTTEN WHAT happiness was. Constant anxiety had compressed her chest like an iron vice. She did everything that Granny Maria advised her: first she warmed up her body in the steam house, sweating; then she sat above the hot stones, pouring water on them, trying to get more hot steam to warm up her lower stomach. She then drank the bitter tea made from the "treasured" dry herbs—but nothing helped. Her strong young body kept the fetus safe inside.

Lena felt disheartened; she did not know what to do and how to tell her mother about her pregnancy. She asked Granny Maria, "Please, don't tell anybody." But the old woman couldn't hold onto the overwhelming news.

Next Sunday morning, while Lena was still in bed, sadly deciding whether or not go home to visit her mother, the door of her dorm room swung open with a kick, and Lena saw her mother, breathing hard, with her gray hair tousled above her shoulders, standing on the threshold.

Surprised, Lena quickly rose up in bed. "Mother?" She got out of bed, hastily pulling down her nightgown. "What happened?"

"And you dare to ask me what happened?" Varya cried out. "You dare to ask me? You have disgraced me in front of the whole village! 'The teacher's daughter is a prostitute!' Was that what I raised you for, denying everything for myself?"

"Mother!"

"She got pregnant by 'Nobody!' Gypsy's blood!" Varya jumped at Lena and struck her cheek with all her might. "Whore! Slut! Don't ever show up in my home again!"

Lena gaped in horror; she defensively extended her hands, trying to shield herself from a new slap. "I am not a whore, mother. I... I simply trusted a man's word."

"How are you going to live now? The factory will throw you out of this room. Who will raise a bastard? Don't count on me, dirty woman. You are the same as your father. Forget you were my daughter..." The infuriated woman cried out words so quickly and desperately that she had no time to take a breath, unable to break off from the blind fury bursting her apart. "Whore... dirty streetwalker..."

Suddenly, with a spasm of coughing, Varya clutched her throat with her hands. She looked like a fish pulled from the water, convulsively catching air with her opened mouth but unable to inhale it more deeply into her lungs. A strong cough smothered her.

"Mom, Mother!" Lena cried. She seized her mother by the shoulders, not knowing how to help. "Calm down, mother..."

Varya, tormented by a coughing spasm, collapsed onto the floor, grabbing at her left shoulder.

"Doctor! I need a doctor!" In horror Lena jumped up and ran down the long corridor, knocking on doors. "Someone call an ambulance! Urgent!"

*　　*　　*

"Heart attack. Your mother is in surgery," a young nurse in a white uniform answered Lena from the Information Desk window at the local hospital. "You must wait."

Lena sat down on a metal chair by the wall. She waited fearfully.

A few hours later an old doctor, a tired-looking man in a surgeon's blue uniform, approached Lena in the waiting room. Lena stood up, "Doctor, how is she?"

The doctor looked at Lena sadly and cleared his throat. In spite of his long years of practice, he was not used to this part of his job. He put his hand on Lena's shoulder, as if she were his daughter. "You have to be strong, Lena."

Lena looked at him, shaking her head in disbelief, "No!"

The doctor sat her down on the chair, "I am sorry. We did what we could... But your mother has died. She had a massive heart attack." He stepped back. "I have to go. I'll ask the nurse to give you some water." He left and closed the heavy metal door behind him.

The nurse brought Lena a glass of water and asked, "When will you take the body?"

Lena didn't hear her. She drank the water, and sat, holding an empty glass, looking straight in front of her with wide-open eyes, not comprehending what had just happened. The nurse silently stood by her, then took the empty glass from Lena's hands and went back to her desk.

The next shift came in, and the young nurse was leaving. She said something to the elderly nurse, who had just arrived, and pointed toward Lena, sitting alone in the waiting room. The aged nurse answered a few phone calls, and then she approached Lena. She sat down beside her and offered sympathetically, "I can call your family for you."

"I don't have anyone," Lena whispered.

"Then your friends or coworkers," the nurse insisted. "I know it was a very hard day for you—"

"How could she die? What am I going to do?" Lena asked with desperation in her voice. "She has died because of me."

"Your mother died because she had a heart problem. Don't blame yourself."

"It's all because of me, because of me," Lena repeated, grabbing her twisted, unbrushed hair in both of her hands, as if she wanted to pull it out.

"Where do you live?"

Lost in her thoughts, Lena didn't answer. The nurse touched Lena's sleeve, repeating her question, "Where do you live?"

"In the dorm," Lena answered slowly, as if under anesthesia, her mind far away.

"Which dorm?"

"The sewing factory."

"I'll call them." The elderly nurse stood up and went back to her desk.

About an hour later Katya, red-faced from the brisk walk, appeared in the waiting room. "Lena!"

Lena didn't turn her head and only said, "Mother... my mother—"

"I know," Katya interrupted, hugging Lena. "Let me ask about their rules." She went to the Information Desk and talked to a nurse.

"She said they can keep the body in the morgue until we can get a coffin," she told Lena upon her return. "We should go now. Get up!" Katya stretched her hand toward Lena, but it was obvious that Lena wasn't in any condition to walk the long distance to their dorm.

"Shit," Katya cursed quietly as she checked her purse for money. "I'll call a taxi." She went to the Information Desk again and asked permission to use their phone.

"We should arrange for funeral supplies early in the morning, the nurse advised me," Katya told Lena while they were riding in the taxi to the dorm.

The next morning Katya and Lena woke up early and went to the local funeral supply store. They were unpleasantly surprised by the crowd outside the store. Experienced Katya immediately suspected what the matter was. "Something isn't right here," she murmured.

Pushing their way through the crowd, the girls entered the store and found absolutely nothing: no people, no supplies, no salesperson. Still stubbornly refusing to accept the monstrous reality, Katya turned to Lena and said, "Probably, there is no reason for the store to keep coffins on display; they are probably stored someplace out back, and here we just pay and get a receipt." To prove her thinking, Katya went to a back door of the store.

The back door opened just in front of her, and a middle-aged woman, wearing a dark-colored work uniform, entered the store. Katya quickly approached the employee and asked politely and softly, unusual for her, "Excuse me. My friend's mother has died. We need a coffin, but—"

"No coffins."

"What do you mean 'no coffins'? How can we bury—"

"The coffins should be here around noon. First come, first served." The woman disappeared behind the closed door.

Katya returned to where Lena was standing, her eyes wide open showing her frustration, and whispered, "It's crazy here! Let's go outside."

Both girls dashed out into the street toward the crowd, trying to find the last person in the line. And yet, even the most bitter and dismal circumstances can hold a ray of light. To their relief there turned out to be two lines in front of the store: the first, which was very long, was for memorial wreaths, while the second, considerably shorter than the first, was for coffins.

"You stay here," Katya told Lena, "and I'll try to find a phone booth to call the factory to find out if they can help us with a truck."

"Thank you," Lena answered quietly. "What would I do without you?"

"That's what friends are for," Katya answered, looking around and asking a person in the line where she could find a phone booth.

"Two blocks from here, by the grocery store," came the answer.

"Do you know by chance how many coffins usually arrive with each shipment?" practical Katya asked the next person in line.

"About twenty."

Katya quickly counted the people in the line in front of them. "We are fifteenth. That's good; we might get a coffin today," she said to Lena and went to call the factory.

Twelve o'clock was approaching, and there were still no coffins. People were nervous, but no one left the line for fear of not getting a coffin. Katya returned and said to Lena, "The factory promised to send the truck here about 4 PM." She looked at Lena's tired face with dark circles under her eyes, and added sympathetically, "There is a little cafeteria two blocks from here. You can get a sandwich, and they have a restroom there. I'll stay in line."

"Thank you," Lena said gratefully, giving Katya money to pay for the coffin. "I do need to use a restroom."

At long last the coffins were delivered. Katya's turn came. What she saw before her was a loose construction of damp, poorly planed boards of great weight and length.

"Excuse me... ah, you know... my friend's mother was a slim woman, not very tall, and light as a bird. This thing here is for a weight lifter..."

"One-meter-eighty. Citizens, all coffins come in standard sizes. Today we have only one-meter-eighties."

"But we don't need a meter-eighty coffin!"

"You don't? Then step aside and get out of the others' way."

"No, no, don't misunderstand me, we'll take it! I just wanted to say—"

"You can talk about it at home. If you're taking it, hand over your money."

They picked up Varya's body at the hospital and delivered it on the truck to the village, where the people helped Lena to bury her mother.

Soon after the funeral, a new teacher moved into Varya's house. Lena brought some of her mother's belongings to Granny Maria. As they stood outside waiting for the bus, Granny Maria looked at Lena's sad face and asked worryingly, "Now that new teacher lives in your house, you won't come to visit me, will you?"

Lena embraced Granny Maria. "I don't know, Granny. I feel so lost." The shock she was experiencing blocked all her emotions and the ability to think clearly.

"I am old and I don't know if God will give me a few more years to live, but you are always welcome here." Granny looked at Lena's stomach and added, "I'll do what I can to help you with the baby."

Lena didn't answer, rushing to move toward the packed bus that had just arrived.

Chapter 22

THE SITUATION AT THE factory that year, along with the disorganization of the whole country, grew increasingly worse and worse. There were days when the factory wouldn't receive materials to work with, and workers were sent home with no pay for that day. Now the women were happy when they could come to the factory and actually have work to do, no matter what they had to sew: uniforms, men's underwear, or just bed sheets.

On one such day, when Olga, Katya, and Lena sat at their work stations, sewing, Olga felt very sick. She worked slowly, from time to time putting her hands on her stomach, as if suffering from sharp cramps. Suddenly she stood up and bent over, screaming and holding her abdomen tightly. Katya touched Olga's shoulder. "What's wrong?"

"My stomach!" The seamstress' face contorted with pain. Katya looked at Olga's hands, squeezing her stomach, then down—and saw blood running onto the floor.

"Someone, call an ambulance!" Katya yelled.

Soon the sound of an ambulance siren was heard outside. The medical personnel came in and put Olga on a stretcher, taking her out from the building. Katya followed, holding Olga's motionless fingers in her hand.

Katya returned from the hospital when their shift was almost over. She took Olga's unfinished work and put it on her table. "I'll finish it all tomorrow; we don't have much work to do anyway." Lena and Katya went downstairs, and stood in the crowd of workers that slowly moved toward the exit. This time the guard was checking the workers' purses and their clothes, touching the women's bodies to make sure there was no hidden material under their garments. Some workers complained, others yelled jokingly, "Hey, man! Why don't you check her boobs also, don't be shy!"

"What happened to Olga?" Lena asked Katya while they waited in line.

"She had complications after an illegal abortion. Olga said it was Peter who forced her to do it."

"How horrible!" Lena whispered.

"Now she won't have a job," Katya said and showed her purse to a guard. The guard patted her down from shoulders to legs and then opened the gate for her to go.

"There are no jobs in this small town, except our factory. How will she survive?" Lena asked with worry, continuing their talk outside the factory.

Katya shrugged her shoulders. "At least she's alive. They removed her uterus, so Olga won't ever have children," she replied.

"But why should Olga lose her job, and not Peter?"

Katya stopped and looked at Lena in astonishment. "Are you really so naïve, or just pretending to be?" Seeing that Lena still didn't understand, she added, "Whoever blamed a man? Olga's pregnancy was her problem, not Peter's."

They walked in silence for a while and then Katya said, "I'm going to the movies. Care to join me?"

"No, thanks. I'll go for a walk. I need some fresh air," Lena answered, turning into the tiny street that led to the river.

*   *   *

All these events—waiting for Arthur to come back, expecting her period and hoping that everything would be all right, the fear of telling the truth to her mother, her mother's death and dealing with the funeral—had resulted in missing the time for safely ending Lena's pregnancy. From the beginning Lena was afraid to go to the factory's doctor, as she knew that information about her pregnancy must be released to the administration and then she would be evicted from the dorm.

Lena knew she could not afford to lose the room because she had no other place to live. She couldn't go back to the village: their house belonged to the school and had been passed on to the new teacher. She was unable to rent a room in Zarecie's private sector as it was too expensive and Lena had no savings, and Varya hadn't left any money for her. The Soviet law about *propiska,* the permanent residence registration, wouldn't allow people to move from the place of their residency to any other city if they had no relatives who would provide a place where they could stay.

Although medical abortions were officially allowed, they were strictly limited. Basically, the doctor could authorize an abortion only for mothers with three or more children, or for women with complicated pregnancies. Lena wouldn't fall under either of these categories. There was no sex education in Soviet schools and contraceptives were not widely available. Young women had to learn through trial and error, or from the advice of others, often paying a high price for unfortunate mistakes that were caused by their lack of knowledge.

The economic situation in the country and the difficulty of getting medical assistance forced many women to go to unqualified people for illegal abortions. Existing government programs provided such limited financial help for child support, that surviving on this money was simply impossible. The bureaucratic system was very resistant in establishing payments to single women, who were often left to survive on their own. It was extremely hard for a woman, who was unable to identify the father of her baby, to obtain help from the government. Single mothers struggled in the "highly moral" communistic society, often being treated poorly and disrespectfully.

Lena's feelings were mixed; she couldn't understand them. Her sickness during the first weeks of pregnancy was so wearisome that she did not think of the child at all. All she wanted was to get over this painful condition in the mornings. She drank the herb tea that Granny Maria had given her, hoping that her period would come, but the herbs didn't help.

Then there was her mother's death and funeral, followed by the despair and fear of abandonment and loneliness. "What to do? How to survive? How will I raise the child?" Lena couldn't find an answer to these questions.

Lena walked to the bank of the mighty river, passing the old shipyard with abandoned boats stored behind the wall. She sat on the hill, looked into the dark water's depth, and wondered if it would be easier to end her life now, by simply jumping from the high rocks. All her problems would be solved immediately; nobody would find her, nobody would know about her shame.

This fear of shame, publicity, and general condemnation was intolerable. Lena hated herself and her life. How could it happen to her, the girl who was always an example for others, "the best of the best," an ideal leader whom everyone aspired to follow?

"Everything is falling apart. If the most powerful country is collapsing, who cares about your life?" a quiet internal voice admonished Lena. "Well, let's say I will be able to live through this shame and dishonor. I'll let people step on me, crush me down, and throw stones at me... And then what?" Lena murmured. She waited for her inner adviser to respond, but the "clever voice" was silent. Lena saw no exit from her situation; she felt as if she stood in front of a high, insurmountable wall.

A cold wave of despair flooded down from the top of her head to her toes, paralyzing her brain, and leaving her with a feeling that she had been insulted. She wanted revenge, but her anger at Arthur meant nothing and was flushed away by overwhelming powerlessness. She had that feeling of defeat from realizing her weakness and uselessness in this world. *Why should I live, for what? Why should I suffer?* She thought.

"You must simply jump from this hill, and all problems will be resolved at once. No one will find you; nobody will know about your shame," Lena's inner voice insisted. She felt tortured by not knowing what the future would bring her. The inability to plan or simply rely on something stable shattered her spirit, which was already weakened by questions and doubt. Fully exhausted, she was almost ready to give up.

Lena lowered herself to the grass on the river bank and sat without moving for hours. The dark glow of the great river caused an inexplicable feeling that seemed to anticipate a special moment. She felt so small and unimportant, as if she was a drop of water in an endless ocean. "Who am I in this world?" she asked herself sadly, but she knew she was still a part, although a small one, of nature's greatness. Lena could sense anxiety and alarm in the water's movement—whether the anxiety and alarm were dying down or, on the contrary, gathering strength, was not for her to know. It was the instant moment in which they were born that stretched out into a long and monotonous existence. And it wasn't for her to know whose force it was, whose power—the land over the water, or the water over the land; the sound of the water was peaceful and soft like a quiet lulling song at her child's cradle.

Lena looked up at the sky and then down at the water, completely hypnotized by its greatness. The rhythmic splash of water by the bank had gradually calmed her down; she observed the opposite side of the river, trying to recognize where the water ended and the sky began.

"Which side has height and which has depth? And where is the boundary between them? Which one of these equal parts contains the consciousness that knows the simplest of the secrets: why do we live? What is a reason for our existence?" Lena asked herself questions which no one had answered yet. She stood up and walked by the river back toward the dorm, looking at the lights on the fishing boats; the gloomy suicidal thoughts had disappeared, as if they had dissolved into the deep waters of the ancient river.

Lena knew that she would need money to take care of the baby, so she tried to use the time she had left until the birth to save as much as she could. With her scanty salary she limited herself in everything. Her normal diet was a potato soup, to which she added fried onions and carrots. She ate this soup twice daily, until it was gone.

At other times she would cook cabbage soup, adding two or three finely cut potatoes and a spoonful of sour cream to her bowl. In the summertime she liked to prepare cold borscht from beets. This cold borscht was a real luxury, especially when she included a fresh cucumber and a boiled egg. Raised in a village, Lena was unpretentious about food—there were days when she would have just a cup of hot tea with a piece of black bread.

One Sunday Lena went to the local flea market. There were hundreds of people forming rows and selling different goods: clothes, towels, soap, toilet paper, packages of food, and cans of marinated vegetables. Lena strolled down every row, looking at the goods and asking for prices. She finally stopped and bought a few skeins of black woolen yarn.

During summer Lena spent time after work in the park. She sat on a bench and knitted a sweater while watching the children play. Later, she wore the wide, oversized sweater that she had made, to hide her growing stomach. She also went to the pharmacy and bought a bandage which helped to flatten her stomach. She spent her days in loneliness, reading in the park, or sitting on the river bank, trying to limit possible contacts and avoid being seen. Her friends thought Lena was grieving the passing of her mother, and tried not to annoy her.

Soon autumn came and brought the cold weather. Now, instead of spending time outside, Lena went to the library and read books about obstetrics. In the beginning Lena had no feelings for her baby; she even thought she could not love this child. Often, when anxious thoughts were attacking her, Lena hated the seed of the man who had used her so callously. *I don't know anything about Arthur. What if he was a former prisoner, who was sentenced for murder? My child might inherit his genes and become a murderer too. What if Arthur was a thief, a bandit, a thug?* In such moments uncontrollable tears rolled down Lena's cheeks. *Why would I love his child?*

Later Lena read in the medical encyclopedia that the chromosomes bearing the genetic information could be incorporated in a random order, and she thought with great hope and tenderness, *What if this child would look like my father, or if it would be a girl who would look exactly like me?* In such moments Lena was eager to see the child. She carried the baby under her heart, knowing that it must survive no matter how hard it would be, and for this purpose her pregnancy must not be discovered. Its birth was the primary goal that Lena needed to achieve, first. What to do after that was the next problem, and Lena wasn't able to think about all of that just yet. All she could rely on for now was hope that when the time came, life itself would resolve everything for the best.

Chapter 23

November 1989, Zarecie

THE LOCALS CALLED ZARECIE "the City of Brides." Like with any other joke, there was some truth in this one too, because there were more women than men at the city's textile production plants. And in this small town, like in any other place, even in that desperate and hungry time, with no salary paid, and empty store shelves, many young girls still dreamed about love and happiness.

November's salary at the sewing factory was two weeks late. It was the last time people had received their money that year. Women grumbled, but they couldn't leave their jobs, and continued working, relying only on the administration's promises that they "would get paid later, and as soon as possible."

In many regions people began to revolt, even starting strikes. Many factories stopped working. The ones that continued to work began paying workers' wages in the form of the goods they produced, such as flour, bread, stockings, soap, clothes, or parts of furniture.

People went to the market, or stood by the railroad stations, waiting for passing trains, and tried to sell their goods, or at least exchange them for food or other household items.

There was a small window in the wall on the second floor of the factory through which the workers received their salary. On pay day dozens of women lined up there waiting for their money.

"It's already five o'clock, knock on the window!" someone ordered in a loud voice. The first woman in the line started knocking on the window, but there was no answer. The conversation of angry and impatient women became louder. More women came to the window and knocked on it; still there was no answer. Then a few women started hammering on the metal door by the closed window with their fists.

The door opened, and a cashier, a tired woman with gray hair, yelled, "What are you hammering on my door for? If I had money, I would give it to you! Go and pound on the director's door!" Without listening to the people, she slammed the door shut.

The next day dozens of women stood together in the factory's meeting hall, bickering. The factory director, in his fifties, with short black hair and wearing a business suit, appeared on the wooden stage and announced, "I have called Moscow. The government knows our problems. We must be patient. The war in Afghanistan is over; and now our economy will do better—"

But the angry women's voices impatiently interrupted him, "We need our money! Or, at least, goods we can sell. We have to feed our children!"

"The government is doing everything possible to send us money," the director replied. "If you want to receive your money in the future, you should continue working. Now, go back to your departments."

Lena stood silently behind the column, listening to the angry voices of the shouting women, her blue eyes seeming too big on her exhausted face. *I have to find money*, she thought. *I must try to get some!*

The winter of 1989 came early and as always, "unexpectedly." Zarecie's streets were buried in snow. In their everyday hunt for food and other goods, people turned to the local market more often. In spite of the cold weather, many would go there trying to sell whatever they could find in their homes; or the goods they had received for their work.

On the following Sunday Lena went to the market. Every so often she stopped by someone who was selling baby clothes, asked for the price, and then she went to the next one, without buying anything. At the very end of the flea market she approached a small store with a handmade sign above the door: "JEWELRY." She stood for a minute in front of it, as if deciding whether or not to go in, and then she pulled the heavy door open and entered.

It was a small room with no windows and lighted by a neon lamp above the long counter where jewelry was displayed under a glass top. An elderly man, looking like a scared crow, bald-headed, with a large hooked nose, and thick-lens glasses, appeared from the back room. He stood behind the counter, hiding his hands in the sleeves of his warm winter jersey.

Lena looked at the jewelry on display, and then she turned to the owner and asked, "May I sell my earrings here?"

The man attentively observed Lena's face, and his eyes fixed on her earrings. "The ones you're wearing? Show them to me," he replied in a squeaky voice.

Lena took off her earrings and handed them to him.

In the back room the man examined the earrings with his jeweler's lens. The next minute his face lighted up with a satisfied smile. He stood up, joyfully rubbing his hands, and then parted the curtains to once again observe Lena, who stood waiting patiently, not even looking at the display of jewelry.

The jeweler came out from his back room, holding the earrings in his palm, and said, "I could give you eight hundred rubles."

"What? That's only about fifteen dollars!" Lena exclaimed in shock. Living in hyper-inflation, people had learned to convert rubles into dollars to have at least something to compare their money to. A year ago, Lena's monthly salary was equal to about eighty dollars, six months later it had dropped to forty, and now she had none.

The old jeweler looked at Lena from her head to her toes as if he was going to buy her. "But…" he paused, giving more weight to his offer. "If you go with me to my back room, you could get more money for your earrings."

Lena's face expressed her aversion. "You… you… dirty prick!" She snatched her earrings from the man's hand and stormed out of the store.

Outside she slowly walked by the rows of the sellers again, stopping by the people who had baby clothes, asking for the prices and going to the next one. Then she turned around and returned to the jewelry store.

The jeweler stood behind the counter and greeted Lena joyfully, "I knew you would be back!"

Lena stood in front of him, biting her lips, realizing his complete power over her. "Yes, I do want to sell my earrings," she spoke slowly. "But… the price you offered me is too low—I can buy nothing… or just only a couple of small items for it!"

"I know, dear, I also don't have much money, and I have to feed my kids too." Now the jeweler's voice sounded soft and disgustingly sweet. He was looking at Lena with greedy eyes.

"But these earrings... They are more than two hundred years old... and they are made from high-quality gold!" Lena begged. "You can't find anything of this quality any more—"

"I know, sweetie, I know. I love your earrings. These antique *serezki* are a piece of art. You should be careful wearing them—there are many bad people around here. Do you know someone else to offer them to?"

"No, I don't," Lena answered quietly, lowering her head.

With his finger, the jeweler lifted up Lena's chin and looked lustfully into her eyes. "Will you go with me, and please me? I'll pay you twenty five dollars then," he whispered.

Lena shook her head and stepped back from him.

The old jeweler looked at Lena's stomach and said with a malicious smile, "Soon you'll need to feed your baby, right? Think of him."

Lena didn't answer. She knew this store was the only place where she could get the money she needed right now. "These earrings are all I have left from my mother," she whispered, and the tears of hopelessness ran down her cheeks.

The jeweler didn't hear her. He went back behind the counter and firmly concluded from there, "Eight hundred rubles—that's my final word. No one will give you a better price in this small town." His voice sounded squeaky again. "Do you want it in rubles or dollars?"

"In rubles. I'll have to spend them today, anyway." Lena took off her earrings and laid them on the counter.

Chapter 24

December 1989, Kiev

SITTING IN HIS UNHEATED apartment, Nevorov called the military commissariat. "I need a job. I have no money left." As he spoke sharply and asked for help, the person on the phone told him to report to the office to receive his retirement documents.

The next morning Nevorov took a *tram* to the center of the city. He quickly found the huge, five-story, gray stone building, and went inside, passing the massive columns by the entrance door.

He went upstairs and found an officer seated at a desk, writing. The officer stood and shook his hand. Then he took a small cardboard document from his desk and gave it to Nevorov, saying, "Congratulations on your retirement, Comrade Colonel."

"Thanks," Nevorov answered.

The officer looked at him. "You don't sound very happy."

"You're right. It's hard to adjust to civilian life after being in Afghanistan for all these years."

"I understand; it must be hard. But I saw from your documents that you asked for permission to stay there when your replacement was due, right?"

"Yes, I did," Nevorov nodded. "I am a soldier. I don't know any other profession. I was trained to fight… and now, what can I do now?"

The officer started flipping through documents and answered without looking at Nevorov, "Take a vacation; you earned it."

"I have no one to spend my vacation with. My wife left me when I was in Afghanistan."

The officer was sympathetic. "I am sorry for your loss, Colonel."

"Life looks so different now. I feel like I am not in the Soviet Union, but in a different country."

"Yes, that's true." The officer gestured toward the door, indicating the end of their conversation.

Nevorov walked to the door, but stopped, holding the handle, and said bitterly, "Leaving for Afghanistan in 1979, I swore to protect the country of the Soviet Republics, my government, and the Communist Party. Now I am back, and we are not building communism anymore; now it is *Perestroika*. Can you tell me, what are we trying to rebuild?"

"This is a question I can't answer, Colonel. I am also a Communist, but the Party we knew is dissolving, and the former General Secretary Gorbachev proposed a new government in the form of a presidential system."

"The fish is rotting from its head..." Nevorov winced in disgust.

"We call it openness, or *glasnost*—"

"What you call 'openness' betrays all the principles of socialism that millions of people have given their lives for," Nevorov interrupted impatiently.

"Yes, glasnost and perestroika—"

But Nevorov didn't listen to the officer. In his soul he already disdained this "rear rat" who had never been in combat.

"What do you mean, 'the Party is dissolving?' Are you saying that nineteen million members of the Communist Party don't exist any more, all these people mean nothing to you? What are you talking about?" Nevorov didn't hide his anger. "And what does '*glasnost*' mean, if no one wants to hear my *glas*, my voice? What does it mean if I can't speak openly, if I have no job, no money, and no one cares?" Nevorov swallowed, then took a deep breath.

The officer didn't answer. He looked down, pretending he was reading his papers.

"So what should I do?" Nevorov repeated his question, now much calmer.

"Take a vacation."

Returning to his apartment, Nevorov sat on the sofa, took out his old address book, and started flipping through it again, as he had done many times before. He felt desperate and useless. When he started at the beginning for the fifth time, he stopped at the same place as he always did: Afanasiev. Until that moment, Nevorov had been determined not to call him. General Afanasiev, with his unusually fast-rising and very successful career, belonged to another world. Afanasiev was married to the daughter of a former member of the Politburo, and had never been through the bloody meat grinder of war, facing the enemies on the front line, as Nevorov did. Victor had always felt uncomfortable after Afanasiev had ordered the urgent delivery to Moscow of the opium that they had found in Afghanistan. The general told Nevorov that this opium would go to the hospitals, but there was a rumor that the bags of opium had never been delivered to the clinics where they were expected.

Afanasiev had always been good to Nevorov, inviting Victor to call him any time. Now he seemed to be the only person with the sort of wide connections in Moscow who might be willing, and able, to help Nevorov find a job.

Nevorov looked at his watch and calculated that with the time difference Afanasiev should be home. He picked up the phone and dialed the number. "Comrade General? Hello, this is Colonel Nevorov speaking."

"Victor? Hello! Many days, many years… are you back home?"

The intonation of the domineering, self-confident voice on the other end of the line brought disturbing tiny goose bumps to the surface of his arms. Nevorov swallowed the lump in his throat and forced himself to continue. "Yes, I am home, General. Kiev is very different now; there is nothing for me to do here. How are you doing?"

Nodding his head, Nevorov listened while Afanasiev bragged about his life in Moscow. Then he answered, "Thank you for the invitation, Comrade General. That is probably exactly what I need right now—just to see my friends, talk to them, and then we'll figure out what to do. You are right, General. I will be in Moscow tomorrow. Thank you."

He hung up the phone, and sat for a minute, thinking. Then Nevorov called the train station and reserved a ticket for the morning train to Moscow. He stood up, took out his military suitcase, and threw in his clothes.

*   *   *

Once on the train, Nevorov sat by the window, drinking hot black tea from a glass in an aluminum holder, observing the villages he was passing. The train stopped at a station and Nevorov saw people rushing to the cars, offering passengers different goods, such as stockings, home-made socks, soap, and toilet paper. This stop lasted about five minutes, and then the train pulled out. On the side of the dirt road that led to the station Nevorov saw a few people standing by some wooden coffins. He turned to the train attendant who came in to pick up his empty glass, and asked, "Why are those people standing by the coffins? What are they doing there?"

The attendant, a woman in a railroad uniform, her eyes red from a sleepless night, responded, "They try to sell the coffins, or exchange them for some food."

"What?" Nevorov asked emotionally. "Why coffins?"

"The local factories don't have money to pay wages, so they compensate the workers in the goods they produce; they call it *barter*. Workers who produce clothes, or soap, or bread are the lucky ones. Those who produce the coffins are having a hard time getting anything in exchange."

"Unbelievable!" Nevorov shook his head, looking out the window while the train was passing a group of despondent people by the side of the road. "In Afghanistan they never told us about these things."

"That's what our life has become now. My neighbor is fifty years old; he lives alone. He became so weak from not eating that he put his coffin in the middle of his living room and laid down in it to wait for his death."

Nevorov covered his head with his hands. He didn't want to hear any more. How could he have even expected that after returning to civilian life he would have to overcome one more obstacle, where death would show its face again? While his soldiers, strong, young, healthy men were dying for the freedom of the Afghan people, his own countrymen were struggling with poverty and hunger.

As a Soviet officer, who with honor carried out his international duty for the Fatherland, he had never imagined that death would appear closer to him in his own country than in Afghanistan, and that the growing crime and corruption of the State machinery would become more dangerous than a Taliban's *stinger*.

Chapter 25

December 1989, Moscow

NEVOROV ARRIVED IN MOSCOW and took a taxi from the train station. He looked out the taxi's window at the busy capital's streets full of hustling people. The taxi drove through Red Square, and Nevorov observed the long, red brick wall surrounding the Kremlin. He listened to the sound of the Great Bell on the Spasskaya Tower, and watched the changing of the guard in front of Lenin's Tomb. The taxi turned onto Tverskaya Street and then onto the Kalininsky Prospect.

General Afanasiev lived in a government-owned apartment on the Kalininsky Prospect, a famous street which housed the Soviet elite.

"Nevorov! Come in!" Afanasiev exclaimed as he opened the door. The men shook hands. Afanasiev had gained weight and looked chubby even in his military uniform. His dark-brown Mongolian eyes had turned into narrow slits and his round face looked like a fully ripened apricot. He was two years younger than Nevorov but had made a meteoric career rise during the Afghanistan war and now was settled comfortably in Moscow.

"Oho! Some people know how to succeed in this life!" Nevorov exclaimed in wonder, going from one room to another, amazed by the expensive furniture that sank gracefully into soft carpets.

"So, you were saying that you can't find a job," the young general said, reminding Nevorov of their telephone conversation, gesturing toward the fancy white-leather armchairs.

"I've never seen such beautiful furniture! I am afraid to even sit down in this chair," Nevorov said in amusement.

"My wife ordered it from Europe through a catalogue." The General smiled indulgently. From under a coffee table he pulled out a mini-bar full of bottles. "Choose, Nevorov. What shall we drink?" Afanasiev showed him the bottles with import labels, one after another. "Brandy, whisky, champagne...?"

Nevorov, confused by this abundance of imports, asked with doubt, "What about our *Stolichnaya?*" He looked at the bottles with bright import labels, then scratched his head. "You, brother, are living... like a king!"

"Ha-ha!" Afanasiev laughed. "I forgot I am with my soldier-brother! I've been stupid; I should have guessed your choice. Nothing is better than our Russian vodka. It's in the kitchen, close by, like a beloved wife," the general grinned, leaving the room. "I'll be back in a few moments."

Afanasiev returned bearing an open bottle of vodka with two glasses in one hand, and a plate with chunks of sausage, bread, and pickles in another.

"This is our way!" Nevorov sighed with relief. "I was concerned. 'Where am I?' I thought."

"It's all right, relax." Afanasiev poured both glasses full of vodka. "Don't you remember who I married?"

Nevorov shot vodka into his mouth, sniffed a piece of rye bread, and then nodded his head. "I do..." He remembered how he and the other officers wondered what the daughter of a member of the Politburo had found in this village guy. Everyone was envious when Afanasiev "won his lucky ticket," as they called his marriage. Nevorov looked around at the walls covered by large pictures, and fixed his eyes on a huge crystal chandelier hanging from a ceiling. "I feel like I am in a museum or theatre. I had no idea that a Communist Party member's apartment could look like this."

Afanasiev took a large drink of vodka and also smelled his piece of rye bread. "Well, just so you know... it's not because of my father-in-law. I have earned everything by myself. But, certainly people knew who I was..."

"Yes, I have heard about your promotion. Congratulations. By the way, how is your new job?"

"I enjoy my new position as it gives me great power and limitless possibilities. I never thought that *Perestroika* could reshape my life so significantly." Afanasiev poured some more vodka into Nevorov's glass, but left his untouched.

"You won't drink another one?" Nevorov asked, seeing that the general didn't refill his glass.

"Not now. I have some work to do yet. Where are you staying?" Afanasiev asked, looking at his watch.

"Nowhere yet. But please don't worry, I'll find a place." He paused and then looked into Afanasiev's eyes. "You didn't answer. What kind of work do you do now, or is it a military secret?" Nevorov repeated his question with a sarcastic grin.

Afanasiev became serious. "You are correct. It is a secret." The general's smile faded.

"You have a secret, even from me, your long time war comrade?" Nevorov asked. "Just yesterday we fought together..."

The general stood and patted Nevorov on the shoulder. "Calm down, don't get so heated up—"

"Heated up? Do you have any idea how civilian people treat me, the war veteran? Do you think I am getting any respect for risking my life in the Afghan desert? No. People look at me like I am an 'untouchable'. They avoid me, don't give me a job. Even the officer at the military commissariat ignored me..."

"Victor! You don't understand. Things have changed here. And changed a lot. It is a work of the media, and the people who protested at Red Square against the war. They showed on TV how the Afghan people 'suffered' because of our intervention there. The media and the West wanted us to stop the war. People were tired, too."

"But we followed an order! Why do people here look at me as if I am a murderer, instead of paying me respect?"

Nevorov was mad and Afanasiev felt he owed an explanation to him. "True, we all followed an order. But people are angry for this war, for their sons' deaths, for hunger and poverty in the country..."

"Is it my fault? Tell me, Afanasiev. We served together, and now, even you, my comrade, treat me like shit—"

"Victor, I know we served together. But now, in fact, you're retired. And I, you know better than anyone else, have taken an oath. I can't release the secret information to you."

"I know." Nevorov sadly lowered his head. "I just got excited, forgot who I am now—an unwanted retiree. I apologize, General," he added, barely able to swallow, as if a stone had risen in his throat. "I must go. Thank you for your hospitality," he said, awkwardly rising from the too-soft armchair and holding out his hand to bid farewell to Afanasiev.

"Wait a minute, Victor, wait. Such a fire you are!" Afanasiev followed Nevorov into the corridor. "Please, understand. I just can't sit here and drink with you now. I must go—I have an appointment."

"Yes I know, I know. You have an important job and I'm sincerely glad for you. But you are the very first person who has told me you are happy with Perestroika. It seems like your soul has also 'reconstructed.'"

Afanasiev acted as if he didn't hear these remarks. "Wait!" He commanded. "You told me on the phone that you wanted to visit some of the men from your battalion. It's a good idea. Even more, I might have a job for you. Do you have a car?"

Nevorov turned to his comrade and answered with a bitter grin, "No. I don't own one. In all the years of service I wasn't able to earn enough money to buy one."

"Here is an address and keys to my other apartment." The general wrote the address on a piece of a paper. "Though why do I write it down? My driver will be here in a minute. He will give you a ride there."

Afanasiev picked up the phone and dialed a number. "By the way, I'll assign this soldier to you as you need. Go visit the men. Talk to them. Put together five or six of your best soldiers. I need you, and them, here in Moscow. Agreed, Colonel?" Afanasiev asked, handing the keys to his apartment to Nevorov.

Victor hesitated, delaying his answer. Then he shook his head as if shaking off an unwelcomed thought, and accepted the keys from Afanasiev's hand.

"Okay, agreed. I'll do what is necessary," he answered. "And how big is your other apartment?"

"Just two bedrooms, but it is located in the historical area near Red Square. It is my private apartment; even my wife doesn't know about it. Do you understand?" Afanasiev winked like a conspirator.

"What?" Nevorov raised his brows. "You have secrets, even from your wife and her papa? You might be a dangerous man!"

"Do you see what kind of private information I share with you? Knowing just that, you could destroy my career with one phone call, isn't that a fact?"

"With such a wife and her papa... You *are* a man!" Nevorov said soberly.

"Yes, and I know that I can trust you. You can live in that apartment as long as you need to. I'm going to buy a bigger one, anyway. If we stick together, this one may become yours as a part of your paycheck. It depends on how business goes. Agreed?"

"Agreed," Nevorov nodded. "I will go to Zarecie first. Remember my commissar, Serega? He lives there. I trust him as I would myself. Together we'll build a team."

"Good plan. Talk to him and bring him, and other men here, to Moscow. Tell them they will be paid well."

"I'll do so. *Specnaz* won't let you down, General."

They clasped palms in a strong handshake.

Chapter 26

IT WAS THE MIDDLE of December, and Lena had everything prepared for her delivery. She packed the baby's items and medical aids into a bag and left it in the factory's locker, ready for departure after her shift. Granny Maria helped her to calculate that the baby would be due in two weeks, and Lena planned to take a vacation starting the next Monday. Granny Maria told her that she had experience in these matters and would help Lena with her delivery. Granny Maria promised to take care of the baby so Lena could go back to work after her vacation.

Katya was absent on Friday and Lena was asked to work a double shift to help with the quota. There was about an hour left until the end of the second shift when she began feeling strong contractions. *It's too early yet*, she thought, continuing to work on the sewing machine. She was wearing the big black sweater she had made to hide her pregnancy. It was cold at the factory, and many people wore layers of clothes to keep them warm, and it didn't look strange that Lena wore an additional working smock which made her look bigger just because of its size.

So far no one had made any comments about Lena's appearance, and she was very happy about how she had managed her situation. Suddenly, she stopped working and put her hand on her stomach, her face contorted from the pain. She whispered quietly to herself, "One, two, three... Oh. The cramps are too frequent." Lena was worried she might not be able to finish the shift. She sighed deeply and continued her work, convulsively clenching her teeth. Suddenly she stopped again, thinking, *Something's wet. Oh, no! Did my water break?*

Lena stood up and walked between the rows of working seamstresses, then rushed into the dressing room. By both walls there were lockers where the workers kept their purses and personal belongings. Lena opened her locker and took out her bag.

She then went to the shower room, locking the door behind her. Lena turned on the faucet to check whether water was flowing in the pipes. She set out the items she had brought with her: she put a towel on the floor and covered it with a piece of the baby's bed sheet. Lena dropped to her knees and looked at the dirty wall in front of her, as if she saw an icon of the Savior there. Lena bent to the floor and whispered a prayer that she used to hear from Granny Maria in her childhood, "My God, rescue, save and forgive me my sins. Help me, Father, help me."

Suddenly, she felt a sharp, rolling pain that pressed her down and forced her to her hands and knees. "Oooo-hhh! Oh, mommy!" Lena rolled from her knees onto her side. She then turned over onto her stomach and rose up again on all fours. She pushed.

Lena remembered from the books she had read that she must breathe deeply and rhythmically. She had practiced doing so many times. "One, two, three, breathe in; then slowly breathe out." But now all her skills seemed to disappear. The intolerable pain paralyzed her consciousness, and she didn't know what to do next. She hoped that nature would take over and direct the birth the way it was supposed to go.

She had read that during labor and delivery a mother does what her body compels her to do to bear the child. A mother's body is made to give birth without assistance, as long as there are no complications. Lena tried to count and breathe rhythmically, but the waves of pain and the convulsions grew stronger and stronger, not allowing her to gather her wits. "O-o-o-o…" Lena stayed on her hands and knees and began pushing, trying to squeeze the new creation and the source of her pain and torture from her body. She attempted to determine if the position of the child had changed by pressing and rubbing her abdomen, while whispering to her baby, "Don't you think it's time for me to see you?"

Unable to get to the showers, Lena struggled to reach the sink faucet, and turned on the water full force. "It will be better this way. Who knows, you might be a loud one." Still on her knees, Lena placed her arms on the sink, and pushed again, "U-u-uhhh." She rested for a while and then pushed once again, "U-u-u-hhh." Something wasn't right. The pain was excruciating. It felt as though a rock was thrust against her tailbone, but the child wouldn't appear. Lena reached between her legs and touched the baby's head, felt its hair.

"What's the matter? Why don't you come out?" Lena's breathing was shallow and rapid. She felt tense and frightened. Her shoulders pulled up toward her ears; her neck and shoulder muscles felt tight and rigid. She began to panic and breathed heavily, sucking air into her lungs and expelling it in short, sharp gasps. Pins and needles prickled her fingers; her mouth went numb. When a new wave of sharp pain overwhelmed her, Lena passed out.

The sink overflowed, raining water down on Lena, bringing her back to life. "O-o-o-hhh, this pain!" she cried. "Baby, are you trying to kill me here?" Through sheer willpower Lena gathered her strength, combined with the force of her rage against the father of this child, and prepared to give one final push. She got on her knees again, instinctively feeling that in this position gravity would assist the delivery. Lena reached and grasped the thick hair on the baby's crown. "A-a-a-a!" As she contracted, she pulled the baby out and again collapsed into the darkness. She didn't see her baby gasp spasmodically and then become motionless.

A milder contraction awakened Lena, as her body completed the birth process. *It must be the placenta being expelled,* she thought, as though she were another object, not herself. Her body jolted. She reached for the infant lying at her feet. *Why is my baby silent?* She saw the umbilical cord twisted around her baby's neck. "Oh!" Lena exclaimed with horror, instinctively chewing the cord to remove it from the baby's neck. The infant was already purple and nearly cold.

She pressed the baby to her breast and touched its body with her lips. "Child, why are you cold?" She looked at the baby in horror. "My child cannot be dead." She could barely utter the words. Lena put the baby's body down. "It's a boy. My little boy is dead." She slowly wiped the infant's body with a cloth, and then swaddled him. Lena didn't have time to grieve. She heard the sound of many people walking outside the door. The shift was over. She wiped the floor, and left the shower room, hiding the baby under her sweater.

In the locker room she put on her fur coat and walked toward the exit. It was early morning; the first shift already had begun working, and Lena hoped she would be able to get through the guard booth unnoticed. She held the baby's body, covered by the cloths, with one hand under her sweater. One guard was making the workers open their purses, another one was checking if the women had hidden any of the factory's goods under the coats.

They're checking for theft, Lena realized, with cold sweat running down her spine. She stopped. *I won't be able to get out. I have to hide him now, and then return later.* The thoughts raced in her head. *I have to find a way to get my baby out from here, and bury him.*

Understanding that she wouldn't be able to get through the guard post, Lena turned around and went back inside the building.

Chapter 27

THE DECEMBER MORNING WAS frosty. *Moscow never sleeps,* Nevorov thought, passing in a military jeep through the busy city's street. He looked at the people crowded at the bus stops, who were attacking approaching buses to get inside. He observed the trolleys, stranded by too much snow, with their iced "moustaches" widely sticking upward, and the women-drivers, struggling to re-hook the wires back up to the cables. His eyes followed the young girls, who were laughing cheerfully as they jumped out of the underground Metro in unbuttoned coats, as if having forgotten that it was a damn cold winter outside.

"Ah, youth!" Nevorov involuntarily smiled behind his gray moustache, looking at the carefree girls. *Life is continuing,* he thought, closing his eyes, quickly tired from the brightness of the fresh-fallen snow sparkling under the rising sun.

The first man he wanted to visit was Sergey. There had been three of them, best military friends: Victor, Sergey, and Andrey. He recalled how they even had a nickname—*Three Bogatyrs.* Although Victor was the most senior in rank, Sergey was a lieutenant, and Andrey only a sergeant—that difference had never had any influence on their friendship.

They had served together in Afghanistan for the years which were so intense and tragic that they could be comparable to a lifetime. Tied by blood and the losses they had during the war, they became closer than brothers. Their lives had depended on each other every day, hour, and minute, and frequently each of them had risked his own life for one of the others.

Three Bogatyrs… Now there remained only two of them—himself and Sergey. "How is my fighting comrade doing now?" Nevorov asked himself, wondering what Sergey's life had become, looking blindly at the trees on both sides of the road, covered in snow as if in a heavy white fur coats. Zarecie was about two hundred kilometers northwest of Moscow. Soon he would see his friend.

"This is my native land. I was born and grew up here," the young soldier-driver joyfully told Nevorov, while the military jeep jumped over the forest road covered with roots jutting out of the ground. "I know these places as well as the palm of my hand. In my childhood I used to go hunting here with my father. I'll deliver you, Comrade Colonel, to your friend, by the shortest and fastest way. You don't mind this bumpy road, do you?" the young soldier asked Nevorov, seeing his drawn lips and rigid composure.

"Did you say hunting is good here?" Nevorov asked with a delayed reaction, as if coming out of his dream and not quite hearing what the driver had just said. "Do you have bears here?"

"Definitely! Bears, and deer, and wild boars…" the soldier listed them enthusiastically. "And a whole bunch of different smaller ones—foxes, hares, capercaillies, and black grouses. These places are rural. Basically, it's a region of prisons. Did you know that?"

"Yes, I have heard of this area. It's not safe to live around here." Nevorov said.

He turned to the window, thinking about the life his young driver had led hunting in the woods near his home. He sighed as thoughts of Afghanistan intruded. *Why does it happen to me all the time?* He wondered. *As soon as I start talking to someone here, in the civilian world, pictures of Afghanistan, that hell, immediately enter my mind. And even now— these innocent words about hunting instantly reminded me of the woods in Afghanistan, scattered over the hilly mountains. How attractive and desirable were their silence and shadows, how tempting the fresh mushrooms looked, teasingly sticking out of the grass and easily viewed through military binoculars. Who would suggest that gathering them could be dangerous?*

His mental journeys back to the war happened quite frequently since Nevorov returned home, and were always very painful for him. In these silent conversations with himself, Victor was still looking for answers, evaluating. *What, as a commander, could I have done differently?* While he was no longer in Afghanistan, he was haunted by his life there, re-living incidents—day by day, hour by hour—and speaking to himself seemed to help him cope with his harsh feelings, even today.

I remember some young soldiers who had just arrived in my brigade. After the Instructions, Sergey put them in small groups to guard our camp. Deceived by the pre-dawn silence, a few men decided to slip out to pick some mushrooms. They hadn't reached the nearby woods when they were cut down by the guerillas' gunfire.

Nevorov sighed, remembering how, with a grieving heart, he sent back home the dead bodies of his soldiers that same evening. For some of their mothers, it was the first news they had received from their just-taken-to-the-military-service sons.

How many senseless deaths I have seen in the years of war in Afghanistan, he thought. *Filling out the Certificates of Death at War became an all-too-regular part of my duty during that military service...*

"Where does he live, your friend?" the young soldier asked, turning his head to Nevorov. "What's the address?"

Nevorov was startled from his reverie. He pulled out a piece of paper from his wallet. Folded twice, it had the address of the mother of their deceased friend, Andrey. He gave it to the driver and explained, "Sergey, we called him 'Serega', said that he would take the Death Certificate to deliver in person to Andrey's mother. She was elderly and ill, so we didn't want to send it to her by mail. Sergey took the letter, along with the remains of Andrey's body…" He paused. "I've been told that Sergey decided to reside here. I haven't seen him or heard from him since then."

"So, your best friend was killed in the war?"

"Yes. One of them. There were three of us commanders who served together. We were in Afghanistan for a few years already when Andrey finally received his overdue vacation. It happened right when Serega had been discharged, and Andrey was glad he could accompany Sergey. We all said goodbye to them and were waiting for the transport helicopter.

"The helicopter appeared from behind the mountain to the sound of a mine explosion. Apparently some sheep had strayed into an abandoned mine field and a young Afghan boy was running behind his herd. Andrey reacted immediately. He ran toward the boy, waving and screaming to him to stay where he was. He navigated through the deadly obstacle course with skill and reached the boy quickly. They held hands tightly as Andrey led the boy, step by step, to a safe perimeter. A few meters separated the pair from safety when the second blast cut their hope and his life short."

Nevorov rubbed his eyes with his fingers as if he wanted to wipe away his memories.

"Serega... He was my best soldier. Officially, he was free from duties after being discharged. But he put his backpack on the ground and ran to help. He went all the way to the zone and brought back the boy and the remains of Andrey's body. He felt it was his mission. He had to do this for his friend, so Andrey's mother would be able to bury her son in Russian land."

"And the boy? Did he survive?"

"Yes. The helicopter took the boy straight to the hospital, and he survived. But he lost both legs."

The young soldier was silent. The colonel noticed that the skin of the driver's hands was turning blue, as he tightly gripped the truck's wheel.

"As I said, Serega was the best soldier. He would have sacrificed his own life for any one of us at any time if we needed him."

"Did you say he was discharged?"

"Yes."

"Discharged because of his wounds?" The young solder looked at the colonel.

"No. Because of his illness. Our doctor decided he must be sent home at the same time we sent out the Cargo-200.

"What does the 'Cargo-200' mean?"

"It was a secret code for the pilots to know they needed to bring a big helicopter. 'Cargo-200' meant that we had dead bodies and needed coffins to carry them out."

"Did you have many of them?"

"Yes. There were too many of them at that time. We were trapped in a small desert area, locked in. We had no communication. The radio didn't work. Our helicopters were unable to find us in a narrow canyon between the mountains where we were hiding from the guerillas. All our provisions—food, cigarettes, and water—were extremely low and almost gone. We had to ration everything, saving as much as we could, trying to stay alive and hoping that help would arrive soon. The heat was hell—above 50°C. We felt like we were baking in an oven. The thirst was killing us. One drop of water was as desirable as life itself.

"We were hiding in a small gorge. Surrounding the mountains was desert. Our soldiers found a small stream higher up in the mountains, and we tried to use its water. The guerillas saw us and they staged an ambush there: a few of our soldiers went up to bring back water, but they never returned. A few days later the guerillas made it even worse—they poisoned this stream, possibly by putting corpses into it, I don't know. The fact is that when our people went there and finally returned with water, everyone who drank it was knocked down with a horrible fever. The doctor told us the water was poisoned and forbade us to use it for any purpose. But the soldiers, exhausted by thirst, didn't obey, and in the afternoon they went to the stream to get more water.

"Serega, when he saw them going there, yelled, 'We are going to lose all our fighters this way!' He seized a mortar, and started to fire, hoping to keep our soldiers from getting to the water."

The colonel closed his eyes, breathing heavily. It was clear: he saw this nightmare in his mind now, as if it was happening all over again.

"Do you smoke?" he asked the young soldier, pulling out a pack of cigarettes.

"No, I don't."

"That's good. I doubt I could ever give it up now."

"And what happened next?" the soldier asked, waiting patiently while the colonel deeply inhaled.

"What happened next—" Nevorov paused, appearing to collect his inner strength to continue. "Our soldiers were so exhausted from the heat, hunger, uncertainty, and especially thirst… this thirst was terrifying… it took over their sanity. While screaming, 'We are going to die here, anyway, so it's better at once!' they jumped down into the desired water, through the mortar's fire…

"Serega, when he saw our soldiers fall, knocked down by his fire, threw the mortar away, crying, 'Brothers!! It wasn't me who sent us here!' And he ran away, escaping into the desert.

"For two nights we looked for Lieutenant Sergey and, finally, found him almost dead, behind a boulder. After the doctor examined him, he shook his head sadly, and said, 'Serega is not a fighter any more…'"

Nevorov stopped talking. His face darkened, as if a heavy leaden cloud had been lowered over it. "And in that mountain's stream… where our dead soldiers fell, blood seeped instead of water for a long time after. That's what kind of war it was."

The young soldier kept silent, his morning's smile and cheerfulness completely evaporated. The military jeep trudged along, as if it were carrying the priceless Cargo-200 on its back.

Finally, after turning a few times onto the twisting silent streets of the small town, the car stopped and the soldier said, "We have arrived, Comrade Colonel."

Chapter 28

"WAIT HERE," NEVOROV THREW over his shoulder to the driver, slamming the door of the military jeep.

The colonel glanced at the old, but yet strong, wooden house in front of him. *Well made,* he thought. *Probably built in the last century, of a quality that serves several generations.*

Nevorov followed a well-trampled path down to the house, noticing that the owner took better care of it in comparison to those of his neighbors' homes. The yards of the other houses were completely filled with snow, but here, despite the early hour, the snow had already been cleared. Even the path to the house was carefully sanded, as if the owner had somehow known that visitors would arrive. At the entrance door firewood had been neatly stacked in a woodpile, and from a chimney on the roof dense smoke was ascending, evidence that a fire had already been kindled.

The colonel knocked on the door, but there was no response. He knocked once again and, not hearing any answer, pressed the latch. The heavy oak door opened softly without a sound.

As with many village houses constructed in the nineteenth century, better known as *izba*, this house, too, had only one large room, which simultaneously served all needs. The interior walls were partly finished, planed and smoothed to a height of about two meters. To the right side of the door a typical red-brick wood-burning *pech* anchored the wall; its top doubled as a sleeping area, large enough for two adults. On the left side of this room was a huge chest made from an oak tree in which the grain was stored for the long Russian winter. In the center, by the window, stood a large dining table, clearly used to serve meals for the family. And on the right side, beside the *pech*, was a bed, curtained off from the rest of the room by a military tarp strung on a rope.

Nevorov stepped inside, closing the door. His attention had been captured by the many icons hanging on the wall. In a corner, decorated with white flowers, was the largest one, of Jesus Christ. His holy face was painted so carefully and with such passion that He looked alive. So much love and power emanated from His eyes that Nevorov involuntarily stood quietly, overcome by this greatness.

On the central wall, opposite the entrance door, between two windows, was an icon of the Holy Mother with the Baby Jesus nestled in her arms. The head of the Holy Mother was covered by a veil, symbol of meekness and humility, as well as submission and obedience, so common for the Russian women since Middle Ages through modern time. The Virgin Mary's eyes radiated so much love and tenderness, and Baby Jesus was so pure and serene, that Nevorov sighed deeply, audibly.

He stepped closer to examine the smaller religious icons located on the left wall, looking at them more attentively. He recognized the icons of Sacred Nikolai and George the Triumphant, but the others were unfamiliar to him.

Nevorov approached a table with a thick open book on it. He looked at the cover: *The Bible. Hmm... Strange business,* he thought. Nevorov wasn't sure how to react to what he was seeing around him.

The colonel turned and approached the pech. The fire was flaming inside, and little pieces of coal quietly crackled. Hot potatoes, with appetizing ruddy crusts, looked out from a cast-iron kettle. He swallowed saliva, realizing he hadn't eaten since yesterday.

"Where is the owner?" Nevorov asked aloud, drawing aside the tarp's curtain. He stopped, suddenly stunned by the presence of military precision. It was like stepping back in time and place, as dark in that corner as it had been in the military tents in Afghanistan.

A camouflage net, used for masking guns and tanks, had been nailed to the wall above the window. Seeing the narrow bed tightly covered with a soldier's blanket, and "straight as a string," brought a warm smile to the colonel's face, reminding him how strict Lieutenant Sergey had been with the young soldiers who couldn't make their beds correctly.

There were army boots under the bed, and by the headboard, leaning against the wall, a Kalashnikov carbine.

"Full alertness!" The colonel grinned, with mixed feelings of pride and anxiety, since his friend could immediately be arrested for keeping a weapon, which was prohibited by law. Nevorov shifted his gaze to the wall and stepped forward to take a closer look.

Placed in a wooden frame was the familiar *Instruction to the Soviet Soldier in Afghanistan* which every new recruit received. Nevorov remembered this text by heart but nevertheless re-read it again:

> "Soviet Soldier! Being in the territory of friendly Afghanistan, remember that you are the representative of the Soviet country and its great people. It is an honor to fulfill this great historical mission which has been assigned to you by our Fatherland."

These words, which he had personally repeated to his soldiers, now resonated painfully in his heart. After years of senseless deaths, and all he had gone through, these words now sounded like a sneer, profaning the memory of victims who had given their lives for the wrong reason.

Next to The Instruction, in the same wooden frame, hung a *Certificate of Death*, filled out by the local District Military Office. Nevorov remembered how he had fought back his tears when he had sent the helicopter carrying the remains of their friend Andrey home, and he had said goodbye to Serega, not knowing if he would ever see him again.

"What is taking him so long?" he asked himself and turned around, but the room was still empty. Nevorov read the "Certificate," trying to picture how Andrey's mother had felt, holding in her hands this tiny quarter of a page, this mere scrap of paper.

In the left corner of the Certificate of Death was the Emblem of the Soviet Union—an embossed five-pointed star with a Hammer and Sickle on top of it (precisely the same star sewed on the military peak-caps and soldiers' shoulder-stripes). Under it was a stamp of the Military Office of the town of Zarecie with a date and an address.

The official record read:

"To Citizen Ryabceva Evdokiya Semenovna
living at the address: Podgornaya, 15.

NOTIFICATION #10852

> *Dear Evdokiya Semenovna,*
> *With regret I inform you that your son, the senior sergeant Ryabcev Andrey Ivanovich, carrying out his military duty, true military oath, showing stability and courage, fell in battle on May 22nd, 1984.*

Accept the sincere condolence and sympathy for your grief."

There was a stamp and the signature, *Colonel Egorov.*

"Accept condolence," Nevorov angrily pronounced, swallowing the bitter lump in his throat. "Condolence from the whole world could never replace for this lonely mother the loss of her only son—the support, hope, and consolation in her old age." Nevorov impotently clenched his hands into fists, as he slid his eyes over the military awards and medals hanging on the wall.

The last award, an Order of the Red Star, was granted to Andrey posthumously. The Star was placed on a red ribbon pinned to Andrey's picture, taken before he was sent to Afghanistan. "Andrey, Andrey..." Nevorov touched the picture of his dear friend, stroked the Star of the hero. "Cheerful talker Andrey. If you only knew how much I miss you," he whispered.

"I miss him too," someone said behind his back.

"Serega! You devil, silent as a shadow, as always!" Nevorov joyfully exclaimed, as he turned around at the sound of his friend's familiar voice. But then he stiffened at the unexpected change in Sergey's appearance.

Sergey stepped forward. "Glad to see you alive, Victor. Thank God!" They joined in a strong embrace and stood still for a moment, unable to overcome or hide their strong emotions.

"Serega! What the hell has happened to you?" Nevorov was shocked at how thin his old friend had become. When they embraced, Nevorov had lifted Sergey off the floor effortlessly. "You've become so light! Where has all your weight gone? And why this hair and a beard?" In amazement he touched Sergey's long gray beard that fell to his chest. The old-man hair looked out of place on his thirty-two-year old friend.

"Yes, a beard... But why are we standing?" Pulling a long wooden bench closer, Sergey invited his dear friend to sit. "You can't imagine how glad I am to see you, Victor! What brought you here? Tell me everything."

"It will be a long story to tell." Nevorov smiled into his moustache, relieved to finally know that his best friend was alive, and in good health, despite the changes in his appearance. "Where did you vanish to? I've been here for almost an hour waiting."

"I stood in line for bread at the local grocery store. The bread is delivered only in the morning, once a day, and because of the snow, the delivery truck didn't come for two days, so all the neighborhood had gathered and was waiting by the store. The truck was late, and it took time to unload it. But I've got bread!" Sergey smiled proudly, taking out two loaves of rye bread from a cloth bag.

"Oh. You're hungry, aren't you?" Sergey exclaimed almost with a mother's intonation. "I am hungry, too. I put potatoes into the pech before I went to the store," he said, fishing the pot of potatoes out of the stove with *uhvat*, the long wooden-handled, U-shaped tool used in all peasant houses.

"I have some frozen pork. Breakfast will be ready in seconds!" Sergey cut slices of pork into a heavy cast-iron frying pan and then cracked large eggs in it.

Nevorov chuckled, feeling free and at ease as if returning to his long-forgotten childhood. "Do you need any help?" he asked, taking a bottle of Armenian cognac out of his coat pocket.

"You just sit and relax!" Sergey responded rapidly, while shredding an onion. "I also have some pickles and marinated mushrooms. Do you like mushrooms?"

"Sure! Get everything out! Let's celebrate our return to a peaceful life, brother!" Nevorov answered Sergey, who was bringing in food from *seni*, the small exterior addition to the house where food stayed cold all year long.

"Why did you leave a soldier outside? It's not in your character. What's the matter, Colonel?" Sergey asked reproachfully, bringing the driver in with him.

"Oh, I completely forgot!" Nevorov admitted guiltily. "The memories overcame me. Do they still bother you?" he asked Sergey, simultaneously moving to give some room on the bench to the driver. "You didn't get cold out there, brother?" he asked. "Sorry, I got lost in my past for a while."

"My padded jacket is warm. And *pech* is right here," the driver answered, stopping by the brick stove and stretching his cold hands toward the fire.

"Get some food. Then you can go up on the top of that *pech* and get some sleep on the warm bricks. You have a long way back. When do you need to go?" Sergey asked the driver.

"It depends on Comrade Colonel's order."

"Eat first," Sergey passed a plate with food to the soldier. "You probably haven't had a homemade meal for a long time? Where are you from? And what's your name?"

"Pavel is my name. I used to live not far from here."

"That's good. Maybe on your way back, you can stop by your home and see your parents."

"I don't have anybody. My father died last year. He was killed by a bear," the soldier said, in short phrases, as if reporting to his commander, not showing any feeling in his voice.

"Sorry to hear that," Sergey said.

The soldier didn't answer, just nodded his head, while hungrily falling upon the food. Both officers looked at him with a kind smile. They knew: one who hasn't been in the Army will never understand the difference between military rations and a home-cooked meal.

Chapter 29

LENA WAS LYING IN bed, with the cover pulled up tightly around her, when the dorm's room door flew open. She turned to the wall.

"UU-h! It's so frosty out, so much snow!" Seventeen-year-old Maya exclaimed happily out loud. Before shutting the door, she and Katya shook off snow from their shoes.

"Are you still in bed?" Katya asked, stepping over and uncovering Lena's head, hidden under the blanket. "Are you ill?"

Lena didn't answer.

"And it's so dark already! We walked and walked for two hours up and down the street, with no luck at all," Maya continued laughingly, taking off a long fur coat. "Thanks for your coat, Lena. It is so warm and beautiful! If there had been any man walking down the street, I am sure he would be mine!" Her cheeks were pink from the cold weather. "May I borrow it again sometime?"

Maya stepped closer to the bed and attempted to kiss Lena's cheek, but Lena quickly pulled her blanket up to hide her sobbing. She had no one to share her grief with. No one could ever know. She had gone back to the factory but couldn't find her baby. Somebody had emptied the box full of cloths and her baby was gone. She couldn't forgive herself for leaving the factory in the morning. But she had been so exhausted, and so afraid to be discovered...

The three of them shared the ten square-meter room, Maya had taken Tonya's place. Two of their beds were placed near one wall and the third one was on the opposite side, with an old wardrobe squeezed next to it. Between the beds under the window was a cupboard, which also served as a table. A mirror hung on the door; and a cloth bag outside the window conveniently served as a refrigerator, which they didn't have. There were curtains on the window and a hand-made linen-cloth on the table—the girls tried to keep their room clean and neat.

"Ah, in my old coat, I'll hardly catch anybody," Katya said with disappointment, looking into the mirror. She and Lena had already spent several years together in this room, while working at the factory. "I am short and not beautiful, not like Lena. And I wouldn't be able to save enough money to buy a new fur coat like Lena did," she said, sadly looking at her seven-year-old overcoat with shabby dark marks on it.

"If Lena did it, you could too," Maya said.

"Lena is strong. She always does things right." Katya sat on her bed and unzipped her old winter boots, taking them off. "She was saving her money for two or three years before she bought this fur coat. I can't go hungry as she did; it's too hard for me." She looked at her watch. "It's ten minutes till six! We've almost missed our shower time. Are you going?"

Both Katya and Maya quickly grabbed their bathrobes and towels and left. There were several shower stalls in the room at the end of the corridor. They took off their clothes and entered the stalls side by side. They shared the same piece of soap. Katya passed the soap to Maya and warned, "Use it carefully. It's our last piece of soap, Maya."

"Yes, I know." Maya soaped her sponge. Katya turned off the water and stepped out of the stall. She took a towel and dried herself off.

"The Director told us that we are going through a difficult time now. Perestroika, miners strikes, many factories stopped…" Maya said while adjusting a faucet.

Katya stopped drying off and answered angrily, "Stop talking as if we were at the meeting! We have listened for years to that lie."

Maya didn't hear her, speaking over the running water in the shower. "But they promised it will be over soon; we just have to be patient and try to survive through the winter."

Katya raised her voice. "Right! *This* winter. What about the winter before? And the one that comes after this one?" She turned toward the door, hearing a knock.

"Hurry up! There are people waiting," a woman's voice called out.

The girls returned from the shower, and placed their towels to dry on the radiator under the window. While at the window, Katya opened the small hinged window-pane, reached for the cloth bag, then looked inside to make sure nothing was there. Katya held the empty bag, and looked at Maya. "I forgot we finished everything." She tried to smile. "Or maybe I hoped the birds would share something with us."

Maya opened her cheap purse and pulled out a sandwich. She took a knife and cut every piece in half, saying, "I saved it from my lunch. It's good that they at least give us food when we work."

"Don't worry, they will deduct the cost from your salary, so you aren't going to receive much," Katya said.

Maya scanned the cupboard with hope. "Do we have anything here?" Cockroaches of all sizes ran out in different directions. "I hate these animals!" Maya shouted. "What are they doing here, if there is no food around?"

"They are not animals, but insects," Katya corrected, "and they are hungry as well."

Lena turned on her back and opened her eyes, remembering. *I couldn't find my baby. Someone took him. Now I won't be able to bury him.* She swallowed hard, forcing herself to keep her tears inside. *I needed at least to say good-bye to him, like I would have at his funeral.* She glanced over at her roommates, and then sat up.

"Wait. I bought some food," Lena said, rising from the bed. She had slept in her clothes. Lena's jacket was giving off a bad smell, her long skirt was rumpled, and her black curly hair was carelessly tied with a rubber band. From a brown-cloth bag, which she lifted up from the floor by her bed, Lena pulled out fresh bread, a big piece of sausage, a can of stewed pork, some cheese, and a few candies. The girls looked at all the food with wide-open eyes.

"Where did you get money for that?" Katya asked in amazement.

Lena delayed her answer. She looked down, and then spoke in a quiet voice, "I sold my gold earrings." She pulled out the bottle of vodka.

"Even vodka!" exclaimed Maya. "What are we celebrating?" she asked.

"Celebrating?" Lena thought for a little while. Her eyes were sad. "Mmm. Let's say, it's 'first Sunday' of this week. Let's make it as silly as that." She tried to smile, but looked down again to hide her tears.

"*First* Sunday...?" Maya didn't get the joke.

Katya looked at Lena disapprovingly. "Did you say that you sold the gold earrings, the only heirloom you have had, that has been kept in your family for years? How could it be? You loved your *serezki* so much—"

"Yes, I know. But my mother told me that I could sell them when a black day comes. Isn't it the right time now?" Lena sighed then turned to her roommates. "Let's eat, girls." She opened the bottle of vodka and poured it into the glasses that Maya handed to her. "To your health, friends." Lena drank, then poured some more vodka in her glass, quickly drank it and went back to bed.

"You are not eating?" Katya asked, worried.

"Later, I don't feel well. You eat, girls."

"Maybe you've got a cold." Katya approached Lena in bed, and put her hand on Lena's forehead, checking the temperature. "You're a little hot. Vodka is the best medicine; it will help you." She covered Lena with another blanket.

Katya stepped back to the table, drank her vodka, and put a slice of sausage on a piece of bread. She looked at Maya and said, "To be able to live through all our problems and sorrows, we need something to be able to forget about them. Have a drink, girl! Vodka helps to be strong, trust me." Katya handed Maya a glass. Maya took the glass with uncertainty, but seeing that Katya was watching her, she closed her eyes and drank the vodka.

Katya looked over at Lena, checking to see if she was asleep, and then sat down on Maya's bed. She slowly ate the slice of bread. "Lena's mother died before you came here, in June. Lena has nobody now. She met a very charming man last spring, but he left and didn't come back," Katya added in a quiet voice.

"Every girl dreams about finding a man," Maya nodded. "Oh! I forgot. I bought a newspaper with advertisements today! Here, look. We will find boyfriends for ourselves." Maya took a newspaper from her purse and began reading. She turned the pages, "See, so many of them. And what do these numbers mean?" she asked her roommate.

Katya looked over Maya's shoulder at the newspaper and then took it from her, irritated.

"You're seeking trouble, aren't you? You should find a husband who will stay with you for life and take care of you and your children, not just a man for one night, Maya." Maya looked at Katya with wide open eyes, totally confused by her words.

"Our town is surrounded by prisons. All these numbers are their inmates' post boxes. And look, every one of them is asking for pictures. Can you afford to pay for that many pictures? And do you have the money for envelopes and stamps?" Katya folded the newspaper, put it on the bed, and declared resolutely, "Just forget it!"

Maya didn't respond. She reached for the newspaper and read it silently, while Katya cleaned up the table.

"Look, Katya!" Maya exclaimed. "Here is something about our factory!"

Katya took the paper and read aloud, "Criminal incidents... The body of a new-born baby was found."

She was interrupted by a knock on the door. The door opened, and a girl's face appeared. "Do you, by chance, have any wash soap I could borrow?"

Both Katya and Maya shook their heads. "We don't have any. It is all gone," Katya answered. The door closed, and Katya continued to read. "The police are investigating." She looked at Maya, "Yeah, like they really care about one dead peasant baby and whoever might be his mother."

"Is it possible to give birth without a doctor's help?" Maya whispered.

"Why not?" Katya collected the dishes and walked to the door. Maya opened the door for her and then shut it behind them.

Lena lay on the bed under the blanket, her eyes closed. She heard the door open as Maya and Katya returned from the kitchen down the hall. They put the clean dishes inside the cupboard and then left again. Lena stood up, went to the table, and poured some more vodka into her glass. She quickly drank it. Then she picked up the newspaper, and found the article. *"A body of a dead baby was found."* She began crying. *"The experts determined that the baby was smothered. The police are investigating."*

Suddenly Lena felt terrified. Tears blurred her eyes. She couldn't see a word. She tore the article from the newspaper, crumpled it, and shoved it in her jacket's pocket. She threw the rest of the newspaper on the floor, then grabbed her fur coat, and ran from the room.

It was late and dark outside. Lena quickly walked down the street. Her coat was unbuttoned, her hair disheveled. She cried. She wanted to blame someone for what had happened to her baby. She blamed Arthur, she hated him so much. If she had not met him, this would not have happened.

"How could I have been so foolish? I simply believed him; I wanted to be loved. He was so sincere; I never suspected he might be lying. Why did he do that to me? Why did he deceive me like that?" she asked, walking faster, and faster, and then beginning to run.

Chapter 30

WHEN THE SOLDIER CLIMBED on the top of the red-brick *pech* to sleep, Nevorov reached for the bottle of cognac. "Well, Serega, we should celebrate our safe return."

"You drink, Victor, but I won't," Sergey answered, covering the top of an empty glass with his palm.

The colonel looked at him in wonder. "You, refusing it? What in the hell has happened to you, Serega?"

"You drink, brother. Don't look at me. I'll tell you." Sergey closed his eyes, returning to the past. His voice sounded muffled, as if it was coming from the distance of a different lifetime. "We arrived home in the middle of June. A Cargo-200 was delivered to the local military office. They gave us the military truck, and we put Andrey's coffin on it. A captain from the local military office went with us also.

"We drove to Andrey's house and stopped in front. We lingered for a few minutes outside, smoking and gathering courage to meet his mother, deciding who would be the one to tell her the terrible news."

Sergey looked into Nevorov's eyes. "Do you know, Colonel, how it feels—to bring the body of your fallen friend to his home?" His voice sounded low and frightened.

Nevorov didn't answer, and Sergey continued. "It feels the same as if you are carrying a bomb that is ready to blow up. It causes the same destructive effect for all who live in that house. This is news that kills.

"We stood by the truck and saw that neighbors from the nearby houses began gathering around, wondering what we were there for. Andrey's mother probably sensed something. The door of the house opened and she stepped outside. She saw me in my military uniform, with my officer's shoulder straps, and she suddenly rushed to me, and fell into my chest, crying. 'Andrey! You have returned, my dear son!'"

Sergey broke off, covering his wet eyes with his hand. "She was old. Constant crying and tears, as she waited for her son's return, had nearly blinded her eyes. Only when she embraced me and looked into my face, did she realize that she was mistaken."

Sergey sighed, and looked out the window at the snowflakes that whirled in an amazing dance in the wind's turbulence and, as if finally being exhausted, slowly lowered and silently settled down. Nevorov waited, and Sergey continued. "We took her inside, sat with her on the bench, and then the soldiers brought in that zinc coffin.

"When she saw the coffin, she understood everything, and did not listen to what the local captain read in his 'Condolence'. She rushed to the coffin and fell upon it, scratching the hermetically sealed zinc with her nails and begging us to open it so she could look at her dear son one last time."

Sergey was breathing heavily. He stood up, poured some more hot tea into an aluminum mug and asked, looking at the full glass on the table, "Why don't you drink, Victor?"

Nevorov lifted his glass and said, looking straight into Sergey's eyes, "To the memory of our friend Andrey." And then he drank.

Sergey nodded, gulped hot tea from his mug, and continued. "After the funeral the old woman felt so ill that she couldn't get up from her bed. Because she was so weak, I knew I had to stay with her for a while, to help her until she recovered. I felt that Andrey would like me to do that for his mother. I also didn't have any place to go, so it worked out well for me at that time also." He paused. "You eat, eat. I have more potatoes," Sergey insisted, quickly spooning more hot potatoes from the iron kettle onto his friend's plate.

He looked at Nevorov and asked, "Well, now, how have you been, Victor? I heard you remained in Afghanistan until the very last day. How is your wife, Tamara? She must be glad you have finally returned home safely."

Nevorov took his time to answer. He poured cognac into his glass, and then drank it, not waiting for Sergey. He didn't take any more food. He looked at his comrade's face as if he was studying it, and then said quietly, "She isn't my wife any more. She left me, Sergey."

"Tamara's left? Impossible!" Sergey shouted at what he had just heard. "What happened?"

"Shortly after your retirement, I received a letter from her. She wrote that she was tired of waiting and wanted a divorce," Victor answered. "The divorce papers were enclosed. I signed them. She had the right to be happy. She said she had wasted her youth on me." He sighed again.

Sergey was silent, melancholically sticking his fork into the pieces of potatoes. Then he reached for the bottle of cognac, and suddenly took a long drink straight from the bottle's neck. He put the bottle on the table, and said spitefully. "She isn't the one to blame, Victor. These men in the Kremlin are responsible for everything that has happened. Swine. I feel so small and meaningless after this war… Our lives were just frittered away in that huge political meat grinder!"

There was no reply from Victor. They ate silently, and then Sergey said, "Now you are as alone as I am. Where are you going to live?"

"I haven't decided yet. Thank you. This all-in-one-breakfast-and-dinner was good!" The colonel pushed away his empty plate and took out a pack of cigarettes from his pocket. He lit one, and continued after inhaling deeply, with the pleasure of a long-time smoker, "Yesterday I arrived in Moscow. I visited General Afanasiev."

"You've seen Afanasiev? How is he doing?" Sergey asked with interest.

"He is doing great, became a 'big man' now."

"He's made from different dough. Not as you or me," Sergey grinned.

"He wants me to put back together men from *Specnaz*, those who were trained for the Special Operations in Afghanistan. He said he's got a job for us to do. What do you think, brother?"

Sergey took his time to answer. "I understand your point, Victor," he replied. "It's a very difficult time now. Not what we thought it would be. We thought we would be treated as heroes, not as outcasts. When people see us, the 'Afghans', they blame us for their poverty and losses, not the government. They can't reach those in the Kremlin, but they can express their hate to us. Many of our men sit out there unemployed, same as I am, because there is no work for us. We didn't learn anything else in Afghanistan, except how to kill."

"Would you work with me?" Nevorov looked at his friend with hope. "You are the first one I have approached, brother. In fact, we are more than just brothers. You and I are tied by the blood of all the soldiers we lost in this war."

Sergey stood up from the bench, collected the empty plates, then wiped off the table, and put the Bible back on it. Nevorov smoked, silently observing, giving Serega time to think about his answer. Sergey washed the dishes, and then returned to the table. He sat down, pulled up the Bible, put his right hand on it, and said quietly but firmly, "Forgive me, brother, but I won't." He saw the disappointment on Nevorov's face, and he explained, "I am a Believer. I live by God's commands now, not human ones, Victor. I cannot kill. Please try to understand me."

Nevorov gazed at Sergey as if he were an alien, an unknown entity, "You are a Believer? No way! You are a Communist, remember? Who converted you, Serega? What happened here? This horrible beard, your exhausted body. What's wrong with you, brother? You were my best soldier!"

Instead of answering, Sergey rose, turned his back to Nevorov, and lifted up his shirt. "Do you see that?"

Nevorov stared at three bullet wounds located equal distance from each other in a line above Sergey's thick military belt, at the level of his kidneys.

"Who did this? Where?" Nevorov asked in a disturbed voice.

"Here, the local *milicia* did it."

"Milicia?"

"Yes. They pursued me," Sergey answered. "I decided to stay with Andrey's mother to look after her, to help her out. But do you remember the condition I was in when I retired? My mind was mixed up after all the killing in Afghanistan."

"I remember."

"I don't know how the news spread around here, but the rumor went out that an Afghan soldier had come back, and veterans from everywhere began to gather here all the time. We talked, shared stories about the war, sang our Afghan songs, and smoked. Then somebody brought something else to smoke. Do you remember how priceless that grass was in Afghanistan? Nothing on the earth was dearer than the last toke before going out to battle. Do you remember?"

Nevorov nodded somberly, and Sergey continued, "I was hooked. That grass helped me to calm down; it turned off my horrible memories. And then someone offered me something stronger, some powder. I tried it, and then I could not exist without it. I was taken by drugs, Victor."

Sergey paused. It was the first time he had opened up like this, but he knew he could trust his commander, as he had so many times during the war.

Nevorov listened without interruption, and the lieutenant continued. "Someone betrayed us. I normally received the powder through a waitress at the local restaurant, but the milicia had arranged a sting. I jumped out of a window, and ran through the back yard. They followed me yelling, 'Stop! We'll shoot!'" Sergey looked at his friend and asked with a small grin on his lips, "Can you see me surrendering? You know I would never surrender. Then, they fired." Sergey closed his eyes—at this moment he was there again, and Victor could see that picture in his mind also.

"I know I was holding the package in my hand when I jumped out of the window. I probably dropped it when I fell." Sergey paused, and his arms went down, tightly pressing his stomach, his skinny body bent down as if he had that horrible pain again. He looked at Victor as if expecting his question, and with his head still lowered, went on, "They didn't find the powder, thank God. People brought me home lifeless; I lost a lot of blood. The medic said there was no chance for me to survive, as my kidneys were damaged, so he didn't send me to the hospital. I was left to die on the bench in the middle of this house."

Sergey kept silence for a while, collecting his thoughts, and then continued. "Andrey's mother knelt beside my body for two days, as if I was her own son, crying non-stop, repeating unending prayers. On the third day she asked a neighbor to take her to a monastery. There she begged an old monk to come and pray for me.

"As the monk began reciting his prayers, I opened my eyes. He stood close to my head and asked, looking directly into my eyes, 'Do you believe in God?'"

Sergey looked at Victor. "What would you say if you were on your death-bed?" He didn't wait for the answer and continued, "I barely opened my dry lips, and whispered, 'Yes...' Then I lost consciousness again. I decided that I had already died, as I saw the Lord in white clothes, surrounded by light as bright as the summer sun. The Lord, so great in His majesty, stood in front of me, and there was a cross right near Him. I looked closely and realized that it was Andrey nailed to the cross. My friend, tormented and covered with blood, was dying. I rushed to him, and he looked down at me and whispered barely audible words to me, 'I paid for your life with my blood, brother.'

"I looked up and saw the Lord. His eyes shined on me with such unconditional love, as if I was His only son. God's appearance was so magnificent that, like an innocent baby who reaches his hands to his mother, I instinctively straightened my arms trying to touch His bright clothes. I even stepped closer. But it was the same as if you would step into a cloud—you see it from a distance, but when you are inside, you become a part of that substance. God's love was all around and inside me, and suddenly I felt so incredibly guilty—for myself, for Andrey, for all our soldiers who gave their lives for stupid political reasons. My legs gave away, and I fell before this bright light onto my knees, whispering, 'Forgive me, Father, please, forgive me.'

"I did not hear an answer from the Lord, because I woke up. I opened my eyes and saw the monk, who was still on his knees, praying. He raised his head, looked at me, and saw that my eyes were open. He stood, still glancing directly into my eyes. I also looked into his eyes; they were the color of heavenly blueness, so deep that they made me feel like a tiny fly in the endless sky.

"I couldn't take my eyes from the monk—so much power and authority were in his gaze. And then he commanded me in a loud voice, 'In the name of the Father, Son, and Holy Spirit, I order you to rise and live! Rise!'

"When I heard his voice I felt a strong force pushing me up. As if I were hypnotized, I sat upright on the bench.

"'Stand up and walk!' the old man commanded.

"I got up and walked around the room. The monk watched me, and said with great satisfaction in his voice, 'Praise God, now and forever!' Then he turned and left.

"I went to the window, looked out, and saw the monk walking down the street in his long black habit.

"I checked my back, stretched my hands—nothing hurt. I understood nothing. It was truly a miracle. I approached the bed where Andrey's mother slept, looked at her, and realized that she had died. She had passed away silently, placing her hands on her chest. She had died in her sleep, with a smile on her lips. I knew she had asked God to take her life in exchange for mine.

"We buried Andrey's mother, and after that conversation with God, I felt like I was born again; I became a different person, Victor. My old life was finished, and I began a new one. I studied the Bible, and I live by God's word now. It's most likely that I will take monastic vows and will go to live at that same monastery soon."

Nevorov listened, not interrupting. If it was someone else, not Sergey, telling the story, he would never have believed what he had just heard. But Sergey would never lie; the colonel trusted him as himself. Three fatal bullets—and still survived?

"Have you done X-rays?"

"Yes, I have. All three bullets are gone."

"Impossible!"

"I know that. But here I am sitting alive, in front of you. Do you know about how Jesus raised Lazarus from the dead?"

"M-mm. I have heard something."

"I think that is what happened to me. It was necessary for God that I become a witness to His power and glory. He also healed my brain. You see, I am a normal person now."

"I see."

Nevorov stood up and walked across the room, and then approached the window. "It's getting dark," he said, looking above the white curtains into the street. "It's time for us to go. Do you have the addresses of other Afghan veterans who live in this area?"

"Certainly. I'll write them down for you."

The colonel stepped to the *pech* and woke up the driver, "Get up, Pavel."

Sergey handed Nevorov a paper with a few names and addresses written on it. "I have written down the phone number of my neighbor for you. I don't have a phone, but he lets me use his. So please call if you need me. We are closer than brothers, Victor. We should not lose each other in this crazy world." He embraced his dear friend.

"Thank you for telling me your story, Sergey. I do not know if it was God or any other force, but the main thing is that you are alive. That is what I am most grateful for." Nevorov smiled, looking deeply into his friend's eyes.

"You be cautious there in Moscow," Sergey replied. "Remember the old saying '*overfed swine are worse than hungry wolves.*'"

Nevorov nodded agreeably, shook his friend's hand, and went out.

"Let's go!" he said to Pavel, as he climbed up into the jeep.

Chapter 31

"HEY, ARE YOU BLIND or drunk?" A man's rough voice roared.

Lena reacted with a violent shudder that shocked her back to reality as a huge bear-like man railed her. She had almost bumped her face into his chest, which was blocking her way. Lena tried to go around him, but he spread his arms wide, and gruffly snarled, "Got caught, tiny sparrow?"

Scared, Lena looked behind her, hoping to see passers-by, only to be met by the mortified stares of more drunken hoodlums. The men slowly surrounded her.

Lena could barely recall grabbing her fur coat and running from the dorm. Driven by an uncontrollable need to escape the confinement of her stuffy room, she had rushed from the premises. It was as if, through the sheer force of will and physical momentum, she was trying to break a chain that constrained her. She wanted to free herself from the unrelenting guilt that haunted her. Lena didn't know how long she had wandered through the dark silent streets of the small town, mechanically passing crossroads, turning here and there—not thinking, functioning like a zombie.

She had been reliving the most horrible day of her life, flashing back in her mind again and again to that moment when she had slipped into the factory's shower room and closed the door behind her, locking it, making sure no one could enter.

Like a worn-out film, over and over Lena had scrolled in her head the events of that terrible night, trying to guess how long she had been unconscious and why the child had died. *Was my baby alive when I pulled him out, or was he dead in my womb? If he was alive, could I have possibly rescued him, if I had noticed the cord looped around his neck before I passed out?* As she replayed the tragic event in her mind, she had walked aimlessly down the road, passing through the town to the suburbs, where she now had come across the drunken crowd of miscreants.

They are prisoners! The horrific thought flashed in her mind. Surrounding her was a crowd of drunken, filthy men, with unshaven rough faces. All of them were dressed in identical jerseys and cheap caps with earflaps.

She recalled that the factory's administrator had warned all of the workers to avoid going out on the streets, especially at night, as an amnesty had been declared in the local prisons and the town would be flooded with criminals. Terrified, Lena hoped that she might be able to appeal to the humanity of these men.

"Guys... My mother's ill, I had to go to the central drugstore for medicine… I was in a hurry, because my mother's waiting. I didn't notice you, please excuse me..." she said in a soft voice.

"Ha-ha-ha! She's rushing home to her mom. Such a sweet girl. And where does your mommy live? Over there, in the woods? Where, in the hen-house?"

"Ha-ha-ha" another hoodlum begun to guffaw loudly, moving aside and gesturing toward the woods. "Okay, show us!" They were at the outskirts of the town, and the deserted road led only to the woods.

"I, apparently, got lost..." Lena hoped for some sympathy from the hardened souls of these crude men, but instinctively she knew that she was in trouble.

"Now you'll have to go with us, beautiful maiden!" said the huge man, looking down at her like a wild bear rearing up on its haunches. "We will even bless the occasion with holy water." He pulled a bottle of vodka from the security of his jersey and with a sweeping gesture exhibited it to his circle of friends. "Here's the miracle-water, helps all to be forgotten," he added, winking with an ugly grin.

"Let's go to that woodpile on the roadside. We'll be shielded better from the wind there," offered a mustachioed man.

"Good idea!" the bear-like man agreed. He squeezed Lena's elbow. "Go, go, girl!" Seeing that some of his cohorts were groping her, he gave them a threatening look. "She's mine!"

The rabble herded Lena toward a pile of logs, howling and bellowing obscene songs, while sipping vodka from their bottles.

"And do not resist me," the bear-like one said, as he pushed Lena ahead. "If I slap this bottle against your head, you'll quickly become obedient." To prove his point, the man hit her in the back of the head with the bottle. "That's just to make sure you know what I said." He kicked her, prodding her forward. "Go, go, you wanton slut!"

Lena stumbled and fell into the deep snow. She wanted to fight, to run away, but was guarded tightly by the encircled her prisoners.

"Here! Drink this, you'll get warmer!" The bear extended the bottle to her.

"I don't want it." Lena turned her head away.

"I told you to drink!"

"See, she refuses you!" a cohort laughed.

"Fuck your mother!" The leader jammed the bottle at Lena's face, and poured vodka on her head. "Come on, open your mouth wide, and drink well." He jerked Lena out of the snow and pressed her with his heavy body against the woodpile. "Look, such a beauty I've got! Never in my life have I seen anything better, never tried one in a fur coat... a queen!" Grinning, self-satisfied, he bent his bristly face to Lena's. She turned her head in disgust.

"Are you turning away?" The bear-leader went into a rage. "Ah, you whore!" He slapped Lena's face, splitting her lips and bloodying her nose. "Get on your knees!"

He pressed down on her shoulders with a huge hand, forcing Lena to fall to her knees, while excitedly unbuttoning his fly. "Whore! Turning away from me! Now, take it... Take into your mouth. I've told you, bitch, suck on it!" He shouted spitefully, trying to push his member through Lena's clenched teeth, "Take it now, dirty slut!" Again, he struck Lena on the head so hard that she fell over in the snow.

"Get up, tramp!" The grizzly leader pulled her up by the collar, returning Lena to her knees. "Take this, I said!" He forced his lust-swollen organ into her mouth, and his body shuddered from the years of restrained desire.

Lena gagged, nearly vomiting from the stench emanating from the man's filthy body, tears ran down her cheeks. Never had she experienced such humiliation. Lena's courage, her strength of character, had been crippled by the events of the last few days. The shock she felt from the death of her child had broken her will. She had lost the ability to resist. Somewhere in the depths of her consciousness, Lena understood that her only chance for survival was silent submissiveness.

"I'll help, I'll help!" The mustachioed man said, holding Lena by her collar, keeping her from falling down again. "Here's our beautiful girl," he said in a lusty voice. "Oh, she's a real honey... I'll be next after you, all right?" He glanced at the leader's eyes.

"Okay," nodded the bear-like leader. Finally, his body shook from the pent-up orgasm. He pulled out his penis, watching Lena choking on his sperm, and said to his cohort, "You can have it now."

The mustachioed man's hand trembled as he unbuttoned his fly, and his member sprang from his trousers like a battering ram.

"Oho! That thing is a weapon!" His cohorts began to laugh boisterously. "Are you going to leave anything for us?"

"You'll have it too, don't worry," the mustached one assured, fiercely working his brawny buttocks. "Oh, you, sweetie... So good..."

Other criminals had drawn closer, pushing each other, impatiently unbuttoning their pants. "I'm next!"

"No, I am!"

"Men, let's lay her down," one of them said.

"It's a good idea," the others agreed, throwing her body on the top of the woodpile.

Lena blacked out; her mind tried to escape the ordeal. But the pain in her lower stomach returned her to a conscious state. "A-a-i!"

"She woke up! This is better!" a dark-haired man, feverishly pumping between Lena's legs, joyfully exclaimed. "Why is it so wet?" he asked, pulling out and examining his penis. "*Ptfu*," he spat. "Blood...?"

"Blood is good," mumbled the next man in line, his exposed organ in his hand. "It means she won't get pregnant. Otherwise, how would we know who the father was? We would have to draw straws, ha-ha-ha," he snickered, finishing and giving up his place to the next fellow.

Lena tried to unclench her swollen eyelids but they were too heavy to open them. She wanted it to be over so she could die. She managed to count the glowing tips of the cigarettes blinking on and off through the darkness. *One, two, three...* There were eight. The criminals hastily did their business and stood aside, giving up their place to the next in line. *My God, my God, what are you doing? Why did you send me this punishment?* Lena cried to herself. Before blacking out again, the answer came like a whisper only she could hear: *Retribution.*

"Hey! After all of you there's nothing left for me!" a shabby fellow with spectacles yelled furiously. "It's all worn out! It's like sticking it into a bucket of melted lard." He spoke deliberately, examining Lena's bloody face, and her even bloodier crotch. "Well, help me to turn this young mare over!" he said with a grin. "Here we go, baby!" he screamed joyfully, digging his nails into Lena's thighs.

The bear-like leader turned toward the sound of a train whistle in the distance. "Time's up, guys. The train's coming!"

"And I? What about me?" yelled the last in line, as his cohorts rushed toward the train, but nobody paid any attention to him. "Well, Beauty, give me your fur coat at least," he said, pulling off Lena's coat, flipping over her half-naked, nearly lifeless body into the snow. "It doesn't look like you'll need it anyway. I can sell it… Since I didn't get any of your love," he added, running after his departing buddies.

Chapter 32

Winter's DAYS ARE SHORT in Russia and it was already dark. Nevorov didn't want to return to Moscow without any result. He handed his driver the piece of paper with the addresses Sergey had written down, saying, "Maybe we could visit one more man tonight."

Pavel glanced at the paper and answered with confidence, "These villages are close to each other, so if we stop in one place, I will be able to drive around to gather others and bring them there. That way you can talk to all of them at once."

"Good idea," Nevorov agreed with this plan while they drove away from Sergey's house. The jeep moved slowly, sinking into the deep snow—one who decides to drive in the rural area in a winter time is on his own. The colonel didn't talk, thinking about Sergey's story while looking out the window. He had met Sergey in 1979, right before the war in Afghanistan. *It was so long ago,* he thought. *It was the year when Tamara agreed to marry me. And we went to Yalta for our honeymoon.* His memories drifted him back in time.

Suddenly, the jeep lurched.

"Comrade Colonel, there is something ahead, lying by the woodpile. Do you see it?" the driver interrupted Nevorov's memories.

"What?" Nevorov had forgotten where he was. He hadn't noticed the passage of time. He looked out the window and saw they were approaching the forest outside the town. "What did you say?"

Still looking out the window, the soldier pointed toward something dark lying in the snow by the woodpile. "It might be a deer," he suggested.

"Let's pull over and stop there!" Nevorov ordered. "I would love to bring some game to share with my soldiers."

Pavel smiled, liking the idea, and turned off the road into the field.

Nevorov jumped out of the jeep, and the next minute he yelled to his soldier, "Come here! Quickly!"

Pavel opened the door and saw the colonel holding a bleeding woman in his arms; he rushed to open the passenger's door. Nevorov placed her onto the back seat, and took off his coat, covering her cold body with it.

"Head back to Moscow! Quickly!" Nevorov ordered. "Drive as fast as if you had guerillas following you, shooting at your back. Her life depends on you, soldier."

Pavel pushed down hard on the gas pedal.

Chapter 33

December 1989, Moscow

NEVOROV HEARD THE SOUND of a key in the apartment door's lock and quickly went into the corridor. The door opened wide and Afanasiev appeared, stepping in and stretching out his hand to Nevorov. "How did it go? Have you found good men for me?"

Nevorov shook the offered hand, but his face expressed the surprise he was feeling from the unexpected visit.

"Why are you staring at me, like you aren't glad to see me? Have you forgotten that this is my apartment?" Afanasiev laughed loudly, jingling his keys on the ring. He walked to the living room and sat down in the armchair. He looked at Nevorov, who stood in front of him and said, rubbing his hands, "It's a cold morning! Why are you silent, Victor?"

"The trip was good," Nevorov answered slowly, after a pause, as if he was carefully deciding what to tell him. "I visited Serega. He has changed a lot."

"Will he work?" the general interrupted impatiently.

"Serega?" Nevorov drew in his lips—he was trying to choose his words—and said, "I am not sure about Serega." He paused, and then added reluctantly, "Serega refused to work."

"Refused to work?" the general repeated, raising his eyebrows doubtfully. "He is your best friend, how could he refuse?"

"Yes, he is my best friend, and will always be. But he has changed a lot. He is a Believer now."

"Religion? What rubbish!" Afanasiev's face wrinkled with disgust, but Nevorov said nothing. "Well, it's up to you, Colonel, to decide who will be on your team. Have you spoken to anyone else?"

"Yes. I do have a couple of people in mind," Victor lied, not willing to admit that his trip had been unexpectedly interrupted.

"All right. I've prepared the first mission for you. You will decide how many people and what kind of weapons you might need. I'll explain the task and I will let you plan it. I will supply everything that is necessary."

Nevorov nodded, and Afanasiev continued, "So, how do you like my apartment? Have you found everything you need?" The general got up from the armchair, walked brazenly across the room, and then opened the door into the bedroom. "The view of the Kremlin is especially remarkable from the bedroom... Oh, who is in here?" Afanasiev stared dumbfounded at the thin body lying under a blanket on a sofa.

Nevorov hastily followed the general, "She's a friend of mine, Comrade General. I hope you don't mind."

"A friend? Is she sick, or what?" Afanasiev inspected the vials with medicine that sat on the stool, placed next to the sofa.

"Yes, she caught a cold... She's sleeping now," Nevorov answered with a low murmur, hoping that Afanasiev would leave.

But the general, not paying any attention to Victor's words, approached the sofa and glanced into the girl's face, partly covered by her tangled, long hair. "What the hell!" Afanasiev exclaimed shocked, after he lifted the blanket and quickly dropped it back. The look of the beaten girl's face sickened him. "She is all covered in bloody bruises! How could you put her on my sofa? Where did you find her?!"

"In the woods..."

The stunned general grabbed his head. "Victor, are you crazy or what?" Afanasiev sat down on the nearby chair and stared at Nevorov, demanding an answer.

"What would you have done, Comrade General? Would you have left her out in the snow to die?"

The general rolled his eyes in amazement and then said more calmly, "Thanks at least, that you didn't put her on my bed." Nevorov didn't answer. Afanasiev bent down from the chair, picked up the girl's jacket from the floor and checked the pockets. "Any documents?"

Victor shook his head, "Nothing." *I actually didn't look for any*, he thought.

"Just a small piece of paper," Afanasiev said as he examined attentively the crumbled piece of newspaper he found in the pocket. "Hmm. Interesting." He dropped the jacket on the floor and said, "I see you have some medicine here."

"Yes, I did call an ambulance—she was almost dead," Nevorov answered.

"I'll send my doctor here to check on her; he's the only one I trust. We don't need anybody to know that we have an undocumented woman here."

Nevorov nodded.

"We'll decide later what to do with the girl. We might use her as well." Afanasiev winked significantly at Nevorov, saying, "It appears that this girl got into trouble and should be thankful for her salvation, but enough of that. Are you ready for work, Nevorov?"

Victor looked at the girl, weakened from a fever, and suddenly realized that he had gotten himself into a trap—now wasn't a good time to be arguing with Afanasiev. The girl needed time for her recovery, and in order for him to help her, he had to do whatever Afanasiev ordered. *At least for now,* Victor thought to himself and he answered firmly, "Yes, I am ready, Comrade General!"

"Let's go to the kitchen. I'll describe the task," declared Afanasiev, getting up from the chair and walking out.

Chapter 34

RETRIBUTION. RE–TRI–BU–TION! THE SOUND was deep and heavy, as if resonating from a cast-iron alarm bell, and it echoed in Lena's brain simultaneously with the impact of thudding, beating lashes on her body. *Re-tri-bu-tion… Re-tri-bu-tion.* Her body, tattered in bloody pieces, was burning. Lena saw huge monsters, wearing grinning, ferocious masks with horns, bending over her with sadistic rhythmical persistency, with their hairy hands tirelessly whipping her body. *Re-tri-bu-tion!* On the edge of consciousness, Lena understood: *I am in Hell.*

Muffled, as if from underground, a quiet voice reached her ears. She could not quite comprehend it.

"Doctor, do you think she will survive? She's been unconsciousness for three days."

"I have done what I could. Now, she is in God's power. This night will be critical." It was a different voice.

God, you know the truth! A begging plea flashed somewhere deep in Lena's mind, and then awareness escaped her, and she fell back again into the darkness.

"She will sleep after that injection. She is young; I hope she survives. She's so lucky that you found her, Colonel."

"How old do you think she is?" Nevorov asked.

The doctor looked at Lena again, "She's very young, maybe twenty-three, maximum twenty-six, I think." He paused and then added, "And she's recently given birth."

"What?"

"Yes, her breasts show that, and her uterus is enlarged. I wonder where her child is."

"She had nothing with her when I found her. No child, no money, not even a coat."

"Probably, the men who raped her took it."

"Raped?"

"I apologize. I thought it was my duty to tell you that."

"To be honest, I suspected it. I found her on the road by the woods."

The doctor nodded. "Women who work night shifts and have to go to work at dark are always at risk, if they don't have someone to accompany them. Here, in Moscow, gang-rape has become an ordinary happening, especially now, when everything is falling apart. No one follows the law, and actually there is no law to follow or prosecute. The milicia won't even go to the crime scene when someone is calling, if there is no murder. 'We can't be everywhere,' they say."

Nevorov shook his head, not knowing what to say. He accompanied the doctor, a young man in a white uniform, to the door and then returned to the bedroom. He moved the chair closer to the sofa. The doctor had said that this night would be critical, and Victor decided to stay and watch the girl's condition in case she needed help.

Victor dozed off, but opened his eyes instantly when he heard a weak cough. It was early morning and the room was lit only by pre-dawn light from the window. The girl was in delirium; she cried out, her body writhed under the blanket.

Nevorov stood up, went to the bathroom, wet a towel, and placed it on her forehead. Then he went into the kitchen and brewed a pot of hot fresh tea. He returned to the bedroom with a cup of tea in his hand, sat on the stool by the sofa, and tried to wet the young woman's dry lips with some tea from a spoon.

"You will be all right," he spoke to her softly, taking the girl's hand in his and holding it. She coughed again and slowly opened her eyes.

Lena looked up at the ceiling, then at the man's face, not understanding where she was. "Who are you?" she asked, hardly moving her lips, her voice wracked with fear.

"I am a friend. Don't be afraid. You are safe now," he replied in a kind voice. "Just drink this tea, please." He brought another spoonful of tea to her mouth, nursing her like a baby. Lena closed her eyes and took a sip.

Thank you, God! She's alive, Nevorov thought. And in the next moment he smiled at himself, realizing that the Communist was thanking God!

Chapter 35

AT ABOUT 6 PM Afanasiev sent a car with a driver to the apartment to pick up Nevorov. It was a yellow *Ziguly* sedan that looked the same as thousands of similar taxis in Moscow. The driver knew the address of their destination, and that Nevorov was the one to carry out the assigned task.

They arrived at the apartment building in an area of Moscow unknown to Nevorov, and the driver stopped the car by the entrance. It was dark, the street lamp had been broken, and the street was lit only by light from the windows. Both men sat in the car and smoked, covering the cigarettes' light with their palms. The driver looked attentively into his rear view mirror. A white car drove by them and pulled into a parking spot. A man in a black coat got out of the car, locked it, and walked toward the entrance of the building.

"That's him," the driver said. Nevorov quickly stepped out of the car and followed the man, who opened the entrance door and went inside. Victor slipped in behind him.

A couple of minutes later, Nevorov emerged from the building, hopped back inside the car. The yellow taxi speed away.

Nevorov couldn't sleep that night. Afanasiev's bed was too wide and soft, the white sheets were too clean, the noise of the cars outside the window was too loud, and the sound of the chiming clock on Spasskaya Tower was irritating. Victor was used to far worse noise during battles and could, if necessary, sleep even on stones amid the sound of gunfire, but this peaceful city noise defeated him. The colonel lay on the general's bed, wide awake, with open eyes, thinking about what he had just done, and doubt of the rightness in following his commander's order crept into his mind.

He thought about his last conversation with Afanasiev, and of their different fates, and about the destiny of their country and its beloved capital, Moscow.

Moscow… It was the capital of Russia for almost eight hundred years. And he, Victor, had always been and continued to be a defender of this great country. He had always wanted to be like one of the Great Russian *Bogatyrs*, and he would have been honored to die protecting the Russian people and the Fatherland. Victor loved Moscow, and always proudly admired its history, and he could talk for hours about it. *No troubles or sufferings had ever broken this heroic city,* he thought. Like the mythical Phoenix, Moscow had always revived, becoming even better and stronger. Fires and floods, wars and revolts, epidemics and mutinies—what misfortunes, sorrows, and troubles had not been known by this great city!

The sound of the chiming clock of Spasskaya Tower in Red Square reached his ears again, and then the loud bell began to clang out the time, as if marking significant intervals in the history of the country: "Bom. Bom. Bom…" the bell's loud sound caused an agonizing pain in the colonel's heart. He closed his eyes as he began to match a milestone of Russian history with each chime of the clock.

"One…" 1156. An image of the then-called "China-town" and its wooden Kremlin appeared before his eyes. Yuri Dolgoruki, the founder of Moscow, erected timber walls with a deep moat around the town.

"Two…" 1378. Prince Dmitry Donskoy, sat astride on his white horse, leading his army to fight a Tartar-Mongols Army in the Battle of Kulikovo.

"Three…" 1565. Next there was Czar Ivan Grozny, who united the princedoms around Moscow, seated on his throne surrounded by his *boyars*.

"Four…" 1590. Boris Godunov defeated the Tatars, then Sweden, and Turkey.

"Five…" 1612. Prince Pozharsky and Kuzma Minin rose up against the Polish occupants.

"Six…" 1671. A Cossack's leader, Stepan Razin, was quartered alive in Red Square.

"Seven…" 1698. Czar Peter the Great, and the morning of the *Streltsy* execution on Red Square.

"Eight…" 1917. Bloody fights in Moscow: the Revolution. Lenin restored the capital from Saint-Petersburg back to Moscow.

"Nine…" 1945. June. Red Square and the Great Parade of the Victory in World War II. Glory to the winners!

"Ten…" 1961. April. Triumph and celebration throughout the whole country. The Soviet astronaut Yuri Gagarin became the first person in space!

"Eleven…" 1979. The war in Afghanistan began with the storming of the Tajbeg Palace.

"Twelve…" 1989. The collapse of the Communist Bloc, the fall of the Berlin Wall… The end of all he loved and had fought for many years to protect.

The clock on Spasskaya Tower struck midnight. Nevorov ordered himself to sleep.

The next morning Nevorov was cleaning the gun and silencer that Afanasiev had given him, when the doorbell rang. Victor quickly hid the weapon and opened the door. The soldier Pavel entered, holding several bags in his hands.

"Comrade General ordered me to bring you some food," he said walking straight into the kitchen, where he began emptying the bags.

"Where did you get it?" Nevorov asked Pavel, amazed at the amount of food the soldier was placing on the dining table. There were products beyond his imagination: bacon coated with garlic and black pepper, salami, jars of red and black caviar, calamari, smoked beef, and cans of sprats, condensed milk, and buckwheat.

"This is the food package for a government employee. The general told me to bring it here. He doesn't need it. 'We have plenty of food at home,' he said."

The soldier finally placed on the table a can of instant coffee, a package of Ceylon tea, and two boxes of chocolates. "That's it!" he said with a smile but he couldn't suppress a deep sigh.

"All of it, just for one person?" Nevorov wouldn't believe that in this time of empty stores, some people could live like capitalists.

"Yes, for one person every week on Friday," Pavel replied.

Nevorov followed the soldier's hungry eyes and asked kindly, "Would you like to take something with you?"

"No-no!" Pavel said, backing out of the kitchen. "Thank you, Comrade Colonel, I should go." He rushed to the corridor and left, closing the door.

Nevorov made himself a cup of tea and went into the bedroom. He sat on the chair and looked again at the face of the sleeping girl. Even the bruises and marks on her face from the beating she had endured could not hide her natural beauty. Her long black hair reminded Victor of his wife, whom he had loved so dearly. He didn't dare to find out how Tamara had lived after she left him.

Nevorov felt so much compassion for this poor girl that he bent over her and tried to sweep the wavy hair from her face. She slowly opened her eyes. Victor took his hand off her hair and asked in a quiet voice, "What is your name?"

"Lena." Her whisper was barely audible, and her eyelids closed again as if under severe pressure. He could see that she tried to open her eyes, but it was too great an effort.

As for Lena, all she could see was falling snow in the night, melting snowflakes twirling and swirling, making her dizzy and nauseated. Twirling and swirling… sticky snowflakes… and darkness, and cigarettes' lights… twirling and swirling.

Chapter 36

LENA DIDN'T KNOW HOW many days had passed when she was finally able to keep her eyes open and see clearly. She stared up into the ceiling, at a big white daisy-shaped light fixture. She recalled that she had seen a gray-haired man with tired eyes. She realized she was in someone's home, on someone's sofa, and wearing someone's T-shirt. *He changed my clothes,* she thought in embarrassment. *And I need to use a bathroom.*

She slowly stood up, and shaking from dizziness, tried to make it out the door into the corridor. She went to the bathroom, and then into the kitchen. It was empty. She took a small candy bar from the opened box and returned to the bedroom.

She lay on the sofa and looked up at the ceiling. *I am alive,* she thought. *I didn't die.* She stared at the daisy-like chandelier and murmured, "Daisy… the field full of daisies… I remember them. I hate daisies now…"

The memory of that sunny summer day, and the meadow outside her village, full of blooming daisies, came flooding back to her. It was the last day she saw her father.

Her life had come full circle. Lena had lost everything she had. But why had all of these bad things happened to her, and not to someone else? Didn't her mother tell her it would be better for her to be born fortunate than beautiful? Now Lena knew that it was true, but what could she do? What could she do to change this misfortune? Could she possibly change anything at all?

She looked up at the ceiling.

"Mama…" Lena whispered softly. "Mother! Are you here? Are you watching over me from up there?" Lena burst out sobbing again. "You told me, you told me, and I didn't listen… Oh, mama…"

Lena turned onto her stomach, pressing her face tight into the pillow, trying to stop her tears. She forced herself to stop crying. *I am paying for my stupidity*, she admitted to herself.

"Lena, learn your lesson and don't repeat the same mistakes again." She knew that was what her mother would say to her.

But these men… What they did to me. How have I even survived it? I thought I would die…

"But you didn't die." She heard her mother's voice in her mind, as if Varya was standing beside her. *"You must live on, Lena."*

In that instant, Lena fully realized how much she loved her mother, and how much space Varya had taken in her heart.

Lena had learned her lesson. She didn't make any vows or promises to herself, but the conclusion was forming quietly in her mind and she knew she would be a different person from now on. A different Lena. Now she won't be as naïve as before. She would live as her mother advised her.

Chapter 37

January 1990, Moscow

GENERAL AFANASIEV SAT NAKED as the day he was born, on a wooden bench in the sauna, almost invisible behind the steam. The door opened, and a man who they called Tolyan, quickly slid in.

Tolyan was in his thirties, with the strong muscular body of a former boxing champion; his nose was smashed—it had been broken in sport battles, and his hair was cut very short "so no one could grab me by the hair," as he would say. Tolyan held two switches of green birch twigs in his hand, called *venik*—a must-have attribute of every Russian sauna, or *banya*.

"Is it hot enough for you?" he asked Afanasiev, putting the two *veniks* into a wooden vat filled with hot water to soak. "Let the leaves warm up and soften for a few minutes, and then I'll massage you, Comrade General," Tolyan spoke while pouring hot water onto the red-hot stones. "Are you ready?"

Afanasiev lay down on his stomach, groaning playfully, "You are so strong, Tolyan, be careful with my back!"

Tolyan smiled and answered enthusiastically, "Don't worry! You are going to be a born-again-man after this, and you will feel as good as a baby!" Tolyan started beating Afanasiev with the birch twigs, then ordered him to stand up. He took a bucket full of ice-cold water and threw it over Afanasiev's head.

The general's body flinched, shocked from the cold water shower, but the next moment he exclaimed happily, "Ah! It's good! Really good!" They both sat back down on the bench.

"I heard a new joke today," Tolyan said.

Afanasiev nodded, "Okay."

In their circle Tolyan was a famous joke teller. He remembered hundreds of anecdotes and knew exactly the right one that would fit any occasion, telling them with great artistic mastery. He smiled to himself, predicting his listener's reaction and began an anecdote:

"A professor at the Medical College asks the students a question, 'What part of the human body increases five times at the moment of erotic excitation?'

"The girl at the first desk laughs, covering her mouth with her palm, 'Hi-hi.'

"The professor looks at her disapprovingly. 'Young lady! It is the EYE PUPILS that get five times bigger, and the organ you just thought of increases only two times. Although, not always.'"

"Ha-ha!" Afanasiev laughed, covering his organ, which had shrunk from the cold water, with his palm, "Not always, ah? Ha-ha-ha."

"I promised you that you would feel like a baby!" Tolyan winked and they laughed.

The door opened, and an even bigger man, with a massive, overweight body and a huge stomach hanging almost to his knees, carefully stepped in. Tolyan immediately jumped down from the bench and stood still.

The big man passed him with a quick, "Relax!" and then he shook Afanasiev's hand. "Hello, General!"

"Good evening, Ivan Ivanovich," Afanasiev replied respectfully. The big man climbed onto the bench. Tolyan left, quietly closing the door behind him.

"How is the steam today?" The big man sat on the second bench not risking going higher.

"Very good! I feel like I was born again," Afanasiev answered, getting down. Doing the same as Tolyan had for him, the general ladled out hot water and poured it onto the hot rocks in the corner of the room, "I'll add some steam for you."

"Thanks." The big man was breathing heavily. He stepped down to the lower bench and sat there. "You did a good job with that journalist, Afanasiev. The press is in a panic now and hopefully will stop prying into our business."

Afanasiev nodded, "Yes, it was my man from the specially trained battalion which the Afghans were so fearful of. They even gave this battalion a special name, *'Black Death.'* The men in this group were especially trained in how to kill, even with their bare hands; they know better than anyone else how to win 'a losing battle', as others would call it."

The big man went to a pail and drank some cold water from the ladle. "It is hot in here! I am ready for a massage." He opened the door and called Tolyan back in.

The former boxer appeared, bringing with him a large towel that he put on the bench. "You may lie down, Ivan Ivanovich," he offered with a bowing gesture of hospitality, pointing to the bench. He went to the corner where the wooden vat with hot water was located and took out the *venik*. He shook it, and drops of water flew down from the steamed birch leaves.

"Ohh! I love this smell!" the big man exclaimed joyfully, lying on his stomach on the towel and stretching out his huge body.

"I soaked the *venik* in hot water, and its leaves are now soft and gentle like butterfly wings," Tolyan said, lightly waving the birch twigs in the air and tickling the man's body with the tips of the leaves. Then he began stroking, pressing the birch switch softly against Ivan Ivanovich's body, and in one long wavy move he drew the *venik* from his neck to his toes and back.

Afanasiev sat on the second bench observing Tolyan's massage and thought about Ivan Ivanovich's power over people. It seemed not just Tolyan, but anyone who met him, would stand as straight as a trained soldier in front of this man. Even his physical appearance made people feel fearful. His eyes were very small compared to his big face. Anyone who looked into his eyes felt paralyzed, like a rabbit caught by a cobra's gaze. He never spoke much, but every word he said was meaningful, and he had never had to repeat anything.

It was Afanasiev's father-in-law who had introduced them to each other, a few years ago at someone's birthday party. Ivan Ivanovich had just relocated to Moscow from Siberia. "He is a person you can trust," his father-in-law told Afanasiev, and they never spoke about it again. The general knew very little about Ivan Ivanovich; he was told not to ask questions, and he didn't. The last name of this powerful man was never pronounced out loud, to show respect and distance, everyone called him by his first and patronymic, or father's name, *Ivan Ivanovich*.

Even during the time of strict Communist Party discipline, Ivan Ivanovich had contacts abroad and was able to perform financial operations that no one could even imagine. He knew people at the highest level and was so powerful that it would be dangerous to try to do anything against him, although Afanasiev had no need to do so. He just provided Ivan Ivanovich with information, and he was paid well for that.

"Why are you massaging me as if I were a sissy girl?" Ivan Ivanovich asked Tolyan teasingly, turning onto his back. "Put some strength into it now!" he commanded.

"Certainly!" Tolyan answered readily. "But you must stand up."

Groaning, the big man swung his legs down and stood up from the bench.

"Are you ready?" Tolyan asked. "Hold on now!" he warned, and started lashing the big man violently, first on his back and then lower down on his buttocks and legs.

"Oh! That is good! Good!" Ivan Ivanovich yelled, twitching under the strong boxer's hands. This violent torture was a great pleasure for him, as his body became bright-red from the lashes of the birch twigs.

"Uff! It's enough! Enough!" he finally begged Tolyan to stop. The boxer's face was sweating from the hard work, but he smiled happily. He took a pail of ice-cold water and poured it over the big man's head.

Ivan Ivanovich was *oohing* and *aahing* from pleasure. Then the men left the steam room and dried themselves with the big bath towels that Tolyan had ready for them.

There was a well-appointed sitting room next to the sauna. Both men leaned back in soft comfortable armchairs, their lower bodies wrapped in towels. An open box of Cuban cigars sat on the coffee table. Ivan Ivanovich took a cigar, lit it up, and shifted the box toward Afanasiev. "Try this. A personal gift from Fidel Castro to me." Afanasiev took one, lit it, and inhaled with joy.

The big man began to talk about politics.

"'Misha is getting on my nerves. Why even worry about him? Yes, he's the General Secretary, so what? His era is gone."

Afanasiev looked confused and repeated doubtfully, "Gorbachev's era has gone? What do you mean? He's so popular in the West with his 'Perestroika'…"

The big man twisted his lips ironically and laughed out loud, and then he started coughing because of the smoke. He battled his cough and then continued, "You're young, Afanasiev. Do you really think that it is the *people* who choose a ruler? Don't be naive. People were tired of elderly leaders, so we gave them a younger one. That's it. Now, we need a change again."

In amazement Afanasiev opened his eyes wide; he knew that Ivan Ivanovich never spoke empty words. "And then, what will happen with Perestroika?" he asked, almost in a whisper.

The big man stood up and pressed his cigar down into the ashtray. He smiled, "We'll let Misha get his Nobel Peace Prize. We need to get through the military conversion—very good money is hidden there." Ivan Ivanovich stood and walked around to the other side of the table.

"And what will happen next?" Afanasiev asked impatiently, looking at the big man's back.

"Next? There will be another marionette, my friend, who will make us enormously rich. We have someone in mind already." Ivan Ivanovich stretched his arms up high over his head; his towel fell down onto the floor, and Afanasiev had a chance once again observe the big man's fat ass.

A few minutes later the door opened, and Tolyan rolled in a cart stocked with bottles of alcohol, other beverages, and sandwiches. He overheard the phrase that Ivan Ivanovich was saying while continuing his talk to Afanasiev, "You know, our politicians are mistaken so often—"

"It's a pity they are not on the bombs dismantle squad!" Tolyan responded to him quickly.

The big man and Afanasiev smiled, and the general added, nodding his head in agreement, "If the politicians blew up after every mistake they made, we would have nobody left!"

The three men laughed, and the big man said confidently to Afanasiev, "It's good that you work for the KGB. Everyone knows that no matter how often the government changes, the police will always remain."

Tolyan placed everything from the cart onto the coffee table. Ivan Ivanovich approached the table and looked at the labels on the bottles. He picked up a bottle of cognac and handed it to the boxer. "I'll have *Armenian*, five stars." Afanasiev nodded agreeably, five stars on the cognac label declared its highest quality, and Tolyan would be punished if somehow there would be a bottle with only three stars on it.

Tolyan poured cognac into a crystal glass, then turned to Afanasiev. "And what would you like to drink, Comrade General?"

"The same. Cognac sounds good to me."

"You may have some, too," Ivan Ivanovich told the boxer. Tolyan poured cognac into two other glasses and passed them to Ivan Ivanovich and Afanasiev.

Tolyan lifted his glass. "Do you know why some people write the number seven with a horizontal hyphen in the middle? …Even though computers and typewriters use the usual seven, without a hyphen?"

Afanasiev and the big man drank their cognac and looked back at the boxer smiling, expecting a new anecdote. "Tell us," Afanasiev prompted.

"When Moses came down from Mount Sinai, he began to read the Ten Commandments to his people. When he reached the seventh one, 'Do not commit adultery', the people began to wail: 'Cross out the seven! Cross it out!'"

Both men laughed heartily.

"Now I know why I write the number seven with a hyphen," Afanasiev said.

Ivan Ivanovich took a salmon sandwich and turned to the boxer, "Well, speaking about the Seventh Commandment. What is on your program for us today?"

Tolyan closed his eyes as if he was day-dreaming. His face expressed joy, and his lips rose up almost to his ears in a lustful smile, "Today, I have a new game for you! Just wait."

He went to the door and opened it. Four young girls, pretty as photo models, all wearing high heels and bikinis, entered. With a bowing gesture, Tolyan playfully introduced them to the men. "You remember our sweet girls: Sasha, Masha, Dasha, and Natasha."

Soft music started to play from the built-in stereo system. The girls began to walk around the room, dancing, swirling, and teasingly showing themselves off. Afanasiev and Ivan Ivanovich followed the girls' moves with their eyes and smiled delightfully.

Tolyan, with the gesture of a magician, pulled two black eye strips out of his back pocket and announced, "The rules of our new game are—"

He paused and waited for the men's attention and then continued, "I will cover your eyes with these blindfolds. Our beauties will give you a gentle massage. You'll have to guess the name of the girl who kissed you. If you are right, the next girl will give you a massage. And if you aren't right—"

"We'll get another girl anyway!" Ivan Ivanovich interrupted him impatiently. All three men laughed.

Without delay, Afanasiev stood up and went to lie down onto a huge recliner chair. "I love this game! Come on, girls!" Tolyan placed a black blindfold over Afanasiev's eyes, and the general impatiently opened up his towel.

Ivan Ivanovich also lay back, relaxing in another chair with the blindfold over his eyes. The girls approached them. Two girls stood by the big man; one kissed and massaged his neck from behind, while another kissed his chest, and stomach, and then moved downward.

The big man's face melted with pleasure as he moaned uncontrollably, "Ooo, yes, baby... ohhh." Then he turned his blindfolded face to Afanasiev and asked, "Remember, when you called me from Afghanistan saying we could deliver opium in the coffins?"

"Yes..." Afanasiev answered slowly like in his sleep.

"It was a genius idea, man!"

Both men snickered.

Chapter 38

THE DOCTOR CAME BACK to check on Lena at the end of the week. He was pleasantly surprised at how well she was recovering. She looked much better, and only the puffy yellow circles on her face and the sadness in her eyes bore witness to the horrible events she had gone through.

"You have taken good care of her," the doctor praised Victor with a satisfied smile. He turned to Lena and said, "But you have to finish your antibiotics. You can't stop taking them, even if you feel better. Did you hear me?"

"Yes," Lena nodded. She looked cute wearing the huge, military shirt that Victor had lent her, which almost reached her knees, while his winter underwear served as a pair of long pants for her.

"I'll make sure she takes her medicine," Nevorov confirmed.

"Then, it looks like my job is done here," the doctor concluded, putting a stethoscope into his medical bag.

"Would you like a cup of tea?" Nevorov offered, gesturing toward the kitchen.

"No, no, no! It is winter time, flu season. I have a lot of home visits to do yet," the doctor answered, going to the corridor. "But thank you," he added with a warm smile, putting on his winter coat.

Lena was very grateful to Victor for his kindness and care. She understood that he had saved her life, although she felt somehow awkward because he had seen her unconscious, and had washed her body and changed her clothes. She was surprised to find out that Victor was only in his forties, because his gray hair and wrinkled face made him look much older. She thought of him more as a father, especially after all the care he had provided for her.

"May I help you to cook something?" she asked Victor when he returned after accompanying the doctor to the door.

"Sure," Victor agreed without delay. "What can you cook?"

"Oh, I can cook everything… all kinds of soups, meat, beef stroganoff, pancakes, *pelmeni*—" she began listing.

"*Pelmeni* sound like a great idea!" Victor exclaimed enthusiastically. "I haven't had home-made *pelmeni* since I went to Afghanistan…"

"Afghanistan? You were in Afghanistan?" Lena asked.

"Yes."

"My friend was killed in Afghanistan. He was my fiancé, actually," she added with sadness in her voice.

"Do you know where he served?"

"No, he never wrote about that," she answered.

"True," Nevorov nodded, "they were not allowed to tell. What was his name?"

"Vladimir Starovoitov," Lena answered. "He had straw-colored hair," she added as if it could help Nevorov to think. "Although it was shaved off at the military office…" Her voice faded.

"Volodya…" Nevorov paused, recalling something from the past. And then he took Lena's hand. "Let's go to the kitchen. You promised me home-made *pelmeni*, didn't you?"

"But you'll have to help!" Lena smiled as they walked to the kitchen. "So, did you know Volodya?" she turned to face Victor.

"Yes. I did," He answered slowly. The image of Volodya's body, the guerrillas parading him around the village, it all came into his mind as clearly as if it happened yesterday.

"Please, tell me how did he die?" Lena asked quietly.

"He died as a hero, Lena," Nevorov said gruffly.

Afanasiev arrived in the evening, opening the door with his keys. Nevorov was watching TV in the living room. Afanasiev briefly nodded to Victor, but didn't stop, heading straight toward the bedroom, "Is the girl there?"

"Yes."

"You stay here," the general gestured, stopping Nevorov, who was getting up from his chair. "I want to talk to her, alone." He closed the bedroom door behind him.

Lena was sitting on the sofa, reading a book she had found on the shelf. When Afanasiev entered the room, she closed the book and stood up.

The general stood in front of Lena, observing her body closely, as if he was buying her. Lena felt so uncomfortable under his staring eyes that her body gave an involuntary shake, and goose bumps appeared on her arms. Trying to hide her uneasy feelings, she hugged her arms to her chest as if warming herself. Afanasiev noticed that and grinned. He extended his hand and touched Lena's chin with his index finger, lifting it up, and forcing her to turn her face to the light. This time he was attentively observing her face. Lena closed her eyes under his disturbing look and stepped back from the man.

"So… how do you feel, young lady?" Afanasiev asked, sitting down on the chair, crossing one leg over the other.

"I am doing well, thank you," Lena answered quietly. She sat back down on the sofa and reached for the book she was reading, but she didn't dare open it. Lena would rather avoid any conversation with this man, but she understood she was in his power; actually, she was grateful that he had let her stay in his apartment. Still, she felt there was something unpleasant about him, and she couldn't understand exactly what it was. It couldn't be his appearance—even with his heavy weight Afanasiev was a good looking man, although his uniform would make anyone uncomfortable. Maybe it was the calculating look in his eyes that alarmed her, and the way he narrowed his gaze, as if he was analyzing something in his mind when he was staring at her. Instinctively, Lena felt an aura of danger emanating from this man, and she wanted to stay away from him. She had to force herself to look into Afanasiev's face and even smile a little bit.

"Nevorov told me he found you in the woods. Did you live in Zarecie?" Afanasiev asked with pretended sympathy in his voice.

"Yes, I did."

"And where did you work?" he continued.

"At the sewing factory."

"Hmm. Sewing factory. Isn't that the one mentioned in this article?" Afanasiev pulled out the piece of the newspaper he had found in Lena's jacket. He noticed the quick, fearful blink in Lena's eyes, which she tried to hide behind her long, black eyelashes.

"Yes," Lena nodded her head. Sincerity was part of her character, and she still hadn't learned how to lie. Even now, unconsciously feeling danger around her, she remained true to herself.

Afanasiev smiled widely in satisfaction, "Ha! You know exactly what I'm talking about, don't you? The doctor who treated you told us that you had just recently given birth…"

Lena's body shrank under Afanasiev's piercing look. He stood up from the chair and picked up the phone that was hanging on the wall. "I will call the *milicia* now."

Lena jumped up from the sofa and quickly approached the general. She touched the sleeve of his leather coat and pleaded with tears in her voice, "Please, don't! I didn't kill him."

Afanasiev looked at Lena doubtfully, still holding the receiver in his hand. "You didn't? Then who killed the baby?"

"He died on his own. He was dead at birth. I didn't kill him," Lena answered quickly, biting her lips and trying not to cry.

Afanasiev put the phone back down on the hook, and turned to Lena. He looked at her intently with a long stare, weighing her words, then repeated, "You say you didn't kill him." He paused. Lena felt he was deciding her fate. "Prove it!" Afanasiev demanded harshly.

Lena delayed her response; her eyes quickly filling with tears, her mind seeking an answer. "How can I possibly prove it?"

"The baby was found dead. You can't prove you're innocent. You'll go to prison. That is the law." Afanasiev spoke in short phrases as if chopping them off with an axe, and each word resonated in Lena's head with unbearable pain. "You didn't even bury him," he added his last accusation.

Lena opened her mouth trying to say something, but she only soundlessly curled her lips, overwhelmed with emotion, and fear. She imagined herself standing in front of a judge, unable to defend herself. The tears ran down her cheeks.

Afanasiev turned away from Lena and went to the window. He stood there looking at the Kremlin and letting Lena cry. Lena felt completely hopeless and unprotected; she thought that all she had left now was a prison cell.

A few minutes later Afanasiev turned back to her, and looking at Lena's helpless face, said slowly, "But—" he paused, waiting for her full attention. Lena even stopped sobbing, trying to listen to his quiet voice. "Maybe I could do something for you."

"What?" Lena asked quickly; her eyes were begging the general as if he were God.

"You lost your job, correct?"

"Yes."

"Do you have any relatives who can help you?"

"No."

"Do you have money, jewelry, anything you could sell to be able to buy food?"

"No."

"Do you have any documents with you?"

"No."

Afanasiev rejoiced. A primal instinct that is rudimentary, and hidden inside even civilized men, took over. Every hunter knows this powerful, victorious feeling of superiority that makes men's heads spin fast and feel high without drinking. Like a poor animal caught in a trap, Lena helplessly searched for a way out, but was unable to overcome the man's cruelty.

The game was his and it was just a matter of time—how best to use this latest victim of his. The general went back to the armchair and sat down. He looked relaxed in this chair. Afanasiev started to count on his fingers: "First—no job, second—no relatives, third—no money, fourth—no permission to live and work in Moscow, fifth—no one single document to identify you, and you can't go back to the factory or dorm, because they will arrest you immediately… Hmm." Afanasiev looked at his fist with all five fingers bent down. "What are you going to do, girl?"

Lena was sitting on the sofa covering her face with her hands.

"If the milicia stops you on the street for any reason, and finds out you don't have documents, what do you think they will do?"

"I don't know."

"They will arrest you, stupid!" Afanasiev assured her rudely.

"I could work—" Lena insisted in a quiet voice.

"Work? Where? Not in Moscow. You don't have Moscow residency. Actually, you can't work anywhere without documents. You-do-not-exist," the general spelled out slowly. "Aren't you getting it?"

Tears were running down Lena's cheeks, and she didn't even try to dry them off. She didn't care about the tears, didn't care about her life. All she wanted was to fall back into unconsciousness. Lena knew one thing: she didn't want to go to prison; she would rather die.

"You don't have parents, Lena, but you have a friend," Afanasiev pronounced in an insinuative tone. Lena, it seemed, didn't hear him. "I could help you, if you promised to be a good girl."

Lena was still lost in her thoughts; she didn't react at all. Only now she began realizing how bad her situation was.

The general stood up from the chair, approached Lena, and sat down beside her. He put his hand on her knee, and said, trying to catch Lena's eyes, "I will let you stay here, sleep on this sofa, you will have plenty of food… but you will have to be a good girl and do what I ask you to do, Okay?"

Lena lowered her head, not looking at the general; she didn't answer, as if she didn't care. At this moment she was unable to negotiate and fight for her life; she would agree to anything to escape prison.

Afanasiev stood up from the sofa and said resolutely, "I am hosting a party tomorrow night, and you are invited. All you have to do is to be nice to my guests."

Not waiting for Lena's answer, he stood up and walked to the door. He put his hand on the handle, but stopped and turned toward Lena. He pronounced in an ice-cold threatening voice, "And don't you dare to resist, or tell a single soul about this conversation." He paused and added, "I will be watching you, even if I'm not here." He stepped out of the bedroom, shutting the door behind him.

"What is in the news?" Afanasiev approached Nevorov who was sitting in the living room reading the newspaper, and he sat down in the armchair beside him.

"You didn't tell me the person I killed was a famous journalist," Nevorov said in a hostile voice. His face was angry.

Afanasiev twisted his mouth. "Famous, not famous—it is all relative. Actually, he had shifted from journalism and decided to become a detective. He wanted to know what happened with some portable nuclear devices we'd had in Afghanistan. He was digging around and found some documents no one was supposed to know about. But we have fixed it. Good job, Colonel."

Nevorov put down the newspaper and said nothing. He was unhappy, but there was no sense in arguing now—the journalist was dead. And he, a Soviet officer, had killed an unarmed man. Never in his life had he had any idea that he would do something like this. He would strangle any person who had dared to suggest such a crazy idea to him. And now he had done it. Nevorov hated himself for his blind obedience to his former commander whose orders he used to follow without argument.

"I have to go." Afanasiev moved to the door. "And, I almost forgot. About this girl, Lena. I will send some clothes and a hair-dresser here tomorrow. Both of you must be ready by 8 PM. I'll introduce you to the best people in this city."

Nevorov looked confused, but to avoid the confrontation, he didn't reply, harshly shutting the door behind his commander. He quickly went to the bedroom.

"What did he tell you?" Nevorov asked Lena.

Lena, her face swollen from tears, wasn't able to answer.

"You must trust me, Lena! What's going on here?" Nevorov demanded, hating to see Lena crying.

Already threatened by Afanasiev, Lena was too scared to say a word. She hid her head in the pillow to muffle her sobbing.

Nevorov went to the bathroom and brought Lena a wet towel. He gently touched her face and eyes, trying to calm her down.

"Tell me what happened to you, Lena. I am your friend and I want to help you," Nevorov said, looking deeply into Lena's eyes, as if he wanted to read her mind.

Lena just sighed, unable to answer.

"Trust me, Lena," Nevorov insisted. "Do you believe that you can trust me?" he asked, not knowing how to prove his loyalty to her.

"I will tell you," Lena said quietly. "But later." She pulled the blanket over her. "I am very, very tired now."

"Yes, I can see that. Get some sleep. We will talk later," Nevorov agreed, leaving the bedroom. "Just remember that you can trust me, because I want you to be happy," he said, closing the door.

Happy! She thought to herself. *I don't remember the last time I was happy… No, I do remember. It was in March, when I first met Arthur… but how can I tell Victor about it? Should I tell him the truth?*

Lena closed her eyes, hoping she could sleep, but her memories would not let her rest. She knew, as she had known after her first stinking kiss from the drunken man, when she was eleven that she had passed from one phase of her life to the next.

Chapter 39

THE NEXT DAY A driver arrived with packages of clothes and shoes for Lena and Nevorov. They both looked at the contents and tried on the items to see how they would fit.

"The general has an exact eye! I wonder, how could he guess our sizes so precisely?" Lena asked, trying on one dress after another.

"He used to be an *artillerist*. That profession requires a good eye," Nevorov smiled, seeing how beautiful Lena looked in the luxurious evening dresses.

"Where are we going tonight?" she asked.

"I don't really know, but I hope you'll like it. Afanasiev said there will be 'the best people.'" Nevorov went to the door and admitted a woman who said she was the hair-dresser.

"Does that mean we are also the best people?" Lena asked with a smile, sitting in front of the big mirror and letting the hair-dresser do her job.

Nevorov was elated to see her smile. "Of course we are the best people," he answered, with a reassuring nod of his head. *Yes, we are,* he thought. *And, far better than most of those we'll meet tonight,* he added wryly to himself.

It took a few hours for them to get ready for the party. Victor looked at his watch; it was 7 PM, and Lena had been in the bedroom for quite a while now. *Maybe she fell asleep,* he thought. He knocked on the bedroom door, and opened it.

Lena was lying on the sofa, reading a book, her hair up, clipped with a hand-made decorative hair comb, its edge embedded with an intricate design. The hairdresser's masterful makeup accented the best features of Lena's face with her high cheekbones, making her eyes look larger and brighter. Victor stood silent for a few minutes, admiring her, and then said, "It's time to get ready, Lena."

Lena put down her book but stayed under the blanket. "Please, don't make me go," she said quietly.

Victor's eyebrows shot up. "I thought you liked the dresses, and the jewelry..."

"Yes, I do like them." She paused. "But they aren't mine. And my mother always told me I should wear only what belongs to me... she said that even in the orphanage she would never exchange clothes with the other girls. I don't know how to explain it, but I don't feel right wearing these things."

"But you wear my uniform," Victor teased.

Lena smiled. "That's different. I didn't have anything else to wear. And it's more like borrowing it from my father." She paused again. "What if I lose one of these earrings, or someone steals the necklace? These things are so expensive; I wouldn't be able to pay for them!"

"I'm pretty sure there won't be people like that at the party. And, I'll be beside you. We promised Afanasiev that we would be there by 8 PM. Didn't your mother teach you to keep your word if you give it?" Victor's voice was soft, but insistent.

"Yes, she did." Lena sighed agreeably and put her feet down from the sofa. "I just don't feel like going anywhere and seeing new people, that's all."

Victor came closer and put his hand on her shoulder, sitting down behind Lena. "Do you want to go back home?"

Lena shook her head. Now, after her conversation with Afanasiev, she realized she couldn't go back. "I don't think I have a job there, anymore," she answered.

"Yes, they have probably fired you by now," Victor agreed. "But we could ask the doctor to give you a medical release. We could call your work tomorrow and explain what happened to you. Maybe you still could have your job."

Lena shook her head again. "No. I am pretty sure my job is taken and my room also. They are very strict there." Victor didn't know about the article in the newspaper, and after Afanasiev's threat she was afraid to talk about it.

"I see," Victor nodded. And then he turned to Lena and said passionately, "Listen, your fiancé Volodya was killed, your mother has passed away, your baby has died, you have probably lost your job, and you have no place to live, right?"

"Yes," Lena nodded.

"So. If things are so bad, what can be worse?"

"I don't know." Lena looked sadly at Victor. "My death, maybe," she sighed.

"No. You are too young to die. If things are so bad that nothing could be worse, it means you have flipped the coin, and you are on the good side now!" Nevorov exclaimed victoriously.

Lena smiled at him. "You sound so confident!"

"Of course, I am," he reassured her. "The bad part of your life is behind you now, and from this point on only good things will happen! Get dressed and let's go!" He stood up from the sofa, extending his hand to Lena.

"I love your attitude!" she answered with a sincere smile, giving her hand to Victor, and shaking it firmly, as if in partnership. "All right, Victor. Let's go!"

From Afanasiev's big bed Lena picked a dark-blue dress that accentuated her blue eyes, making their color even deeper. She chose a sapphire necklace with matching earrings and ring to wear with it.

Nevorov looked imposing in his dark tuxedo, and Lena was stunning in her blue dress. They gazed at each other and smiled, anticipating the evening they would spend together.

Lena had never seen Moscow at night. Its high buildings with hundreds of luminous windows, bright decorations, and the big and comfortable limousine captured her imagination. She felt excited and tried to hide her nervousness, moving closer to Nevorov's strong body in the car's back seat.

The car stopped at the entrance to a large, brightly lit hotel. The driver opened the door and Nevorov stepped out, walked behind the car and offered his hand to Lena. Accompanied by an attendant, they entered the building and followed him to a huge ballroom.

The room was crowded with people in small groups talking to each other, soft music was playing, and waitresses offered beverages and appetizers. Lena felt like she had suddenly stepped into a different world, one she had fantasized about in her childhood. She looked up at the heavy crystal chandeliers, so huge and bright with hundreds of bulbs. A white marble staircase led down to the dance floor, and Lena held tightly to Victor's elbow, afraid she might slip on her high heels.

"How do you like it here?" Afanasiev suddenly appeared in front of them.

"It reminds me of the fairy tale about Cinderella, when she went to the ball for a short hour," Lena answered, smiling shyly.

"Why just for an hour? I promise it will be longer," Afanasiev laughed, appraising Lena from top to toe. "I have to admit, you look like a princess, my dear." He whispered into Nevorov's ear, "I wasn't mistaken; she is a V.I.P. girl!"

Afanasiev took Lena's hand and led her away from Nevorov. "Let me introduce you to my guests."

Nevorov watched with uneasy eyes as Afanasiev glided across the hall, showing off Lena as if she were a trophy. He frowned as he saw him stop and place Lena's hand in that of another man.

"This is Mister Frank," Afanasiev said to Lena. "He is visiting here from the USA." Frank, a dark-skinned man in his late forties, politely took Lena's hand. The orchestra started playing a waltz.

"Shall we dance?" Frank asked Lena with a warm smile. Lena nodded and followed him to the center of the room. They didn't talk. Frank, although he was a little heavy, moved quickly and easily, like a professional who had spent years on the dance floor. Lena enjoyed dancing with him, feeling his strong hands, and easily following his quick movements. They belonged to the music, completely. They danced one number after another; Frank wouldn't let her go.

Finally the orchestra took a break. Frank gestured to his interpreter, a small Chinese man in his thirties, to come closer. He said something in English, and the interpreter translated, "Frank invites you for a private dinner."

Lena looked toward Afanasiev, who was standing by the opposite wall. The General nodded his head, as if he knew what Frank was asking about, and Lena followed the interpreter.

Chapter 40

Growing up in a village and then living in a small town, Lena had never experienced city life. She had never even been to a good restaurant. The only one she had ever known was the old parlor where she ate the ice-cream with Arthur, and it couldn't compare with this place.

Lena, the interpreter, and Mr. Frank sat in a booth together in the upper class restaurant of Moscow's best hotel, and Lena was at a loss as to how to behave accordingly. A handsome waiter served the food. Lena could not imagine that men would work as food servers. That was women's work, she thought. The men she knew would consider such a job beneath their dignity. She watched in amazement as dish after dish arrived, noticeably shocked at seeing so much food at one time.

Frank observed Lena and then said something to his interpreter. "Is anything wrong with the food? Don't you like what we ordered?" the interpreter translated into Russian.

Lena's face flushed red, ashamed at being caught, "Oh, no, no. Sorry. Everything is good. "

They began eating. Frank watched Lena with admiration, and then spoke to the Chinese man again.

The interpreter asked, "Could you tell Frank a little bit about yourself? Where do you work?"

Lena shrugged her shoulders, not ready for conversation, and tried to smile politely. She looked confused, not knowing what to say and how to behave with this foreigner.

"I am just a simple provincial girl," she answered modestly. "And what about you? Where are you from and where did you learn our language so well?" she asked the interpreter in Russian. She had never spoken with foreigners before and was fascinated to meet both of them.

"I studied business at the Moscow University for five years through a student exchange program," the interpreter explained. "The Soviet Union helps China in many ways, especially in economic development. And now I am working on my Doctorate here and translating helps me to get by during this difficult transition time."

"Your Russian is perfect!" Lena exclaimed.

Both men smiled back politely, and then Frank spoke again.

"Frank invites you to have coffee and dessert in his room," the Chinese man translated.

The three of them went up to the third floor and then walked along the red-carpeted long corridor to the room. Frank opened the door and invited them in. There was a double bed in the middle of the room; the bed covers, night lamp, and curtains were a deep burgundy color. There was a bottle of *Soviet* champagne and a box of fine chocolates on the coffee table by the window. With a gesture of hospitality, Frank invited Lena to the table.

"I'd like to taste this Russian wine and chocolates with you," he said and opened the bottle of champagne, filling the wine glasses. He then lifted up both glasses, offering one to Lena, and asked, raising an eyebrow and wrinkling his forehead, "How do they say it in Russian? *'Na zdorov'e?'*" He drank and waited for Lena. Lena sipped from her glass a little bit, and then she smiled and drank it all. "This wine is good, isn't it?" Frank asked with a smile, gesturing to the interpreter to leave.

Frank opened the box of candies and offered it to Lena. Lena took one and put it in her mouth, savoring its tender velvety texture. Frank approached Lena, and hugging her tight with his hand above her shoulder, looked closely into her eyes. "You are so beautiful!" He tried to kiss Lena on her lips, but she turned her head away in surprise, and his kiss landed on her cheek. He made another attempt, but Lena turned around and fled to the door.

She opened it and quickly ran down the corridor to the staircase, but in the next moment she was rudely stopped by a strong man's hand.

"Where are you going, girl?" An athletic man with a shaved head grasped Lena's shoulder.

He must have been standing at the end of the corridor. Lena realized. *Afanasiev's promise to watch me was real.* She didn't answer, but instead tried to free herself from the man's strong grip. The man forcefully dragged Lena back to Frank's room, opened the door, and threw her inside. And then he closed the door.

Lena fell on the floor, and her head hit a corner of the bed. Frank bent over her. "Oh, my God! What did that man do to you?" Frank helped Lena get up, and guided her to a chair. He sat her down and stood in front of her. "Should I call the police, or the service desk?" he asked, but the next moment he realized he couldn't call anywhere. By the hotel rules, he was not allowed to have a guest in the room after 11 PM; so, if he wanted Lena to stay, he had to be quiet.

Frank stood up and locked the door. Then he sat on his bed and looked at Lena. She was crying. Her hair was tangled, and her mascara was smeared over her face. He noticed that there was a scratch on her forehead with some blood on it.

He went into the bathroom, wet a towel, and brought it to Lena. "Here, let me clean this for you."

He carefully wiped her head, but Lena took the towel from him and went into the bathroom.

A few minutes later she came from the bathroom and sat on the chair. She had cleaned up her face, wiped her tears, and fixed her hair, but she looked sad. The good mood she had been in when he met her downstairs had disappeared. She sat on the chair quietly, with her hands clasped together on her lap, looking down at them.

Frank stepped to her, knelt down, placed his hands on top of hers, and held them in his. After a few minutes he asked softly, "Can you talk to me? Do you speak any English?"

Lena sighed and said slowly, recalling her lessons in school, "I do not speak English very well."

"And your name is…" Frank couldn't remember it without his interpreter's help.

"Lena."

"Yes. Lie-na. Beautiful name."

Lena smiled a little at how he forced his tongue trying to pronounce the unfamiliar word.

"Is it your nickname or real name? How your parents call you?"

"My father called me Lenochka, or Elenushka, and my mother called me Alena."

"Li-ena-Li-e-no-chka-A-ly-o-na," Frank repeated, trying the sound of these new words, rolling them in his mouth, as if it was a sweet caramel candy from his childhood. "Liena-Lienochka-Alyona!" he repeated. "I like all of them!"

Lena couldn't resist his sentimental personality.

Frank sat down on the floor, crossing his legs beneath him. "Tell me your story, Li-ena. Do you work?" Frank tried to speak very slowly.

"No," she shook her head. And then she added, "Now, no."

"Are you a student?"

"No."

Frank looked puzzled. "No? Why not? Do your parents live in Moscow?"

She shook her head again, "No. Died."

"They are dead? Both?" Frank exclaimed, thinking he hadn't heard it right.

"Yes, both." Lena didn't want to go into details. She didn't know if her father was alive or dead.

Frank paused, thinking of what else he wanted to ask. This girl looked so sad, and she probably had a good reason for that, at least based on what he had just learned.

"I want you to trust me," he said. "What can I do to make you smile?" Frank stood up and thought for a minute.

Lena didn't react.

Frank looked around his room, and not finding anything better, went to the radio that was on the wall and turned it on. The Army Choir was singing the popular song *Yablocko*.

Frank smiled widely and exclaimed joyfully, "I know this song! I've seen *The Sailors Dance* at the theater!" He put his hands on his hips, squatting, and kicking his legs out alternately, while pretending to mouth the words to the song.

Lena burst into laughter. Frank lost his balance and fell onto the floor. Lena rose to help him get up, still laughing.

They sat down and drank some more champagne, and then Frank continued his questions. "Where do you live, Li-ena?"

"I live in Zarecie."

"What is that? A city? A town?"

"It is a very small town." Lena noticed the notebook that was lying on the night stand; she gestured toward it and asked, "May I use it? Do you have a pencil?"

"Oh, yes!" Frank gave Lena the notebook and a pencil.

With a few quick strokes, Lena drew a few peasant houses, covered with snow, and a well with a bucket hanging above it. "This is my village, Rizovka," she said, tearing out the page and giving it to Frank.

"Oh! You draw so fast and so well!" he exclaimed with admiration after looking at the page.

Then Lena drew a summer meadow, full of flowers, and a little girl with daisies in her hands. "This is me," she said.

On the next page she drew the forest and children picking mushrooms. "Oh! Mushrooms!" Frank exclaimed watching while Lena was drawing. "I love mushrooms!"

"I like them too," Lena answered. She circled one of the children in her picture and said, "This is Volodya. Killed in Afghanistan."

"Oh," Frank sighed, taking the picture. "You are so talented, Li-ena!" He couldn't stop repeating it.

Then she drew a small woman with a tired face. "My mother, Varya. She died. Heart."

Frank just nodded his head, not wanting to take on all the sadness he felt for this girl.

Lena drew a picture of her factory and the women working on the sewing machines. Then she started to draw her baby, but she stopped and quickly scratched it out, so Frank couldn't recognize what was there. "This is all," she said.

Frank noticed that Lena had destroyed the last drawing. He understood there was something she didn't want to share with him. He looked through the pages again, amazed at how much he had learned in a short period of time. In these minutes he felt a strong and unexplainable, almost visceral, connection to this Russian girl; she seemed unaware of her strong power to attract people. Her graceful posture reminded him of ancient goddess. At the same time, there was so much pain in her dark blue eyes that he felt a desire to know her better, to be able to understand her secret.

Frank went to the night stand and picked up a Bible. He sat back in his chair and showed it to Lena.

"Do you believe in God, Li-ena?"

Lena took the Bible, flipped a few pages of the book, and then handed it back to Frank. She shrugged, and shook her head, showing that she didn't know the book.

Frank looked at his watch, then picked up the phone and dialed a short number. "Come up here," he said.

A couple of minutes later there was a knock on the door. Frank opened it, and the interpreter walked into the room.

"Frank wants to know if you believe in God," he translated to Lena.

Lena thought for a few moments. Officially, she was an atheist because religion, *the opium of the masses*, by Marxism-Leninism theory, didn't exist in the Soviet Union. But, on the other hand, she had lived in a small village where people still kept the old traditions and, although unofficially, followed the Orthodox church calendar in their everyday life. She knew a prayer she had heard from Granny Maria, and she had even prayed herself, hoping God would help her when she was giving birth. But He hadn't... *God didn't save my baby.* Lena thought, and answered honestly, not looking at Frank, "I don't know."

"I want to read it with you, Lena," Frank said softly. He opened the Bible, and began flipping the pages, trying to decide what Psalm or Scripture would help him to say what he wanted to communicate to Lena. "But before that..." He looked at his interpreter and asked, "Can you explain to me why she has so many names?"

The interpreter raised his eyebrows. "Many names?"

"Like Li-ena, Li-enochka, Alena?"

"Oh, that. It's easy. It's just because in Russian language, you can use different variations of the person's name—but it's still the same name! It depends on who you are talking to. If you speak to a little girl, you call her Lenochka. If you address a lady, call her Elena, and in official settings you would add patronymic, meaning father's name. So, we would call you Elena...?" the interpreter looked at Lena.

"Elena Kyrilovna," she answered.

Frank smiled. "How interesting! But why do they need all these different names?"

The interpreter kept smiling. He liked to demonstrate his knowledge, although he wasn't a linguist. "Russians like playing with words. By changing little parts of a word—like prefix, suffix, or ending—they create many different meanings. Their language is very powerful, *the great and mighty*, they say. Right, Lena?" He addressed Lena with a smile.

"Yes," Lena nodded. "And we have many jokes based on word play!" she said, turning to the interpreter.

"Which aren't easy to get, if you aren't fluent in language," the interpreter noted. "It's practically impossible to translate their jokes into English."

"So... If Frank was a Russian name, what would you do to it, Lena?" Frank questioned with curiosity.

Lena squinted her eyes and paused in this mental exercise, "Mmm... Frank, Franya...?" There were not too many combinations for this foreign name.

"And to show love and affection...?" The interpreter tried to help her.

"Franechka, or Ranechka...?" it didn't sound right to Lena's ear, but Frank's face showed his satisfaction.

"And notice that every Russian name has a meaning. Parents are always very careful in choosing the name, because it could affect the baby's fate." The interpreter said.

"Wow!" Frank exclaimed. "And what does your name mean, Lena?"

"My mother told me, it means 'the wise one', other say it means 'chosen.'"

"Fascinating! It's simply fascinating," Frank admitted. "But please, listen to this," he said, opening the Bible to a Psalm he wanted to read.

*   *   *

A few hours later there were still many people downstairs in the ballroom. Even more women had appeared, all of them young and pretty. Sasha, Masha, Dasha, and Natasha were among the crowd; they were chatting with different men, drinking wine and laughing.

Nevorov and Afanasiev stood by the wall talking. Afanasiev looked at his watch, "It's been three hours now. I told you she is 'a pro.' But I will give him this night for free."

Nevorov was puzzled, "What are you talking about?"

Afanasiev looked tired. He ignored the question; he was ready to leave. "Wait here for Lena. When the American brings her back, he might want to talk to you. If he asks for another night, show him this amount." Afanasiev ripped off a piece of paper from his notebook, wrote down a figure, and gave it to Nevorov.

Nevorov became angry. "Are you forcing Lena to sleep with him?"

"Don't get so worked up, Colonel. Was she a virgin when you found her? The American will stay here for two weeks. Bring me the money he pays you. You know where to find me, don't you?"

"Yes, I know."

Afanasiev left. Nevorov followed him with his eyes, and then spat on the marble floor.

Smiling, Frank returned Lena to Nevorov at about three in the morning. Hating his role, Nevorov nevertheless followed Afanasiev's instructions and handed Frank the note Afanasiev gave him. They agreed they would meet again tomorrow.

On the ride back to the apartment, Nevorov studied Lena's face, trying to read her emotions, but she avoided looking at him directly. It was obvious to him that she was not as tired as he was.

"So, how was the American?" Victor asked Lena after a long silence while he was trying to decide if it was appropriate to ask this question or not, hating to see Lena becoming a fallen woman.

Lena shrugged her shoulders, "He was okay." She paused and then added, "He read to me from a Bible."

"What did he do?" Nevorov turned to Lena, not understanding her answer.

"He read the Bible, the religious book, to me."

"In English?"

Lena nodded, "Yes, and his interpreter translated it for me."

Nevorov scratched the back of his head, "Hmm. These Americans are strange people!"

"Yes, they are," Lena nodded in agreement. And then she burst out laughing, and covered her mouth with her hand, trying to stop but not successfully.

"What?" Victor asked her.

"You know…" Lena was having a hard time talking while keeping herself from laughing, "I have never seen a black man before."

"So…?"

"And I was surprised to see that his palm was as light as mine!"

"Ha-ha!" Nevorov laughed. "I bet the bottoms of his feet are white too." He hugged Lena, feeling relieved that nothing bad had happened to her this night. He would rather have her reading the Bible with this strange American than doing what he had envisioned.

Chapter 41

IN THE EVENING NEVOROV called a taxi and took Lena back to the hotel. The taxi stopped by the hotel's entrance, and they saw the interpreter, who was waiting for them. Victor got out, and the interpreter gave him a package with money, and then he opened the other door, helped Lena get out, and accompanied her inside the hotel.

Frank was standing in the hall; he was smiling, pleased to see Lena again. Frank invited her to the restaurant for dinner.

"What would you like to eat?" he asked Lena after they found a table. "I want to eat something you choose."

Lena smiled, and after reading the menu, ordered a salad Napoleon, beef-stroganoff with buckwheat, and Turkish-style coffee with *Arbat* ice-cream for desert.

"I also like *golubci*, and *pelmeni*, and many other things, but we can't have all of them at once," she said apologetically.

"Don't worry, we'll try them next time," Frank reassured her, while reading with interest the long list of entrees on the menu. "Can you cook any of these?" he asked.

"Oh, yes, definitely. Every woman knows how to prepare food; we learn it from our mothers and grandmothers."

"If I invite you to visit me in the USA, would you cook all these things for me?"

Lena just smiled politely.

"I love Russian food. I've been in many countries and I am able to compare," he said.

The interpreter added after he translated, "Yes, Russian cuisine is great." He excused himself from having desert and started to leave.

"I'll call you later," Frank said, sipping his coffee. "Oh, it's too strong!" he exclaimed, raising his eyebrows at Lena.

"It is normal coffee," Lena answered, not even suspecting that coffee could be different—they had always had strong coffee in their local coffee shop. Lena loved ice-cream, and this kind looked especially good: five scoops of different flavors, topped with nuts and fruits and covered with honey. It was simply delicious. Lena's face melted into a smile as sweet as the ice-cream melting in her mouth, "Mmm…"

Frank finished his ice-cream, put his elbows on the table, rested his chin on his hands, and watched Lena with admiration as she ate her desert. They went upstairs to his room after that.

"I went to the bookstore and bought an English-Russian dictionary," Frank said proudly, after they sat down in his room. "Now I can speak Russian with you!" he declared cheerfully. He flipped several pages, looking for a few words, and then pronounced slowly in Russian, *"Ya Lubit Ti."*

Lena laughed at his pronunciation, and then corrected him, *"Ya Lublu Tebya!"*

Full of joy, Frank jumped up and kissed Lena on her cheek. "I love you too!"

*   *   *

Victor picked up Lena the following morning and took her back to Afanasiev's apartment. He then walked to Lubyanka Square, a few blocks away from the Kremlin. He stopped by the statue of Felix Dzerzinsky, the founder of *Ve-Che-Ka,* the current KGB. The dull, massive sandstone building was referred to as "one of the tallest" in Moscow, since "Siberia could be seen from it" as people bitterly joked. The biggest Moscow prison was contained in its basement, famous for being impossible to escape from and also for its staff's cruelty. A clock centered in the uppermost band of the façade read a quarter till nine.

Nevorov opened the door and was stopped by a soldier in uniform guarding the entrance. He pronounced Afanasiev's name, and the soldier directed him to the counter to receive a pass. A few minutes later he went upstairs to the fifth floor, then down a corridor with many doors, curiously looking at people in uniforms carrying file folders in and out of their offices. He finally found the door with Afanasiev's name on it, and knocked.

"Come in!" he heard the General's voice, and he opened the door.

It was a large room, maybe 10x10 meters, with ceilings about three meters high. Afanasiev was sitting behind a huge redwood desk full of papers. There were five different colored phones on his desk. Another long desk stood perpendicular to his, with eight chairs on each side. A large portrait of Mikhail Gorbachev hung on the wall above the general's desk. There were bookshelves on both sides of the walls, filled with the books of the Communist Party Directives.

Nevorov approached Afanasiev and gave him the package he had received from the American the night before. Afanasiev quickly opened it and looked through the hundred dollar banknotes, exclaiming joyfully, "Oho! This is generous. He has paid for the whole week in advance! Great! This Lena is like a magic 'gold fish' for us!"

"The American also asked if he could invite Lena to visit him..." Nevorov replied.

Afanasiev began laughing loudly. "To visit him? In America? Ha-ha-ha! It will cost him a fortune!" He paused, thinking, and added, "But if he wants..." Afanasiev wrote an amount on a sheet of paper and handed it to Nevorov.

Victor looked at the figure, and his eyes became enormous. He responded explosively, "No way! No man could afford it. Have a conscience!"

Afanasiev smiled. "Conscience? What is a conscience? Conscience is the word that cowards use, and we are not cowards, right?" He stood up, went around his desk, approached Nevorov, and tapped him on the shoulder. "The American is hooked, so he will pay. Take the money and make copies of his passport and his airplane ticket. We'll do the rest."

Nevorov turned to leave.

"By the way..." Afanasiev's voice stopped him. "You can ask him for more, and anything you receive above this amount will be your bonus."

Nevorov puckered his face in disgust and opened the door.

Nevorov was in a bad mood when he returned to Afanasiev's apartment, but after seeing Lena's face his heart softened a little bit.

"I cooked *borscht* for you," she said with a smile, helping Victor to put his coat into the closet. "And some *cutlets*."

"Good. I am hungry," he admitted.

"I can see it," Lena said. "Your eyes look angry. And 'men are angry if they are hungry,' my mother used to say. She told me that a good wife should always feed her husband first, and only *after* he ate should a woman talk to him."

"Your mother was right," Victor nodded, quickly washing his hands, impatiently looking at the table where the borscht was steaming in a big ceramic bowl.

"And what is it that you needed to talk to me about?" he asked a short time later after quickly emptying a plate filled with mashed potatoes and two big cutlets covered with rich gravy.

"I can't decide what to wear tonight," Lena said.

"Really?" Victor lit his cigarette and followed Lena into the living room. He sat in the armchair and looked at Lena, who brought in her dresses to show him.

"Frank has seen me already in the blue and in the black. And I don't really like the red one, it's too bright. What shall I wear tonight, Victor?"

He smiled into his gray mustache, thinking of how quickly a woman could go from "I don't need these dresses" to "I don't have anything to wear."

"You like this American, don't you?" he asked.

Lena stopped looking at the dresses, and became serious. "Frank is very kind to me, Victor. He talks about God and reads me stories from the Bible. It warms my heart when I hear them. I feel safe with him." She paused. "I might wear this black one again, with a fur. He said he likes seeing me in fur."

"The American told me he wants to invite you to visit him. Would you go?"

Lena placed the dresses down on the sofa, approached Victor, knelt down by him, and looked closely into his eyes, "Do you think Afanasiev would let me go?"

Victor's face became hard. "Let's go and take pictures for your passport."

Chapter 42

FRANK HAD MET IVAN Ivanovich in Switzerland. His banker had introduced them to each other, telling him that a representative from the Soviet Union was looking for Western businessmen who were interested in buying Russian goods and natural resources from his country. Frank had talked to Ivan Ivanovich and was amazed at the low prices the Russian offered, because he was bypassing the Soviet Ministry of Foreign Trade. Frank couldn't miss this lucky chance, and agreed to visit a few plants and refineries in the Siberian region with Ivan Ivanovich.

Russia currently had the world's monopoly on raising sable in its natural habitat, living only in the Siberian climate. Moreover, Russian scientists had been able to raise sable in captivity and even managed to breed new black sable which became the most valuable article at fur actions. The Soviet fur industry produced approximately fifteen million pelts annually, and there was a great potential in its future development.

During his visit to Siberia, Frank made some valuable connections and now was waiting in Moscow for samples of fur coats to be delivered for shipment to the auction houses in Europe, and to complete all the necessary paperwork for concluding his business in Moscow. He was enjoying his time in the Russian capital, seeing its famous sights, and visiting world famous museums and theaters.

Frank met Lena at 6 PM in the hotel's lobby and told Nevorov that in the morning his interpreter would have all the necessary copies of the documents and all the money that Victor requested. Frank took Lena to his room, while talking quickly about his day. "Li-ena! I have seen so many interesting things in Moscow today," he shared excitedly with her.

"I went to Red Square again—I love that place. There was a long line of people trying to get inside Lenin's Mausoleum. I didn't want to wait in line—it was too cold, but I managed to go inside the Kremlin's wall, and I saw the Palace of the Patriarch, the Armory Museum, and the Tsar-Bell. Then I saw the changing of the guard—it was great! The British have a similar ceremony; I saw it in London. After that I took pictures of the Spasskaya Tower, and the statue of Minin and Pozarsky, and St. Bazil's Cathedral. Oh, Li-ena! It is all so beautiful, so unbelievably beautiful…" He was opening the door of his room, letting her in, as he kept talking.

"There are eight small churches around the main dome and all have paths to each other. The architecture is mixed up and the colors are different, but formed all together in one entity, it is simply magnificent!"

He finally stopped and, not being able to hold back his feelings, quickly kissed Lena on her cheek. "I love Moscow! Don't you?"

"Yes," she said, smiling at his childish behavior.

"Sit down, please, sit down." Frank put Lena in a chair. "And in the afternoon… do you know where I was in the afternoon?" he asked, looking at Lena, while unzipping his bag and getting out a small package.

"No, I don't know."

"Do you believe in fate, Li-ena?" His face was serious now.

Lena shrugged her shoulders, indicating her doubt, but then she said, "Yes…"

"I do believe in God and I believe that He ultimately controls what we describe as fate. Oh, Li-ena!" Frank exclaimed emotionally. "I believe that everything happens for a reason. Even the fact that I met you has happened because God has both a perfect and permissive will for both of us." He said. "'The Lord shall preserve thy going out and thy coming in from this time forth, and even for evermore,' as Psalm 121 says," he quoted.

Lena looked at him, attentively, trying to catch up with his words.

"Listen, Li-ena, listen," he continued. "I went to the Tretyakov Art Gallery!" Frank paused. "And do you know what I saw there?"

"No," Lena shook her head.

"Oh, Li-ena… you won't believe it, as I couldn't believe my own eyes!" Frank sat down on the bed, holding a small package in his hands. Lena was looking at him questioningly.

Frank paused, and then he shouted out, "I saw you, Li-ena!"

"Me?"

"Yes." I entered the hall, and there was a picture on the wall… and when I saw it, I just stood frozen in front of it. I couldn't believe my eyes. How could it be, Li-ena?"

She looked at him, not understanding what he was talking about.

Frank opened the package he was holding in his hand; it was a collection of postcards he had bought at the Tretyakov Gallery kiosk. He flipped through the pictures, then took one out and showed it to Lena. "Look. This one."

Lena looked at the picture and nodded. "Ivan Kramskoi, *A Stranger*," she said. "I know this picture."

"You know it? Is she your relative, a great grandmother or something? Look at her eyes, and eyelashes, cheekbones, and her look—it's exactly the way you looked at me when we met, Li-ena! Who is this woman?"

"A Stranger," Lena repeated. "No one knows who she is."

"But her eyes and hair are exactly like yours, Li-ena! Although a tour guide said she was half-gypsy."

"And I am, too."

"Her grace, charm, and posture, and this aristocratic gaze… the two of you look like twin sisters; it's simply fascinating." Frank passionately kissed the picture he was holding in his hand, and then put it back into the envelope. He went to the window and looked out at the falling snow. "I want you to go out with me and show me your Moscow, Li-ena. Would you do that?"

Lena looked confused and didn't know what to answer. She stood up and went to the window too. Frank hugged her, and they stood quietly looking at the night city. "Would you like to go outside with me?" he repeated his question.

"It's too cold. I don't have a coat," she answered quietly.

"Oh." Frank looked at Lena's evening dress. He hadn't realized that she had jumped out of the taxi and gone straight into the hotel. "Yes. It is cold out there, no doubt about that," he admitted. "But wait, I can help you!" he smiled victoriously. He took a key from his night stand and said, "You will be surprised!" He gestured toward the door, inviting Lena to follow him.

They went out and he unlocked the room next to his.

Lena stood still in amazement at the scene before her: there were mountains of fur coats on the bed, in the chairs, on the coffee table, and the closet was full of them also. "Ah!" was all she could say.

"Choose the one that you like the most, my dear Princess," Frank gestured around the room with a king's generosity. "Which fur would you prefer? Here are all kinds of them: mouton, broadtail and Persian lamb, sable, mink, lynx, red and black fox, squirrel, and even beaver and sea otter." He smiled widely, enjoying Lena's amazed reaction.

Lena carefully sat on the side of the bed and gently touched the beautiful fur. She liked the gray mink, and the black fox with white highlights in it. She liked the rough texture of the broadtail lamb, but wouldn't choose anything that belonged to the sea animals. She sighed and looked at Frank. "I don't know."

Frank watched her closely and noticed her choices. "Try this one," he said, offering Lena the gray mink and holding the black fox coat in his other hand. She tried on several coats, and they finally agreed on the long sable, trimmed with leather. It looked very elegant on Lena's tall figure and accentuated her beautiful black hair.

"Now we are ready!" Frank exclaimed happily, but he noticed that Lena was looking down at her feet. "Oh! You need winter boots too. We'll buy them at the gift shop downstairs. It is still open," he added, quickly checking the time on his watch.

Lena and Frank spent the evening together, walking through the Moscow streets, stopping here and there, looking down from bridges into the dark water of the Moscow River, talking and laughing, and throwing snowballs at each other, and then making a little snow man on the side of a street, placing him there to guard a street light.

∗   ∗   ∗

Nevorov was already waiting downstairs when Frank and Lena arrived at the hotel in a taxi.

"Oho!" Nevorov whistled in wonder at seeing the "new" Lena. "That's quite a coat!"

Lena just smiled in response. "Frank gave it to me."

Frank kissed Lena on the cheek. "I'll be waiting for you tomorrow at 6 PM, Li-ena! We will go to the *Bolshoi* Theater."

Lena nodded to him and got into the taxi with Nevorov. "Bolshoi Theater! What a wonderful idea!" she whispered. "I've never been to the theater and we will go there tomorrow…" She smiled, covering her face with her new fur coat's collar. *Bolshoi Theater!*

Chapter 43

NEXT MORNING, FRANK'S INTERPRETER apologetically explained to Nevorov that they needed more time to come up with such a big amount of cash. He told Nevorov that everything would be ready in the early afternoon. He also asked for Victor's passport and a phone number. Victor thought it was a fair request, and gave them his passport and his phone number in Kiev, because Afanasiev told Victor never tell or indicate to anyone that they knew each other.

Victor received the sealed package with the money and copies of Frank's documents at 2 PM, as promised. The package was fat, and Victor could hardly squeeze it into the inner pocket of his leather coat, and it protruded on the left side of his chest. Victor had never had so much money in his hands. Actually, there was enough cash for him to go back to Kiev and buy a new apartment or even a small house somewhere in a village. These naive Americans hadn't even kept his passport; they had just made a copy of it and returned his original. Of course, the milicia would search for him, but with his survival experience he would be able to hide. He could take this money and go somewhere south or east, or even overseas. With so much money he could easily change his name, get new documents, and start a new life. Didn't he deserve to have a good life? Nevorov was so hot, he was sweating, even though the temperature was 25 below zero Celsius.

Nevorov stopped walking. He was only a block away from Lubyanka, when his legs suddenly weakened, and he couldn't take another step. His heart was pounding heavily and his pulse was racing so hard that he couldn't breathe. Victor sat down on a bench in the park he was passing through, not even sweeping off the snow. He took out a pack of cigarettes and lit one. His hands trembled, and he broke a few matches before he could finally inhale.

"Got a smoke?" A filthy disheveled man with a strong odor of cheap alcohol stopped, scarcely keeping his balance, in front of Nevorov.

"Yes." Victor reached to his pocket again.

"You're not stopping here! Go, go!" A country-looking woman in her fifties, dressed in a cheap synthetic winter coat, insulted the man, harshly beating on his back with her purse, pushing him forward.

The man almost fell under her blows, but he stretched out his hands to Victor, grabbing his shoulder.

"Just take them all," Victor said, quickly giving the man his cigarettes and matches, helping him back on his feet.

The woman grabbed the man's elbow, directing him away from Victor. "You'll smoke when we get home. Go now!"

Nevorov sadly watched the couple walk away. Somehow the drunken man reminded him of his father, who had been an alcoholic and died in his late forties. People don't live long in Russia, "life is too hard; no one can survive it," as someone had once joked bitterly. It was his mother who had raised the three children, with no support at all from her husband; and he, Victor, the oldest one, was always her help and hope. His youngest sister was still living with their mother in her one-bedroom apartment, with her husband and two kids. Her husband was paralyzed now, and the last three years he spent in bed. He had been a miner, and his back had been broken when rocks fell on him in the coal mine. Victor's sister worked as a clerk at the post office, and they hardly made ends meet, even with his mother's small pension added.

Victor had visited them after his return from Afghanistan, but couldn't stay long because there was no room for him to sleep there. He gave his mother all his money and returned to Kiev.

The cigarette burned down to his fingers, and he threw it under his feet. After smoking, he could think more clearly. He had two options, even three, actually. He could be as poor as other people, who live honestly only on the money that the government pays them, which was hardly enough to survive. Or, he could steal the money he had in his pocket and begin a new life. Victor started to cough uncontrollably from the sick feeling this idea created in his body. Steal? Steal from his friend? He couldn't tolerate the idea, wondering how this thought could even enter his mind. He had never stolen a thing, even anything small. His conscience would not let him do so.

But what is conscience? Only cowards hide behind the word 'conscience', Afanasiev's voice clearly sounded in his mind. *And we are not cowards.* Victor felt something was wrong with that statement, but he was having a hard time figuring out exactly what it was. He knew he wasn't a coward. But he also knew that he had a conscience, and he had always been proud of that. And now Afanasiev, his former commander, whom he ought to trust and whose commands he must follow without doubt and argument, had told him that "conscience" was not a word for them. How could it be? Victor was lost. After all of his years in military service, with the harsh training and iron discipline which demanded his obedience to his commander, now Victor's heart and his conscience were railing against everything he had believed in. Nevorov looked at his watch; he needed to go.

Then there was an option three: listen to Afanasiev, do what he asked him to do, and maybe one day he would have an apartment in the center of Moscow, and money, and a sweet wife. He could have it all, if only he would forget what the word "conscience" meant. Nevorov sighed deeply, then stood up and slowly walked toward Lubyanka.

*   *   *

Afanasiev sat at his desk, writing. Nevorov approached the general, took the package out of his pocket, and handed it to him. "Here is everything you wanted."

Afanasiev took the package and threw it in his drawer.

"You won't count it? There is a lot of money in there!" Nevorov asked nervously.

Afanasiev stood up and shook Nevorov's hand, "I trust you, Victor; good job." He paused. "Now go home and forget about this American. He will be gone in a few days."

Victor didn't understand him. "Forget? What do you mean 'forget?' Are you going to do what you promised or not?"

Afanasiev puckered his lips, "Don't tell me you care about this capitalist or his money. By the way, did you get anything for yourself?"

Nevorov's eyes flared in rage as he grabbed Afanasiev by the collar of his uniform. "No, I didn't get any for myself; I don't steal money from people. No matter who they are: Russians, Afghans, or Americans."

Afanasiev tried to free himself, but couldn't. Nevorov held him with a death grip. "And you'll let Lena go free, since you have received all of this money for her."

The general's face became red from lack of oxygen, but he managed to whisper angrily, "You just want her in your bed, don't you?"

Nevorov suddenly opened his fingers and dropped Afanasiev. He looked into Afanasiev's face and his voice was like steel. "I want her to be free, Afanasiev. And you better do what you promised to that American, otherwise—you know me."

The general straightened his uniform and tried to smile, "All right, Victor, I was joking. We'll do everything as it is supposed to be."

"That's better," Nevorov replied and he left the room.

Afanasiev went back to his desk, picked up one of the phones that connected him directly to his staff, and said, "Do you see the man who just left my office?" He paused, went to the window and looked out, then confirmed, "Yes, the one in a black leather coat and a brown muskrat winter hat. Right. He just turned. Take care of him."

Afanasiev went back to his desk, sat down in his chair, closed his eyes, and remained sitting there for a long time. Then he opened the drawer, pulled out the package Nevorov gave him, took the money out of it, and put it into his brief case.

Nevorov walked down the street. He was angry and didn't see the man in a cloth cap and a long gray overcoat who was following him. Victor stopped at the intersection, waiting for a green light. Two women in black clothes stopped next to him, also waiting for the signal. When the light changed, Nevorov walked behind them. The women turned the corner, going in the direction of a nearby church. Somehow, without thinking, Nevorov followed. Only when he stood on the gray concrete steps did he realize he was in front of a church. He paused for a moment, wondering at himself, and then he went inside.

The church was nicely decorated. Victor hadn't been inside a church since his early childhood, when he was secretly baptized by his grandmother. Following the women, he passed the booth where candles were sold, and stood by the column looking at the altar from a distance. The priest was reading from the Bible.

Nevorov listened, barely understanding the old Slavic language, but the whole ceremony sounded so peaceful and so comforting to him, that he said to himself, "Maybe Serega was right. Maybe God is all we have left." He stood for the whole service, listening to the psalms of the choir singing from the balcony, and reliving his whole life in his mind. He realized that at the end it will be he, Victor, who will answer in front of God. *There is no authority higher than God,* he thought, *and no one can stand between us and tell me what to do. No one can force me to turn a weapon against my people, whom I swore to defend. My conscience is God's voice within me, and I can't ignore it.* The simple and clear decision that he hadn't been able to find before, formed in his mind.

"I know what I'll do," he said to himself, leaving the church. "Thank you, God." He quickly walked toward Afanasiev's apartment, using short cuts through the dark streets of central Moscow.

He was walking fast, remembering that Lena was waiting for him, and he still hadn't noticed the man in the cloth cap who was following him, reaching for something hidden under his overcoat.

*   *   *

Frank was waiting for Lena at the front door of the hotel, impatiently looking at his watch. The interpreter approached him and said with a worried tone in his voice, "Sir, I couldn't reach Nevorov at the phone number he gave us. Would you like to go in? It is cold out here."

Frank just gestured, "No, I will wait outside." Then he asked, "Are you sure you translated it correctly? Maybe they are waiting for us at the theater?"

The interpreter shrugged his shoulders, "Yes, sir. I'm sure."

"I will go there, and you wait here," Frank instructed.

"Yes, sir," the interpreter replied.

Frank waved at a passing taxi and told the driver, "To the Bolshoi Theater!"

Lena, dressed in the red evening gown, stood at the window looking out onto the nighttime city. The sound of chimes could be heard from the clock on Spasskaya Tower. She counted the peals of the bell, "One, two, three... ten." She worried. *Why is Victor so late? Where is he?*

Chapter 44

LENA WAS AWAKENED BY the noise of the early morning city buses and honking cars from the street; it was 6 AM. She had fallen asleep, in her evening dress, while sitting in the chair waiting for Victor. Her shoes were lying on the floor. Lena stretched out her numb feet and looked at the empty sofa.

"Victor?" she called out loudly, but there was no response. Yesterday's worries returned. *Where is he?* she thought, getting up and going to the bedroom. She stood silently for a few minutes, looking around for signs that would give her a clue where Victor could be; then she went around the bed, and opened the drawers of the night stand, but nothing was inside. She looked out the window onto the busy street, and saw only the rushing cars.

She walked into the kitchen. There she also looked out the window that was facing the other street. She gazed at every person walking on the street, but Victor wasn't among them. Then she turned around, looked at the empty kitchen counters—no note, no empty tea cup, nothing.

With growing anxiety, Lena went out to the entrance hall and tried to open the door, but it was locked from the outside; she had no key. Sudden fear overcame her and she hopelessly slid against the door onto the floor. *I'm locked in; I can't open the door. Frank was waiting for me. Now he must think I'm a liar. Where is Victor? What am I going to do?* Lena sat there for a long time, hugging her knees and looking at the same spot on the wall; and then she finally got up and went into the living room.

She sat down on the sofa by the phone, picked up the receiver, and put it back down. Her mind was racing. *Who can I call? The hotel? How will I find Frank? I don't even know his last name. And what would I say? Frank can't help me anyway. He might call the milicia, and they would arrest me. Afanasiev? I have no number to call him, either. All I can do is to wait until he decides to come here.*

Lena got up and started pacing around the room. She approached the window, opened it, and looked down. *It's the fifth floor—if I jumped down, I would be dead on the icy concrete. I can't escape from here,* she realized with growing panic. Cold air filled the room, and she quickly closed the window.

There must be a way out, she chided herself. *I must not panic. What can I do, what can I do?* She went to the bedroom again, sat on the bed; her mind was searching for a solution. She glanced around the room, and her eyes stopped at the wardrobe. She stood up, approached the wardrobe, and for no particular reason, opened it. She began to mechanically sort through the men's shirts and suits inside of it, her couple of dresses, Victor's uniform. She took out Nevorov's uniform jacket, and checked its pockets. *Maybe he has a spare key in his pocket...* She found no key but there was a small piece of paper in the inner pocket. She looked at the paper: Sergey's address. *Victor told me about him.* Lena looked on the other side of the paper: a phone number!

She ran to the telephone and dialed the number. "I need to speak to Sergey. Yes, your neighbor." She paused, waiting while the neighbor went out and found Sergey.

A few minutes later a man's voice answered, "Hello."

"Sergey? My name is Lena. Victor Nevorov told me to call you if anything happened to him." She listened, and then continued, "He didn't come home last night. It has never happened before. Yes. Could you please come here and help?"

Lena changed from her evening dress into the jeans and T-shirt that Victor had bought for her. She was trying to occupy herself by doing something, but she was so nervous that finally she just sat on the carpet by the sofa in the living room, clutching her knees, and waiting. She looked at the clock on the wall: it showed 5:45 PM. Suddenly, the door bell rang. Lena jumped up and ran to the door.

"Who's there?" she asked, looking through the peephole, but seeing only the stairs behind it.

"It is Sergey," the man's voice answered.

"I can't open the door! I'm locked in," Lena yelled through the metal door, almost crying. Sergey didn't answer, but in a few moments she heard a faint metal sound behind the door. She saw that the bolt was turning, and then, the door opened.

"How did you do that?" Lena whispered, one hand covering her mouth in amazement. She looked at Sergey's gray hair and beard and was so shocked by his appearance, that she covered her mouth with her other hand, too. "Oh!"

Sergey closed the door, and extended his hand to Lena, "I am Sergey. So where did Victor go?"

"I don't know. He told me he was going to see Afanasiev. And afterward we were going to the Bolshoi Theater with Frank, but Victor didn't come back."

Sergey scowled. "I know Afanasiev, but who's Frank?"

Lena hesitated. Sergey put down his backpack and said, "Let's go to the kitchen. You must tell me everything you know."

Sergey quickly glanced over the light brown wooden furniture, the gas stove, and the square dining table by the window. There was a teapot, two empty tea cups, and two empty plates on the table.

They had hot tea with honey and Lena told Sergey what she knew about Victor, Frank, and Afanasiev. He then asked her to tell him about her life. It was the first time Lena had met Sergey, but his appearance, and especially the kindness shining from his dark eyes, comforted her, and she told him everything—even the worst parts.

"We all have had hard lives," Sergey said. "But it seems like you have had more troubles than most of us. It must have been very hard for you to lose your baby."

"Yes," Lena whispered, full of emotions.

Sergey put down his empty cup, and folded his hands together as if for a prayer. And, in the same way as Frank had asked her a few days ago, he asked, "Do you believe in God, Lena?"

This time, after her nightly Bible readings with Frank, and thinking about her life, she responded more easily. "Yes, I do."

"Let me pray for you, Lena," he said. "God loves you, and He will never leave you. Remember that."

Sergey prayed quietly, and Lena recited a simple prayer, the only one she knew. She asked God to help her, to free her from Afanasiev, and… she didn't know what else to ask, so she just repeated again and again, "God, help me, please help!"

Sergey stood up, took the bag he had brought with him, and went into the bathroom.

Lena cleaned up the table and washed the cups. She couldn't suppress her amazement when Sergey reappeared. He looked very different: his hair and his beard were shaved off completely; he wore a black uniform, and was holding a black face mask in his hand. Lena caught herself thinking that he was young and handsome.

"You're a different person now," she exclaimed with a smile.

"Victor tried to help you, and I'll have to find out what happened to him."

"Thank, you, Sergey. But what can you do?"

"I have a few friends here. We were in Afghanistan together; they will help me find Victor."

They left the kitchen and walked to the corridor. Sergey stood by the front door, ready to leave. Lena came closer, took his hand in hers, and said, looking closely into Sergey's eyes, "Sereza, I'm afraid. Please, come back!"

Sergey nodded, and then kissed her lightly on her lips. Their gazes lingered on each other. Lena didn't want him to leave. She tightly squeezed Sergey's hand, and then suddenly she took his head in her hands and kissed him long and passionately. Sergey was the one who freed them from the kiss.

"I must go, Lena," he said softly but firmly. He glanced at her once again, and then added, opening the door, "I'll buy you another pair of earrings, I promise."

"Just come back!" she whispered, closing the door behind him.

Chapter 45

LENA SLEPT ON THE sofa in the living room, covered tightly with a blanket. She dreamed of a bright sunny day. She wore a light summer dress and was walking with Sergey, holding his hand. They talked and laughed. Sergey stopped and wanted to kiss Lena, but she playfully ran away from him. Sergey followed her, and caught her near a birch tree. He grabbed Lena by one hand, but she hid behind the tree. Sergey grabbed her other hand, but the tree trunk was between them, not allowing them to kiss.

They began whirling around the tree, laughing. Finally, Sergey caught Lena and slowly lowered her down onto the grass. They kissed, and kissed, and kissed. Then they lay on their backs under the tree, looking up into the sky. Sergey stood up and picked the golden-yellow flowers growing down from the birch tree like hundreds of golden earrings. He playfully hung them on Lena's ears. "Here are your golden earrings."

Lena smiled, she liked his joke. "I've got *serezki* from Serezki," she replied with joy.

"Yes. Something precious for my precious! Do you like them?" Sergey asked, and his voice sounded like music to her.

"I love them," she laughed, enjoying the tender touch of his palm on her cheek.

Lena opened her eyes. Sergey was standing in front of her, watching her sleep.

"Ah! You came so quietly!" she said and jumped from under the blanket, quickly putting her robe on. "Where is Victor? Have you found him?"

Sergey sadly shook his head. "They killed Victor, Lena."

"What? Killed?" she screamed out in horror.

"They did what they used to do to all good people in this country. A single hero can't fight the system; that's why many people are trying to escape."

Sergey pulled from his pocket a white envelope, opened it, and took out a passport and an airplane ticket. "The American is leaving tomorrow morning, right?"

"Yes."

"You need to go with him, Lena. Here is a passport with an American visa and a ticket for you. Thank God, Afanasiev was a coward and had your documents made 'just in case'. You told me that you wanted to go, didn't you?"

Lena looked at Sergey confused, "Yes, I wanted to... but... couldn't I go with you?"

Sergey took Lena's hand and looked into her blue eyes for a few seconds as if he was trying to read her mind. Then he spoke slowly, weighing every word, trying not to hurt Lena's feelings. "You are very nice and very beautiful, Lena. And I wish I could make you happy..."

"Why can't we—"

"We can't. I promised God that I wouldn't kill anymore. But I did kill, last night." He sighed. "I can't live in this world, Lena. I can't stand it."

Lena looked at him with her eyes wide open. Sergey held Lena's hand in his. "I want you to be happy. You will start a new life in America. At least you will be free there."

"Freedom... is consciousness of necessity," Lena responded slowly and routinely, as if she were under hypnosis. She took her hand off his and stepped back.

"What?"

"Remember, we learned it in school? 'Freedom is consciousness of necessity,' as Marxism-Leninism taught us."

"Yes, Lena. I do remember. I used to be a good student, and a Communist." Sergey paused. "Everything in the world takes place according to the laws of the eternal truths... necessities and only through the exercise of reason is our freedom realized."

"*Reason?* What reason are you talking about? Are you saying that Victor was killed for a reason?"

"Yes, for a reason. Since everything takes place by necessity, true human freedom cannot exist in heroic opposition to the inevitable order of things."

"I don't understand you."

"I've been thinking a lot about this, Lena. After the October revolution we turned away from God, and now we are paying our price."

"God..." she pouted, unable to argue and giving up this battle.

"Yes, God. The Russian people have always believed in God, and Christianity existed here for thousands of years. And then one man came and declared religion as the *opium of the masses...*"

"Yes, Lenin and Karl Marx said so."

"And now we pay our price for that."

Lena didn't answer.

"We are slowly coming back, Lena. Only God can save us. And my mission is to pray for my country and for my people."

"I would pray with you," she said quietly.

Sergey sighed. This conversation wasn't easy for him. Lena was very attractive and sensitive, but his faith firmly controlled his passion. "I can't have a family, Lena. I have to serve God. There are people in the monastery near where I live who pray day and night for the salvation of our country, and I must be there with them."

Lena was silent. She looked into Sergey's eyes, and she could feel his passion and love for the people and country which he had sworn to defend. She nodded. It seemed she understood him, and respected his decision.

"I've got something for you," Sergey said and took a small box from his inner pocket.

Her face brightened in a smile when he opened it. "Oh! *Serezki!* Exactly the same as I've seen in my dream."

Sergey looked at Lena and said kindly, "I'm glad you like them."

Lena nodded, "Yes, I love them! Thank you!" She paused, then added quietly, "I wish I could go with you, Sereza..."

"You must go with Frank, Lena. It's dangerous for you to stay here any longer." He took the earrings from the box and held them on his palm.

"I want to give you these earrings, Lena. And let them be not for a black day, but for a happy one. All right?"

Lena's eyes filled with tears, as she nodded, "Yes..."

*   *   *

At the hotel Sergey went to the front desk and talked to one of the young receptionists. She responded with a pleasant smile, and then dialed a phone number.

Sergey returned to Lena, and they stood in the vestibule waiting. The elevator door opened and Frank appeared. He saw Lena, and a big smile lit up his face; he ran toward her, "Li-ena! I'm so glad to see you!" Frank hugged her happily.

"This is Sergey." Lena turned to introduce Sergey, but he had disappeared.

It was an early gray morning when Lena and Frank arrived at the main entrance of a Moscow airport. Frank got out of the taxi and opened the door for Lena. They entered the airport building, and went to the departure zone. Soon they were seated together on the airplane.

Lena sat by the window, quiet and pensive. She was wearing her new earrings, touching them from time to time. Frank sat next to her, reading *The Moscow News*. On the front page there was photo of Afanasiev under a banner headline, "Political Assassination! General Afanasiev killed in his bed. His wife did not even hear the killer."

The plane began backing up. Lena looked out the window as it turned, maneuvering, and slowly passed by the airport terminal. She tried to memorize with one last glance all the details of that piece of her native land. She said "good bye" to the snow, and the dark trees, and the gray sky… and suddenly, on the balcony, she saw a solitary figure. The distance between them slowly increased, and Lena turned her head, continuing to stare at him: the man standing there wore a monk's black habit.

Lena closed her eyes, trying to hold back uncontrollable tears that began rolling down her cheeks as she whispered, "Sereza, Serezenka…"